Fire in My Soul

Angie Daniels

Published by Caramel Kisses Ink, 2019.

The Fire in my Soul

Angie Daniels

ACKNOWLEDGEMENTS

To my homegirls Tonya Houston, Kim Ashcraft, and Novia
Mearidy,
your friendships have meant the world to me.

The Fire in my Soul
Angie Daniels

Prologue

I NEEDED A CIGARETTE, but there's one problem with that thought.

I don't smoke.

I slipped from underneath the blanket and rose to my feet. No point in lying there any longer. Sleep wasn't going to come easy tonight, which was nothing new. A quick look down at the clock on the nightstand confirmed what I already knew.

It was two o'clock in the morning.

As I blew out a long shaky breath. I made my way downstairs, heading to the kitchen. A cup of chai tea was just what I needed. Although a shot of gin probably would be a lot better. Only I didn't have anything in the house to drink.

"Then tea it is," I mumbled to myself.

I made my way into the kitchen, padding across the floor with bare feet. Within minutes I had a mug inside the microwave heating for two minutes. While I waited, I leaned against the countertop. Thoughts started racing through my mind again.

"Find your real mother."

I couldn't let it go. No matter how much I tried to shake it. The not knowing was driving me insane.

"What does that mean?" I shouted. "Mommy, what does that mean?"

Night after night. It was the same thing. The same thoughts. They nagged at me, kept me tossing and turning. Wondering and confused since my parents had been killed in a hit-and-run accident.

5

"Keke, you need to know the truth."

What did she mean?

The microwave chimed, jarring me from my thoughts. I retrieved the blue mug with the phrase *True Diva* personalized on the front. I dipped in a tea bag followed by two sugar cubes. It was something my mother had done, so naturally I would do the same.

Was she your mother?

Just thinking about her and my father caused my chest to hurt. Time would heal my wounds, but only one thing would erase the anger and resentment, the sleepless nights, and the feelings of uncertainty—answers to the questions that haunted me.

Find your mother.

Only seconds before my mother, Olivia Hart, closed her eyes for the last time, she'd breathed those three words that had changed my life forever.

"I'm so sorry."

Stroking my mother's hand, I tried to comfort her the best way I knew how. "Mommy, there's no reason to apologize. The accident wasn't your fault."

"No...please listen." Olivia signaled me to come closer. I leaned forward as she took another deep, shaky breath. "Find... your mother."

"W-what do you mean, find my mother? I-I thought **you** *were my mother."*

"I'm sorry..." Olivia gasped, struggling to catch her breath. "You need...to know... the truth." With that, her fingers loosened their hold and she was gone.

I swallowed hard and wiped away the hot tears trickling down my cheeks. Constantly, day after day, I relived the same scenario. That's why I couldn't sleep at night. That's why most days I couldn't think.

Was she telling me the truth?

Mommy and Daddy were gone but left so many unanswered questions. Two people I had known all my life as my parents. Now I had doubts about our relationship. Even though we resembled, I had even started questioning my connection to my father. Was I adopted?

Combing fingers through my hair, I reached down for the mug and carried it into the living room where I curled onto the couch with my feet tucked beneath me.

You've got to pull yourself together.

I was tired. I looked much worse.

You look a hot mess!

That was true. I couldn't remember the last time I'd used any makeup to enhance my cinnamon-colored complexion. Even my natural chestnut curls were an unruly mess and long overdue for a trim. This morning I noticed the dark circles that had settled beneath my eyes, a result of too many sleepless nights. I had to get myself together. But I knew now that wouldn't happen until I got my answers.

In search of a plausible explanation, I had broached the subject with both my aunt and uncle on two separate occasions. Not only had they told me I'd misunderstood my mother's last words, but my uncle went as far as to confirm I was indeed his brother's biological child.

"You are a Hart," he said in that deep husky voice of his.

Why would Olivia tell you to find your real mother if it wasn't true?

The uncertainty made it impossible to simply let it go.

Find your mother.

The echo of Olivia Hart's words slid around the edge of my mind. My parents had been tough, no-nonsense and believed in preparing me for the ugly world surrounding me. Olivia showed very little warmth. Consumed by my father's political career, I had, at times, wondered if my mother even remembered she had a daughter because neither of them spent much time with me. And when they did, they expected nothing less than perfection. Nothing I had ever done was good enough. My relationship with my mother had been a tough one. I'd tried to do all the right things: staying out of trouble, getting good grades and graduating at the top of my class. I even waited until in college to date. However, it had never been enough. Olivia had been quick to judge and had rarely given praise or affection. I could count the number of times she had bestowed a kiss or a loving word of encouragement.

My father was a kind man, but he seemed to have left most of the childrearing to his wife. It wasn't until I opened my employment agency three years ago that Olivia had finally told me she was proud to have me as a daughter. For the first time, I'd felt loved. Now I was alone.

Or was I?

If my mother had been telling the truth, there was another woman out there who might be looking for me. Maybe I would finally discover what I felt I'd been missing all my life. Maybe I would finally feel like I belonged somewhere.

A gush of spring air rushed through the half-opened window. I reached for a flannel blanket at the foot of the couch and covered my feet. I'd spent so many nights in the very same spot crying, shaking with resentment at her for not telling me before...before it was too late to ask questions.

My mother had been many things: dominating, outspoken, and strict, but she had never been a liar. If Olivia said to find my mother, then she was telling me the truth. She wasn't my biological mother.

Then why is everyone else lying? The question stabbed at my heart.

Deep down I believed there had to be something no one wanted me to know, something they preferred to keep a secret.

But I was determined to find out what that could be.

Chapter 1

I SAUNTERED THROUGH the double doors of the Holiday Inn Executive Center. My black strappy high heels lightly tapping across the gleaming lobby floor. As I wheeled a rolling briefcase, I followed the signs directing me to a large banquet room at the rear of the hotel. Through a maze of partitions, I found booth number eighteen where Staffing Solutions was assigned.

"Hi, Calaine."

Turning in the direction of the familiar voice, I spotted Jasmine Bates, a recruiter for Oscar Mayer, setting up a display at the next booth.

"Hey, Jazz," I greeted with a warm smile. Maneuvering the rolling bag behind the table, I leaned it against the blue partition wall as I added, "I see you're still trying to do my job."

Jasmine's blue eyes sparkled. "You know my boss still believes if I work harder, we won't need to keep contracting a staffing agency to fill our shifts." She rolled her eyes heavenward and spoke with an exaggerated sigh, "I told her that just isn't possible, but she doesn't believe me. So here I am."

I laughed aloud. Staffing Solutions had been supplying laborers to Oscar Mayer ever since I adopted a temp-to-hire practice. As soon as my staff specialists filled a job order, Jasmine was calling for another. After two years, the local plant was now one of my largest clients. Like most employment agencies, Staffing Solutions did the background checks, drug testing and handled the payroll. Then, in compliance with a service agreement in their contract, the temporary worker had the opportunity of becoming a permanent Oscar Mayer employee after ninety days of continuous employment. The program was a great success. However, since her transfer to the Columbia, Missouri plant, Vice President Torri Moretti had been searching for ways to cut recruitment costs in half by the end of the year, which ultimately meant eliminating the temp-to-hire program.

I shrugged. "As much as I hate to lose your business, it can't hurt to try. However, it won't be long before your plant has filtered through every male or female between the ages of eighteen and twenty-five in our little city," I teased.

"Then I guess we'll have to start recruiting in the next town," Jasmine replied. She and I erupted with laughter.

Even with competitive wages, the turnover rate at Oscar Mayer was still high. It also hadn't helped that the city's unemployment rate was at an all-time low.

While we continued to chitchat, I prepared for the crowd that would soon fill the conference center for the annual Chamber of Commerce sponsored event. Applicants liked the idea of being interviewed on the spot by some of the city's top employers. Last year's turnout had been tremendous, and it was anticipated this year was going to be just as successful.

I unloaded a large display, applications for employment, and several brochures, putting them on the table along with personalized pens and a dish of peppermints. Several other recruiters arrived, and within the next half hour all fifty booths were occupied. A short, petite event assistant came around with a clipboard, making sure everything was in order. She handed each of us a nametag. I was pinning mine to my lapel when someone strolling through the door caught my attention.

Damn!

Dressed in a tasteful charcoal gray suit that had been cut to fit him perfectly, the dark handsome man walked with an air of lazy confidence and swag. He was the epitome of hot and sexy with a large solid build that stood well over six feet, exuding strength and charisma. Even from across the conference room floor, I could feel the power that coiled within him, which rather unexpectedly made my blood tingle and my nipples harden.

"Damn, who is that?" Jasmine murmured under her breath.

I shook my head. "I've never seen him before."

"Oh my!" she moaned. "It's creatures like *that* that make being married so difficult."

I nodded and murmured absently, "It's men who look like *that* who make being single a true blessing." As he walked over to speak to one of the program coordinators, I caught myself admiring his stance. His legs were parted, emphasizing the size of his thighs. *And maybe something else,* I thought with a snicker. He was built like a professional football player with wide shoulders and large forearms. Goodness! He satisfied my sudden craving for chocolate.

As my eyes followed him, a smile crept to his lips that caused my eyes to narrow curiously. There was something about that smile that was familiar. While I continued to watch him, I wondered where had I seen that fascinating creature before? A pair of expensive Ray-Ban sunglasses shielding his eyes prevented me from seeing his entire face. Nonetheless, he sported short twisted locs while a neatly trimmed mustache and goatee accentuated full, luscious lips that had me wondering if he could kiss. Something told me he was probably good at everything he did.

"You're salivating."

Blinking, I turned my head to see Jasmine laughing at me.

"Goodness, was it that obvious?" I asked, giggling along with her.

"Oh it's obvious. And I don't blame you one bit."

A quick sweep of the room, I noticed several other recruiters staring in his direction.

Yep, the hottie was eye candy.

I went back to setting up my table, and yet I kept my eyes on him. I watched as he pinned his nametag above his suit jacket pocket, then reached down to retrieve his briefcase. Turning, he began to move in my direction with a confident, bow-legged strut that caused me to still. It wasn't until he removed his sunglasses that the blood drained from my face at the impact of his amazing eyes. It wasn't because of the penetrating shades of brown, gold, and green. It was because I knew them all too well.

"David?"

Hearing his name, David stopped in mid-stride. His head reared back, and I noticed his eyes fixed on mine. My heartbeat quickened as he began to peruse the length of me, taking his sweet time. I was glad I had worn my favorite blue suit. The jacket had a belt that emphasized a small waist. The skirt ended mid-thigh, baring long legs that traveled all the way down to my high heels.

When he'd last seen me, my hair had been long. Now it was short, sleek and sophisticated. My staff told me the new look emphasized my high cheekbones and full-painted lips.

As soon as he was done taking it all in, David walked toward me with a mixture of surprise and recognition. "Hello, Calaine. What a *pleasant* surprise."

My gaze was locked in the depths of his arresting eyes. "Same here," I managed to say, barely recognizing my own voice. The sound of my name rolling off his tongue caused my body to respond in a way I'd rather not dwell upon. However, before I could pull myself together, David snaked an arm around my waist. The unexpected contact sent a tiny shock through me. He pressed a tingling kiss upon a tender spot just below my ear, causing me to gasp.

"It's so good to see you." He was practically growling.

I swallowed and pushed away from the heat his closeness sparked. I wasn't sure which was more disturbing, the rough bedroom quality of his vibrant voice or the impact of his warm lips against my skin.

"How have you been?" he asked.

"Fine."

"Yes you are," he rumbled under his breath. That line was so tired and dated and yet my stomach did a somersault.

There was a glint of masculine appreciation in his eyes as they slowly perused my body, causing my skin to prickle. Despite the suit, I felt naked. An emotion I hadn't experienced since college flowed through my veins. It couldn't be. Yet for several seconds my heart thumped uncontrollably. *Snap out of it!* At forty-four, I was not about to react like a lovesick teenager.

"What are you doing back in Columbia?" I asked, breaking the spell. "Last I heard you were living in New Orleans."

"You've been checking on me," he teased.

"Not hardly," I snorted. He was so cocky. David chuckled while I tried to ignore another delicious shiver.

He pointed to the banner displaying the University of Missouri's black and gold logo. "I've been back for almost a month. They made me an offer I couldn't refuse." Glancing down, I read his nametag. *Director, Human Resources Services.*

"I'm impressed."

"Thank you," he said with a husky sensual tone that sent my nerves into a tailspin.

I had almost forgotten Jasmine was standing beside me until I heard her politely clear her throat. Stepping forward, the petite beauty barely came to his shoulder as she said cordially, "Jasmine Bates. Pleased to meet you."

"David Soul," he said, and while they shook hands, I watched him lick his lips.

Jasmine fingered her hair that looked as if it had blown in the wind on the drive over and cooed, "So you're the new bigwig on campus. I interviewed for that job."

"So did half the city," I interjected with the roll of my eyes. I didn't, but several of my colleagues had.

David pinned us with his gaze. Lips parting, he revealed a dazzling display of straight white teeth as he said, "Then I guess I was the lucky one." He winked, then turned and moved to set up his booth.

The moment his back was turned, Jasmine nudged me in the side. Tilting my head, I met her gaze as Jasmine mouthed something I pretended not to understand. *Uh-uh.* Hell no. I knew what Jasmine was alluding to and wasn't about to go there.

With a silly smirk, Jasmine sashayed around my table and over to David's, batting her eyelashes shamelessly. "So, how do you know Calaine?" she asked.

My pulse skittered.

David stopped what he was doing. His slow smile taunted while his eyes twinkled mischievously like a little boy with a secret. I gasped inwardly. *He wouldn't dare!*

"I used to date her roommate in college," he replied.

I blew out a breath of relief that sounded more like a snort as I said, "Along with most of the females on campus."

David chuckled and I noticed his teeth were strong and white, making me wonder if they'd been bleached. There was just no way that man could still look that damn good after all these years.

One could only hope.

Jasmine squealed. "It sounds to me like the two of you have a lot of catching up to do. Feel free to take lunch together. I don't mind watching all three stations."

I gave an unladylike grunt. Jasmine was watching us curiously and must have read something in my body language that had given her the impression David and I were more than friends. I swallowed.

If she only knew.

At one time, David and I shared a subtle, yet strong connection. And there was no way I was spending any time with him. *Alone*. One of the event coordinators opened the double doors and the crowd started coming through saving me from responding.

The University of Missouri or Mizzou as they were referenced, was Columbia's largest employer, which guaranteed a continuous flow of interested applicants in our direction. Just as I hoped, we were too busy handing out pens and applications for Jasmine to ask any further embarrassing questions.

In between prospects I found my eyes drifting without my control over to David, reminding me of the bad taste he had left in my mouth years ago.

As my thoughts filtered back to the first time we met, I realized I had been no more prepared to see him now than I had been then. David had been the first man I'd ever fallen for. What I hadn't expected was to have fallen flat on my face.

It was during summer welcome... twenty-five years ago. I was touring the Student Union when David came strutting down the hall with his hazel eyes and irresistible grin. I remembered his faint mustache and a short, fade haircut. My body had acknowledged him with a shiver of excitement. There was something about him I liked. I liked a lot.

Since we'd both majored in Business Administration, we had several classes together. David took his education serious, but his free time was spent chasing females. Girls didn't care. He had a magnetic charm that won him the hearts of many across campus. Even I wasted countless hours I could have better spent studying for an exam, watching him in action. Loving him from afar for almost a year until one day, he stopped me after class.

I remember my heart thumping so hard I could barely catch my breath. I was screaming inside "Yasss! He's finally noticed me." Only instead of asking me out, he asked me to introduce him to my roommate, Donna.

I refused, but David badgered me incessantly until he had worn me down, using my weakness— chai tea.

Donna went out with him a few times, but she had grown up a strong believer of saving her virginity for her wedding night. I had gotten a kick out of David trying to work his charm. He spent more time hanging around our dorm waiting for Donna than he did spending time with her. David soon discovered being an accountant was much more important to Donna than dating.

I blinked my eyes vigorously, returning to the present and tried to focus my attention on something else but found the attempt unsuccessful. While David went through the routine of meet and greet, I continued to watch him out of the corner of my eyes. I soon realized that for the first time in quite a while, I found myself drawn to a man.

Desperate for a distraction, I focused on the group heading in my direction while trying to draw him from my mind. However, as soon as they moved on to the next booth, my vision shifted to David again. I stared at him, admiring the way his dimples deepened when he said, 'hello.' The fullness of his lips as he spoke. The way he listened attentively as questions were being asked, and how he took the time to respond to each interested applicant with a level of professionalism that amazed me.

Watching him conduct himself maturely made me feel all tingly inside. For the first time in forever, I was reminded of how long it had been since I had been with a man. *Too long.* That's it. I was horny. That's all it was. Nothing more.

While David was handing out brochures and talking about career opportunities at Mizzou, I wondered if he had ever married. *Yeah right.* I seriously doubted he had learned the meaning of commitment. Men like him never do.

I pulled my eyes away to greet another round of candidates. After providing each of them with an application, I moved behind my table to grab another stack of brochures.

Listening to David explain the university's application process, I had to admit he knew his stuff. Not that I should have been surprised. David had always strived to be the best at whatever he did. The more challenging the situation, the better. Unfortunately, in college he had decided to add women to that list. The rumor around campus had been that David was an excellent kisser and an even better lover. Normally, I would have dismissed college gossip, but the kissing part was one thing I had personally experienced.

When he turned, I quickly averted my gaze, pretending I was straightening up my table. I didn't want to think of him. I didn't want to remember the taste of him on my tongue. Why was I fantasizing about the feel of his tongue exploring my mouth? David might be a wonderful lover, but that was one road I had never journeyed. I had known him well and physical contact was one thing I had certainly tried to avoid. However, images of him sitting in front of a fireplace with a baby on one knee demanded presence in my scrambled mind. Why was I thinking about sex, babies and David all in the same screwed-up daydream? David Soul married? Never.

Although, he would have been everything Olivia and James would have expected in a son-in-law—intelligent, confident, educated, career-driven, and if he was still as tight with the dollar as he had been in college, then he was financially stable. Yep, my parents hadn't cared much for David the college student, but they would have approved of the man he had become. In my book, that meant he was very wrong for me.

I briefly closed my eyes, willing the painful memories away. Why did I have to think about my parents' dislike in my choices in men? I didn't want to think about them. Not today. Not in front of all these people. Holding my breath, I let it out slowly. I still felt the threat of tears.

"Jasmine, I'll be right back. Can you watch my table?"

"Absolutely." She waved off my concern without looking my way and went back to speaking to an attendee.

As I started for the bathroom, David intercepted me with an iron grip to my wrist. I sucked in a breath as a tingling sensation ran through me.

"Where are you running off to?" he murmured.

I tried not to look directly at him. "To the ladies' room, if you don't mind."

"My bad. I thought maybe you were trying to sneak off to lunch without me."

Forgetting about the telltale signs, my head came up and met his direct gaze, our eyes fusing for several seconds. "I don't plan to have lunch with you. Not today or any other day. Now if you'll excuse me, I have something more important to attend to."

David started to release me when his eyebrows shot up. "Keke, is something wrong?"

I shook my head. I didn't want his kindness. Not now. Not when I was trying so hard to hold the tears in. *I won't cry. I won't.* I tried to blink back the burn of tears that blindsided me. I didn't want to give in to them. Not in front of David. Nevertheless, hot tears rose to the surface and clouded my vision.

David swallowed, visibly. "You never were any good at lying." He signaled to Jasmine that we were taking a break, then slid a possessive arm around my waist and guided me in the direction of the lobby.

The hotel lobby had created a cozy atmosphere with couches and chairs that surrounded an electric fireplace surrounded by a wall of mosaic glass tiles.

"Have a seat."

I sat and David moved beside me. He didn't speak. Just licked his damn lips.

I was so embarrassed, I hunched over with both elbows resting on my knees. David reached into the front pocket of his jacket, removed a white handkerchief and handed it to me.

"Thanks," I said as I dabbed under each eye.

David put his index finger beneath my chin and tilted my head so I couldn't avoid his speculative gaze. There was no hiding the tears I was sure glistened in my eyes. "Are you going to tell me what's bothering you?" he asked, genuine concern etching worry lines on his face.

Closing my eyes, I squeezed the handkerchief until my knuckles turned white, then took a deep breath and whispered, "My parents were killed in a car accident a couple of months ago."

In a sympathetic tone, he replied, "I'm sorry. I had no idea."

"My father was killed instantly. My mother passed away at the hospital." I swallowed hard, then opened my eyes again. Something in his warm expression encouraged me to continue. "It's still hard to believe they're no longer here." I stared off in the distance as fresh tears began to surface. I blinked them away.

When David reached over and squeezed my hand, I felt a surge of warmth. Years had passed, yet he was sitting next to me treating me as if I was his little sister. It should have irritated me, but instead I found his concern comforting.

I told him about the hit-and-run accident with a drunk driver that had taken their lives. Avoiding eye contact, I focused on the front entrance where several people had entered dressed in what appeared to be their Sunday's best, eager to find employment. While I spoke, David listened attentively. Feeling the heat of his watchful eyes, I suddenly felt uncomfortable. I pushed a strand of hair away from my forehead. If I were lucky, David would go back inside and leave me alone.

No such luck.

He gave my hand another comforting squeeze. "How are you *really* holding up?"

Again, a glimmer of warmth flooded my body. Unable to look directly at him, afraid that he might see my reaction, I stared down at my heels. "I've been taking things one day at a time." I forced a cheer that I did not feel into my voice. Now that I had answered his questions, I hoped he would get back to work. I didn't want his sympathy.

"I remember your parents," he said. "They were good people."

The corner of my mouth ticked at the very memory of his brief encounter with my parents. "*Good people*?" I repeated with abrupt humor. David wagged his brow suggestively, causing me to laugh uncontrollably. He, too, joined in.

I reached up and dabbed the corners of my eyes. "I guess you've forgotten that my father threatened to kill you." I giggled at David who grimaced in good humor.

I would never forget the time David came to the dorm looking for Donna. Just getting out of the shower and wrapped in a bath towel, I had let him in. We were sitting on my bed discussing midterm grades when my parents had come knocking at the door.

"I will never forget the looks on their faces."

His dark eyes smoldered. "I imagine we *did* look suspicious."

"What would you think if you found your daughter sitting on her bed half-dressed beside a horny college student?"

Still laughing, I turned and looked up into those beautiful eyes again. Big mistake. Even after all these years, David was still yummy. The air around me began to sizzle. Despite all the reasons I could come up with for not wanting to be attracted to him, I felt an intense ache in my chest that caused my nipples to bead as they rubbed against the fabric of my blouse. Thank goodness I was wearing a jacket.

My gaze dropped to his lips, and he licked them as if they were dry. It was something he used to do all the time and drove me crazy. Now it caused a reaction in me that made me squeeze my thighs tightly together. For a heartbeat I wanted to feel his lips pressed against my own.

Breaking the magnetic pull, I whipped my head around and stared toward the door again. Silence enveloped us. I fingered the fabric of my jacket, hoping David would say something or just go away.

As if he could read my thoughts, David said, "I hope you know I'm your friend. If you need anything, just let me know."

"Uh-huh. Sure," I murmured as my last attempt to resuscitate reason. Why was my body reacting in such a traitorous way to David?

"Look at me," he drawled softly, giving me his full attention. "I mean it."

Desire continued to course through my veins in hot spurts of awareness. I felt myself being pulled in by his charm as I grew all soft and warm inside. David elicited feelings I had long forgotten. Another wave of longing coursed through me. For almost a heartbeat, a part of me wanted him to take me in his arms and tell me everything was going to be all right. The other part of me knew better. There was no way I was going to fall into that trap. The smartest thing to do was to put some distance between us so I could regain my senses.

And get my ass back to work.

"We need to get back to work," I finally said. In an effort to try to keep my mind on track, I stood. As I turned away, David reached out and gently touched my hand.

"Why the rush?" he asked with a quick glance down at the watch encircling his thick wrist. "We've plenty of time."

"Because I have a job to do," I murmured. His touch was making it almost impossible to get my body back under control.

Releasing me, he chuckled knowingly. "I see you're still running away from uncomfortable situations."

"I am not!"

"You are too," he retorted. "I can see that delicious pulse throbbing at your throat. I still make you nervous." The expression on David's face told me he was thinking about the last time I had run away.

Cocky bastard.

"If you're not afraid, then prove it and have lunch with me." He smiled that wonderful heart-melting smile I remembered, and I had to look away to keep from returning it.

Chin lifted aggressively, I spat, "I don't have to prove myself to you." How could I have only seconds ago thought I was attracted to him? David hadn't changed a bit. He still had that same wolfish gleam in his eye.

Frowning, I said, "I'll see you inside." With that, I pivoted on my heels and departed.

I HAD BEEN WATCHING a Lakers' game for the past hour and didn't have the slightest idea who'd scored. Any other evening the team would have had my undivided attention, but tonight my mind was a million miles away.

While lying across my bed, I found myself thinking about how much my life had changed. Prior seasons I had shared with McKinley. We would spend evenings curled up on the couch with a bowl of popcorn, rooting for rival teams. While I was a diehard Lakers fan, McKinley's heart belonged to the Sixers.

Shifting uncomfortably, I was surprised McKinley had come to mind. I hadn't thought about my ex-boyfriend in ages. Maybe it was because I was feeling so lonely.

I reached for the remote and increased the volume, hoping the excitement of the game would drown out my thoughts.

So much for wishful thinking.

I really was lonely but unprepared to do anything about it. As long as I felt a void in my life, how could my future be certain? I could never marry until I found out where I came from. Not until I knew something about my family history. It was too late to bring a child into the world, however, the very thought of spending the rest of my life alone frightened me. I had hoped to have married and had babies. At one time, I even believed I had found my soulmate only to discover I had been wrong.

I met Detective McKinley Clark at a Policemen's Ball shortly after opening my agency. The first thing I had noticed was that he looked impeccably handsome in uniform. It was love at first sight, and it wasn't long before we were sharing an apartment. I had thought everything was going wonderfully until McKinley began to complain that I spent too much time at work. Because I was the boss, he didn't think I had to work quite so hard. As a result, my job was the topic of several arguments. No matter how hard I tried to explain it, McKinley never understood that I had to work hard to get what I wanted. I would not have gotten as far if I hadn't.

Trying to be sensitive to his needs, I had decided one afternoon to leave work earlier than usual and surprise him. I would never forget finding him in an uncompromising position with his co-worker, Christine.

I'd chuckled lightly at the memory of the woman rushing out his office half-dressed after I threatened to snatch that tired weave out her head. It pleased me to know I could finally find humor in a once awkward situation. My feelings for McKinley died a long time ago. He had since relocated to Phoenix. Too often, he called hoping to rekindle our relationship, but I declined, finding that along the way I had gotten over the pain of losing him.

Since then I rarely dated. Instead, I spent all my time and energy establishing my agency and hadn't missed being in the company of a man until today. Seeing David stirred feelings I had thought long since dead. Damn him! I scowled as I reached for a pillow.

I'd been thinking about him ever since I saw him at the job fair, and for the love of God, I couldn't understand why. It wasn't as if I was the least bit interested in him. Sure, David was gorgeous, but the man was a dog.

Nevertheless, first-hand knowledge of his reputation did little to calm the desire stirring inside. I didn't want to remember the tender way he had kissed me in college. Or the feelings of uneasiness after that night and all the other times we had run into one another on campus thereafter.

However, after today, it would be almost impossible to forget the feel of his hard body pressed against mine, his hot wet lips that brushed my skin, the mustache that grazed my neck, or the intense look in his sexy gold-green eyes. Even now my cheeks burned with the memories.

Clutching the pillow close to my chest, I blinked several times, then made another failed attempt at watching the game.

The emotions he had stirred was the way *any* woman would have responded to a handsome man, David included. The man was yummy, so it was a physical attraction, nothing more. If I could help it, I would never have to see him again.

Closing my eyes, I could do nothing to fight the memory of his masculine scent that flooded my senses. My lids sprung open and after swearing under my breath, I tossed the pillow across the room.

The next time I decided to take a chance on love, it wouldn't be with a heartbreaker named David Soul.

Chapter 2

THE NEXT DAY, I PULLED my Toyota Avalon into the circle drive of what I had once considered home. Staring out my windshield, the two-story Dutch Colonial-style home gave me the chills. The house was large, formal and lacking in warmth. I was certain that when my parents had the house designed, family living was not in mind.

It made me smile to see the tulips were in full bloom and the lawn was green and lush. However, I scowled as I discovered newspapers scattered across the front porch. I had contacted the *Columbia Tribune* weeks ago asking them to cancel the subscription. It appeared they were slow at getting around to my request.

After taking a deep breath filled with the scent of freshly mowed grass, I opened the door and stepped out the car. My legs felt like Jell-O as I moved up the walkway to the stairs beneath a covered porch. I checked the mailbox and found several pieces of junk mail. The rest had been forwarded to my house months ago.

Opening the door, I stepped into the two-story foyer that was centered by a graceful curved staircase. The faint odor of furniture polish reached me, a clear indicator that Silvia had made their monthly cleaning schedule.

Moving to the right, I entered the living room where uncomfortable Queen Anne furnishings surrounded a red brick fireplace. The walls were eggshell white while the floors were bamboo cherry with a scattering of Persian rugs. I dropped my purse onto a floral chair, then shrugged out of my brown sweater and laid it across the burgundy sofa.

I walked over to the distressed wooden mantel and studied several photographs. With feelings of dismay, I wondered why I had never noticed the lack of resemblance before. Why? I asked myself for the hundredth time. Why had my mother waited until her death to tell me the truth?

Hanging over the fireplace was a large mirror. I tried to avoid looking at my reflection but couldn't. Comparing my image to the photographs, I found myself looking for similarities. The more I looked, the clearer it became.

Silly girl.

There was no denying I was a Hart.

My father and I shared several of the same features such as complexion, widespread nutmeg colored eyes and full lips, while Olivia and I had none.

Running a nervous hand across my hair, I turned away. Mentally, I had tried all day to prepare myself for this visit. I thought I could come here alone, but now I wasn't so sure.

You must find out the truth!

Yes, I had to find answers, otherwise I would never be able to get on with my life.

After a few more seconds of coaxing, I moved back out to the foyer and followed another Persian rug that ran the length of the hall and ascended the staircase.

I stopped at the first door on the right and turned the knob. Staring at the large canopy bed and frilly pink curtains, my lips twitched. Dozens of stuffed animals were still in a net that hung in the corner. Directly below, several volumes of *Nancy Drew Mysteries* filled a small white bookshelf. The room had once been my personal refuge from a dysfunctional family life where having dinner together around a large formal table felt more like a pathetic ritual. I was still haunted with memories of talking to my dolls or spending hours sitting in the window reading. Sometimes I had created my own make-believe world while other times I dreamed of turning eighteen and gaining my independence.

When Olivia suggested I live on campus, I jumped at the opportunity to escape. College had been the best time of my life. Nothing had ever felt as good as freedom.

Shutting the door with a loud click, I moved past the other three rooms to the end of the hall where my parents had slept. My heart jumped as I stepped into the master suite. For several seconds, I stood motionless in the doorway of the sitting room as I took it all in.

The room was still just as my parents had left it.

Silvia, their housekeeper, had worked that unforgettable morning as she had for over thirty years. The sheets had been changed and the bed made. A handmade imported bedspread covered the king size mattress, and matching draperies were drawn over the windows. My mother had been an interior decorator, so the room reeked of her traditional style. There was a large cherry-wood poster bed with a matching chest of drawers, and an armoire that stood as it always had in the far-right corner of the room. I moved over to the large bed. The massive wooden frame stood well over two feet off the ground. Lowering onto the mattress, I remembered when I was smaller how my feet had dangled over the side. It had taken the help of a footstool to climb in or out.

Next to the bed, on the nightstand was my father's watch. He had forgotten it that morning. I reached over, picked it up and read the inscription on the back. *I love you Daddy.* Tears flooded my eyes. I had given it to him for his last birthday. I swiped a forearm across my face, my cotton shirt wiping away the tears.

"You can do this," I whispered.

Leaning over, I reached for the phone and dialed.

"Hello," answered a deep robust voice after the first ring.

"Uncle Tad?"

"Keke, what's the matter?" Thaddeus Hart knew me all too well.

I swallowed back the painful lump in my throat as I said, "I'm over at the house." I didn't even have to tell him which house.

I heard him swear, then sigh. "I thought we'd agreed we would go together?"

Even though he and my father were brothers, I felt uncomfortable having someone else rummaging through my parents' belongings. "I know, but I need to do this myself."

"Are you sure?" Thaddeus didn't sound totally convinced. He knew I was stubborn and tended to let pride stand in my way.

Closing my eyes, I pictured the concerned look in his large brown eyes and the frown upon his full lips. I pinched the bridge of my nose, willing away the tears. "Yes...I'm sure. I just needed to hear your voice."

"You know you can call me anytime." There was a noticeable pause before he suggested, "Why don't you let me take you out to dinner this evening?"

I sniffed. As usual, my uncle was trying to cheer me up. I shifted the phone to my other ear and replied, "All right."

He sighed with relief. "I'll pick you up around seven."

"I'll be ready."

"Love you," he said.

Those two words meant the world to me. "I love you too."

I hung up the phone and took a deep breath, then glanced around the room again. An antique clock on the wall had stopped some time ago. The time still read seven-thirteen. Its soothing chime had helped me sleep on numerous occasions.

I remembered one time when I was five, Grandma Bradley had slipped and broke her hip. Olivia had gone to spend the weekend with her mother. There had been a terrible storm that night, and I had been too afraid to fall asleep. I raced into my parents' room where my father had lifted me up and onto his bed beside him. While stroking my hair, he had spent hours comforting me with stories, some he made up and some he didn't until I drifted off to sleep.

The memories brought along my first smile all day. I had loved my father. Whenever Olivia wasn't around, he always seemed so much more relaxed and at ease. Those were my favorite times. My father had been my favorite. I couldn't help wondering if that was why it had been so hard for my mother to reach out to me.

Because she isn't your mother.

My heart lurched and I jumped up from the bed. I was on a mission. It was time to find out the truth.

"Now where do I begin?" I mumbled aloud.

Deciding to slowly work my way around the entire room, I moved to my parents' closet. I looked past a row of designer labeled clothing and grabbed a stack of photo albums that were on the top shelf. Carrying them over to the bed, I took a seat and opened the first one.

I was soon reminded of happier times when my parents, Uncle Thaddeus and Aunt Alma, and I had vacationed together. We had gone to Disneyland one year, then spent several days on the beach in the Bahamas the next. Sitting cross-legged, I found myself laughing at pictures of me on my seventh birthday in their backyard. My dad rented a pony that had ruined my cake.

Moments passed before I finally picked up the last album. It was large and old. With the back of my hand, I dusted off the cover and opened it. Looking inside, I realized I had never seen any of the photos before and was surprised to find captured moments of my parents together in their early years. I was in awe at how young and beautiful my mother had been—mahogany long legs and shoulder length silky black hair. She was smiling and appeared happy. I frowned. How come I never remembered my mother that way? Olivia had always been so serious and stern.

There were also photographs of her as a child all the way to her twenty-second birthday. It was a large celebration. I saw pictures of my grandparents, who were deceased; my mother's sister, Aunt Greta; and several cousins who had all taken part in the celebration. I studied a close-up of Olivia dressed in a beautiful lavender dress and caught myself grinning. She was such a beautiful woman when she smiled.

As I began to turn the page, my hand froze as something clicked in my mind. I flipped back to the inscription at the bottom of the photograph. April 23, 1975.

I was born in May.

Quickly, I flipped back through all the photos of my mother's birthday party again. Her dress was form-fitting, revealing every curve.

She wasn't pregnant.

"Oh my God!"

For the next several hours, I combed every corner of my parents' room frantically trying to find answers. Finally, in the bottom of my mom's dresser I found a small fireproof box that was locked. Heart pounding fiercely, I raced downstairs with the box in my hand, then reached into my purse to retrieve a large ring of keys that had belonged to my mother. Finding a small silver key, I nervously tried several times until it opened. I lifted the lid and looked inside.

There were pieces of jewelry, several hundred dollars in cash and numerous pictures. I skimmed through them until I found a picture of my mother holding a baby wrapped in a blanket. *That must have been me.* On the back was scribbled 1975, confirming my suspicion. As I thumbed through the stack, I found a picture that caught my attention. Resting an elbow on my knee, I stared.

The photograph was of six young women in nursing uniforms standing under a large awning that read School of Nursing. I looked closely at the photograph to see if any of them looked familiar. They did not.

Freshman class of 1973.

There was something eerie about the photo. Who were these women?

I set it aside while I finished rummaging through the last of the items. At the very bottom of the box was a carbon copy of a cashier's check made out to my parents for twenty-five thousand dollars. It had been drawn by Uncle Thaddeus. My pulse lurched.

Why had he given them so much money?

I closed the box and leaned back against the couch. Sitting quietly for several seconds, I had the strangest feeling I had stumbled onto something. I reached for the photo and stared at the six women again. They were all beautiful black women smiling proudly at the camera. *1973.* Two years before I was born. Something about the picture kept drawing me to it. What was it? Flipping the photo over, in faint letters I found scribbled in poor penmanship, *for Calaine.* A chill washed over me. Could one of these women be my mother?

There was only one way to find out.

I LOVED CC'S CITY BROILER. It had been one of my favorite places since I first tasted their ribeye. Now whenever I needed a night to unwind, I dropped in.

"How's work?" Thaddeus asked, trying to break the silence. I had been quiet since he'd arrived at my house to pick me up.

I smiled adoringly at the handsomely distinguished man sitting across from me. Thaddeus had been aging slowly for years. His hair was completely gray now, adding character to his otherwise pale face.

Tilting my chin, I smiled at him. "Business has been better than ever. I've had over fifty job orders this week."

"That's wonderful, sweetheart." He smiled, causing the fine lines around his brown eyes to crinkle.

It wasn't until the waiter arrived for our orders that Thaddeus reached for his menu and studied the selections. I didn't have to. I already knew it by heart. I ordered a ribeye and a large house salad while my uncle ordered a fifteen-ounce T-bone steak.

When our waiter departed, Thaddeus reached across the table and grasped my hand. "I know going to my brother's house was difficult for you. That's why Alma and I want to help. We would be more than happy to help you pack up the house and put it on the market."

"I know, and I appreciate your offer. I just need a little more time."

"I'm very proud of you," he said, and as if an afterthought, he added, "and so was my brother and his wife."

A slight frown marred my forehead. "They had a hard time showing it." This wasn't the first time we'd had that discussion.

He squeezed my hand once more before he released it. "People express things differently. They may not have been very affectionate with you, but then how often do you remember seeing them show affection to one another?" he reminded.

Staring across at him, I took a moment to think about what he said. He did have a point. My parents had rarely showed affection, even to each other. I could probably count on my hands the number of times I had seen my parents kiss, which was usually during the holiday season when several dozen guests were around.

I closed my eyelids briefly. "You're right." I nodded, not trusting myself to speak again until the waiter returned with my margarita. I smelled the tequila before I brought the salted rim to my lips and took several sips. Once I felt better under control, I reached into my purse and removed the carbon copy receipt. "Uncle Tad, can you tell me what this was for?"

He accepted the piece of paper from my hand and looked down at it. "Where'd you find this?" he asked with a speculative glance.

"In my mom's drawer," I responded, then waited for an answer.

"It was a gift. I gave your parents twenty-five thousand when you were born to put towards your college fund."

"Oh," I answered, lips compressed with disappointment. That was not at all the answer I had been expecting. Instead, I had expected the money to have been for something else, something that would have explained who I really was.

He studied me. "Why the long face? I'm your uncle. Since Alma and I couldn't have any children, you were all we had to spoil."

I nodded hard, trying to will away tears. Reaching for my glass, I took another sip, then reached into my purse again.

"Do you know who they are?"

Thaddeus stared down at the photograph and the color in his beige face drained.

My heart thumped with excitement. "You know who they are, don't you?"

Thaddeus rubbed his clean-shaven jaw as he spoke. "I taught all of them that year. The nursing school was still part of the medical school until around 1976 when it became its own separate entity." His voice suddenly sounded softer, almost far away. "Those were the most determined bunch of women I had ever met. This one here," he pointed to the woman on the end. "She was smart enough to have gone on to become a doctor." He paused. "What a shame."

"What do you mean?" I questioned.

"I heard she committed suicide. I never heard why." He stared long and thoughtful, then continued. "Eventually they each started drifting apart. I can't remember, but I don't believe they all graduated. I think one or two of them even dropped out the program by the end of the second year." He continued to examine the photo until our food arrived.

I stared across the table at Thaddeus. As he carved his medium-well steak, my mind was reeling with all the information he had given me. I shifted nervously on the bench, then launched into what was really on my mind. "Could one of those women have been my mother?"

Thaddeus nearly choked on his food. His expression held surprise. "What?"

I repeated the question even though his reaction was a clear indication that I was on to something.

Thaddeus lowered his knife. "Sweetheart," he began as he tried to regain his composure. "As I have told you before, Olivia's your mother."

He was lying. "No, she wasn't," I countered. "I've seen pictures of her twenty-second birthday party, and she was *not* pregnant."

Thaddeus averted his gaze to his plate. I could tell by his silence the photographs were never meant for me to see.

I leaned closer. "Tell me the truth... did my father have an affair?"

Glancing up again, he looked at me with somber eyes and said, "Calaine, you need to let this go."

"I can't," I persisted, then lowered my voice as if I was afraid someone at the next table might overhear. "I know Olivia wasn't my mother. I feel it in my bones. I think I have always felt it. So stop lying to me. Please, Uncle Tad, I have a right to know the truth."

When Thaddeus finally spoke, he had to clear his throat twice before he could get the words out. "Some things are better left alone. The past is the past. There's no point in stirring up memories that might be painful."

"So Olivia wasn't my mother?" I asked as if I hadn't heard a word he'd said. I saw the struggle in his expression and felt it within myself. "Please tell me," I murmured, then held my breath as if bracing myself against my worst fear.

Concern shadowed his eyes as he shook his head and said, "No, she wasn't your mother. After three miscarriages, Olivia was too afraid to try again."

"Oh, my God! It was true," I gasped. His admission sent my heart rate into a sprint. Taking a deep breath, I tried to slow down the pounding in my chest.

"But believe me when I tell you, Olivia loved you as if you were her own child."

It all made sense now. "It was hard for her to love me because I was Daddy's love child," I mumbled absently.

"Calaine, just leave it alone," he pleaded.

There was no denying his concern, the worried look in his eyes was quite apparent, but I had every right to know the truth. "I can't." Toying with my salad, I knew there was no way I was going to be able to get anything down. Dropping my fork, I clutched my stomach, afraid that I might be sick. "Do you know who my mother is ...was?"

Thaddeus shook his head and replied, "No, I don't."

I breathed a sigh of relief. Good answer. If he had, I would have felt betrayed by him as well.

At my prolonged silence, my uncle leaned in close and said, "It takes a strong woman to raise another woman's child. She didn't have to do it."

Yes, she did. I didn't say it aloud, but I was thinking it. As the wife of a prestigious member of the community, there was no way Olivia would have given that up and faced humiliation in front of her peers. I should have felt grateful for that. Instead, I felt as if I had spent my entire life paying for my father's sins. Had my mother agreed to raise my husband's love child just so she would have had the pleasure of throwing it back in my father's face?

I groaned inwardly. I didn't know who I was anymore. The only people who knew the truth were either dead or not talking.

"I want you to help me find her."

Thaddeus studied my expression and sighed. "All right. I'll see what I can do to help you."

IT WAS AFTER EIGHT o'clock when I returned home.

My small three-bedroom ranch style home was nothing like the elegance I was raised in. *My* home looked lived in. Olivia had insisted on decorating the place for me, but I stood firm and refused. This was my house and it reflected my own personal taste. No Queen Anne furnishings or cherry woods, and no expensive artifacts or paintings.

Two floral overstuffed couches were in front of a big-screen television. A glass-topped coffee table was in the middle, scattered with magazines I never had time to read. Everything else I had either found at a garage sale or had bought at Wal-Mart. The rest of the furnishing was sparse, but it was just the way I liked it. I believed furniture wasn't meant just for showcasing. If I didn't need it, I didn't buy it.

I kicked off my shoes, dropped my keys and purse on the coffee table and padded into the kitchen to put my doggy bag in the refrigerator. Closing the refrigerator, I glanced down at my cell phone and discovered I had missed a call and a voicemail message. I tapped the phone and brought it to my ear.

"Hey, Keke, this is Donna. Give me a call when you get this message. I'm going to be in Columbia at the end of the month and I want to reserve your couch."

With a smile, I dialed her number, then stepped out onto a small wooden deck. I took a seat and propped my feet on the railing, then dialed. After several rings, Donna's raspy voice came through the line.

"Hey, girl. I thought maybe you were out on a date," she teased.

I snorted into the receiver. "Not hardly. I was out with Uncle Tad."

"How have you been?"

"As well as expected." We hadn't seen each other since my parents' funeral. Donna had flown in and helped with the arrangements. "Guess who's back in town?"

"Who?"

"David."

Donna paused a moment as the name registered. "*My* David?"

"Yes, *your* David," I chuckled, finding her possessive claim quite amusing. "And you better lower your voice before Bruce hears you."

There was a brief silence before Donna replied, "He moved out."

"When? Why?"

"Irreconcilable differences. Lately, the two of us have been disagreeing on a lot of issues. Bruce was the one who finally decided it would be better if he moved back in with his brother. I agreed." When her explanation was met by my silence, she added, "Hey, it's better now than after we had gotten married. Don't worry. I'm actually enjoying single life again."

I wasn't convinced. Donna and Bruce had been together for almost four years and had planned to marry in the fall. The fact that Donna was being evasive proved that she really wasn't taking the break-up well. Nevertheless, I decided to wait and broach the subject when the two of us were face-to-face. For now I would just play along. "Maybe it's time to rekindle your relationship with David."

Feminine laughter came through the phone. "Hmmm, maybe it is. I can't wait to find out if he's lost that arrogant attitude."

I grunted. "Not as far as I could tell."

"Good." Donna sounded pleased. "I had always found it so sexy. A weekend of being wined and dined sounds quite appealing. Tell David I'm looking forward to catching up."

I giggled. "I'll tell him. See you soon." I hung up feeling a great deal better.

Donna was one of my closest friends. We shared just about everything.

While staring off at the diamond-studded sky, I took a deep breath. I had yet to share Olivia's confession with Donna. I would eventually. Right now, I needed time to get used to the idea.

Olivia really wasn't my mother. So who is?

The dull ache of not knowing was killing me.

Chapter 3

I ADJOURNED A WEEKLY meeting with my sales team and headed down the corridor to my office. With my sales manager, Debbie's, persistence, we had finally landed a contract with State Farm Insurance. I was ecstatic at the possibilities. They were one of the city's top five employers. Staffing Solutions had already received an order in the Claims department for a receptionist. Since it was our first order, we had to make sure it was filled with one of our best employees. My staffing supervisor, Sherrie, was already on the job. I had confidence in her ability to find the most qualified candidate.

I entered the last room on the left and crossed the rose-carpeted floor toward my desk, then reached for a bottle of Smart water from the dorm-sized refrigerator.

As I took a seat in a large leather chair behind my desk, I reached into my purse for something for a persistent headache when I spotted the photograph. I removed it and stared down at the six women again. I must have looked at it a dozen times, trying to find a resemblance, and they each had something I could identify with. One woman's hair, the other's eyes, two of the women and I shared the same complexion. She could be any one of them.

Why did Olivia save this picture for me?

One of them had to be my mother. What other explanation could there be? I had debated asking Aunt Greta but declined since she'd been an emotional wreck since my mother's death, and I didn't want to bring up any painful memories. But I couldn't ignore that she, too, had lied to me about my birth. I wanted—I needed—to know the truth. I would give Aunt Greta a little more time to deal with the loss of her sister. I gave an impatient sigh. In the meantime, I was going to have to find answers on my own. First things first, I had to find out the names of each of the six women.

"Excuse me, Calaine." My receptionist's voice came through the intercom startling me. I had been so absorbed I'd almost forgotten I was still at work.

I pushed the button on my intercom. "Yes, Norma?"

"David Soul is here to see you."

The mere thought of him standing in my lobby made my pulse leap. What could he possibly want? Part of me was anxious to find out what he wanted while the other half wanted him to stay as far away from me as possible. Although... regardless of how much I tried to deny it, David had changed. At the recruitment fair, I'd sensed the changes twenty-five years had made in him. David seemed to be a stronger, more mature individual.

Why do you care?

I don't care...not really.

"Would you like me to send him back?" Norma asked, interrupting my thoughts.

Before I had a chance to talk myself out of it, I heard myself say, "Sure, go ahead." Quickly, I reached inside my drawer for a small mirror and checked my hair and face, then put it away. I smoothed the front of my soft gray suit and straightened in my seat. Taking a deep breath, I reached for a pen and stared down at a report, pretending to appear busy. A moment later, I heard a slight rap on the open door.

"Calaine."

By the time I raised my head to acknowledge his presence, David had already crossed the short distance and was standing over my desk, grinning and flashing white teeth. Once again, his yummy good looks caught me off guard. I regretted looking up at his face and the tremor that raced through me.

David was dressed impeccably. This time his slacks were gray and pleated, accompanied by a black single button jacket that spanned his shoulders. I could feel the aura of him from where I was sitting. He had a male magnetism that seemed to reach across the desk and touch me. I tried to shake it off, categorizing it simply as a woman's response to a man, nothing more.

"Hello, David. What are you doing here?"

"I came to see you, Keke."

His smile was warm and slow while his voice flowed through my blood like fine wine. If I were a lesser woman, I would have sat there drinking him in, losing track of the time. Instead, I pulled myself together and forced my full lips to twist in an unwelcoming manner. "I would prefer if you'd call me Calaine."

David cocked a sexy eyebrow and gave me an appraising once-over, before his gaze lowered to my lips. "Why? Have you outgrown the nickname?" he teased.

"No." I briefly closed my eyes and sighed. *It just sounds so damn sexy when you say it.* "It just sounds unprofessional."

David seated himself in a leather chair across from my desk. "Tell you what...I'll only use it when we're alone," he growled.

I picked up the meaning in his words. Ignoring my heart that was pumping wildly against my ribs, I cleared my throat and asked as naturally as I could manage, "As you can see, I'm very busy."

"I want to have lunch with you."

"I can't."

"Why?"

"Because I'm working."

"Then let's make it about work. I have a proposal for you." David licked his lips, drawing my attention to his mouth. It reminded me of the time we had shared a pitcher of Jungle Juice and ended up rolling around ...

Quickly, I averted my gaze to meet his direct stare. "What kind of proposal?"

"Subcontracting our secretarial pool."

"*What*?" I couldn't possibly have heard him right. I had been trying for years to get my foot in the door at Mizzou. However, due to budget restraints the only temporary employees the purchasing department would authorize were from their own in-house temporary services.

"What happened to SOS?"

"Nothing. Secretarial and Office Support Services is still in full swing. However, until the hiring freeze is lifted on campus, we can't keep up with the needs of our departments. So in the interim, the department has decided to subcontract with any agencies willing to lower their bill rates to reflect ours."

My mind was reeling at the amount of business the merger could generate. "I'm sure we can come to an agreement."

David stretched his long legs out in front of him, then leaned over and reached into his briefcase. Removing several sheets of paper, he held them out to me. "I've had a chance to look over your rates and—"

"How do you know what my rates are?" I asked after accepting the sheet of paper in his proffered hand and looked up with surprise.

"I have my ways," David stated confidently as he handed me another sheet of paper. "Here are the rates we are willing to pay which would cut your current mark-up by twenty percent."

He's so cocky. I gave him a pointed stare before I looked over the rates classified in every category from an executive assistant to a medical records clerk. "I'm impressed."

David gave a low confident rumble. "I thought you would be. We'd also like to include a sixty-day liquidation clause."

Brow raised, I sat back on my chair. "Our current liquidation is no fee after ninety days."

Crossing his arms over his jacket, David smirked as he said a little too confidently, "I know. But with the volume of business the university can bring you, I would hope you would be willing to modify your terms as you have done at Oscar Mayer."

I just bet. Irritation sparked. Jasmine and her big mouth. He had somehow managed to wiggle out the details of their contract. Our contracts were *supposed* to be confidential.

"If there's a hiring freeze on campus, what difference does it make how the liquidation clause has been written?"

"There are always ways around things. In hardship situations, we have authorized departments to fill vacant slots. However, that's handled on a case-by-case basis, and only our vice chancellor can approve those requests."

I took a few minutes to glance through the report he had given me. Despite the compromises, the opportunity was too good to be true. Two major accounts in one day! Wait until my staff hears about this! "Shouldn't I be dealing directly with Joann? After all she is the manager of SOS."

"You should and you shall. Nevertheless, I'm the boss and she's so overwhelmed at the present, I told her I'd be more than happy to assist," he replied with that predatory smile of his.

I just bet.

I groaned, seething inward at his confident smile. I wasn't about to be intimidated by his charm. The contract was like dangling meat in front of a hungry lion, and he knew that every temporary agency in the city would jump through hoops for the chance to work with the university. Me included. Or, so he thought.

I folded my arms and tipped my head to one side as if I was considering his proposal. "I'll have to give it some thought, then discuss with my team. I'll get back with you in a couple of days."

His jaws sagged slightly. "Very well. When you're ready, I'll have purchasing put together a contract that we'll both be pleased with."

"Very good." Lowering the papers, I laced my fingers and smiled across the desk at him. "Thanks for considering me."

"You're welcome. I've heard nothing but great things about your company. Your customer service values are commendable."

"Thank you," I replied with pride. "I've learned a long time ago customer services can take you a long way." Adopting a practice of customer satisfaction was essential to the success of any business. Staffing Solutions had an eight-hour guarantee. If a customer was dissatisfied, they were offered a replacement and the first eight hours were of no charge. "I'll have my sales manager schedule an appointment with you or Joann so we can go over the proposal in more detail."

Relaxing in the chair, David nodded in agreement. However, he didn't look in any rush to leave. Silence hung between us.

"Well, I need to get back to work."

He glanced down at his expensive watch. "How about lunch?"

"N-no thank you. I've got a t-thousand things to do."

David flashed a half smile. "I'm asking for a lunch between friends, nothing more."

"I can't."

"You can't or you won't?" he asked with a wicked smile.

My gaze moved back to his eyes. "Do we have to go through this again?" I frowned. He never gives up.

"How about a business lunch? We can discuss the terms in further detail," he persisted.

"I really can't."

David leaned across my desk. "Are you afraid to be alone with me?"

Oh for Pete's Sake! Once David set his mind to something, it was easier to find front-door parking at the mall than it was to change his mind.

I also didn't like the way those brilliant eyes of his made me shiver inside. It was difficult enough trying to keep from squirming in my seat beneath his scrutiny.

"Afraid? Why would you say that?" I finally managed to say.

David took a moment longer than I expected before answering. "It's just an observation. We used to be very close and then things changed." He paused, then continued, hesitantly. "I was just wondering if it had anything to do with..." He purposely allowed his voice to trail off.

"Absolutely not!" I shot back. "Now if you'd excuse me." I tried to hide the nervous flutter of my hand by rearranging a stack of papers on an otherwise neat desk and instead sent the pile sliding onto the floor. With a curse, I reached down to pick them up.

David had moved around my desk to help, despite my protest that I didn't need his assistance. I reached for a stack and underneath was the old photograph. David grabbed it before I could.

Looking down at the women, he asked, "What are you doing with a photo of my mother?"

Chapter 4

THE STACK OF PAPERS slipped from between my fingers and fluttered back onto the floor. Even though my heart felt like I was running a marathon, I couldn't move. I was afraid my ears were playing tricks.

"One of those women is your mother?" I whispered. *This is it! The photograph was already beginning to paint a story.*

David nodded. "Yes, this lovely woman right here." He pointed to the fair-skinned petite woman in the middle. "With that Afro I almost didn't recognize her." He chuckled absently. Glancing up from the photo his expression sobered as his eyes met mine. "Is something wrong?"

"No, nothing." The shock of the discovery hit me full force. I couldn't breathe. I felt faint. With a shaky hand, I took the photo from him and slowly lowered into my chair. Breathing hard, I found my throat suddenly dry. Reaching for my water bottle, I took a long swig and wished it was something, much stronger.

"Are you going to tell me why you look like you've just seen a ghost?" he asked with obvious concern written on his face.

I didn't answer. Not yet. I needed a few more minutes to pull myself together. My pulse was racing. Talk about a small world. One of those six women was David's mother. One of the women I suspected to be my biological mother was *his* mother. Strange thoughts continued to race through my mind, then I gasped inwardly as a possibility emerged. What if we were... No, I didn't even want to go there.

"Calaine," he called, breaking into my thoughts.

I blinked and watched David return to his seat. I studied his face and realized I was searching for similarities in our features. "How old are you?" I blurted out as I felt the screams of frustration at the back of my throat.

"What does my age have to do with anything?"

"Just answer the question," I demanded with a hint of hysteria. "I need to know," I added softly.

David hesitated, probably shocked at my cray-cray behavior before answering, "I'm six months older than you. Why?"

My eyes narrowed suspiciously. "How do you know how old I am?"

"For crying out loud, Calaine! Have you forgotten we went to school together?" He barked with laughter that lacked humor.

While nodding, memories of Donna decorating our dorm room registered in my mind. I even remembered the cake she had bought in honor of David's birthday.

I slumped back against my chair and sighed with relief. Thank God for small miracles.

This was starting to turn into a nightmare. First, I discovered Olivia wasn't really my mother and now the only connection I have with her past, I had to share with David, of all people.

"I would like to help," he said.

"What?" I asked suspiciously. "Help me with what?"

"With whatever is on your mind. I could tell at the job fair that something other than your parents' deaths was bothering you. I have the same suspicion even now."

"How would you know?" I snapped. "You don't know anything about me!"

"I know more than you think. I'd know even more if you would just talk to me. Come on, Calaine. You still haven't told me why you have a picture of my mother."

I looked over and wondered if I could share my dilemma with him. But I needed to talk to someone.

"Please, Keke, talk to me."

I pulled in my lower lip and after a moment blurted, "I'm trying to find my birth mother."

"I thought..." David's voice trailed off, confused by my words before his dark brow shot up with surprise. "Mrs. Hart wasn't your mother?"

I swallowed back an emotion so consuming I couldn't put a name to it and sadly shook my head.

"Oh damn." His voice softened. "How long have you known?"

I blew out a shaky breath. "I didn't find out until a couple of months ago." Leaning back in my chair, I shared my mother's last words, and the conversation I'd had with my uncle two nights prior.

David raked a hand across his locs. "I'm so sorry, Calaine. I couldn't begin to imagine what you're going through. You must really be having a hard time right now."

"You don't know the half of it." I leaned forward, folding my arms on the desk. "How would you feel to know the life you had lived was not really your life at all? It has all been a lie."

"How can you say that?" David gaped. "You weren't adopted. You grew up with your father."

I shook my head with dismay. "It's not the same. I never had a close relationship with my mother. I never felt loved and accepted. I never had long talks and shopping trips like all my friends have with their mothers." My voice came off thick with a knot of emotion that clogged my throat.

I remembered all the weekends Donna's mother had spent at the mall shopping for hours with her, even the times they spent on the phone sharing and gossiping like best friends.

"My real mother is out there somewhere. I might even have another family I know nothing about... a sister, maybe even a brother." I reached for the photo and looked down at the women as I said, "All I know is that one of these women is my mother."

"How can you be so sure?"

"I feel it in my bones."

"Well, I can at least guarantee you *that* woman is not your mother."

I looked up and grinned at his attempt to cheer me up and caught David studying me.

"You didn't think you and I could have possibly been brother and sister, did you?"

I shrugged. "I just had to be certain." If he was my brother, it would have been more than I would have been able to handle in one lifetime. "You always did try to act like you were my big brother."

"Somebody had to protect you from the big bad wolf."

I felt warm at his comment. Sisterly love was the last thing I felt when I was around him. *Who was going to protect my heart from him?* The rich, deep gold of his eyes shone in the bright afternoon sun, pulling me into their depths. My gaze drifted to his wide mouth, and the pink tongue that suddenly darted across his lower lip. That habit was driving me crazy! I felt the urge to rise from my seat, lean across the desk and entwine my tongue with his.

"Is there anyone else you can ask about your birth?"

Regaining my common sense, I shook my head and glanced down at the photograph again. "Only my mother's sister, but I don't think she's going to be much help." Shaking my head, I murmured, "They should have told me the truth!"

David rounded the desk in two strides and came to me, placing a comforting hand to my shoulder. "There's no point in driving yourself crazy trying to understand why. I'm sure your parents had their reasons. Maybe your mother wanted to make sure you never thought any less of your father or her as anyone other than your natural mother. If you were the result of..." he cleared his throat, "...of an affair, then I can understand why your mother never wanted you to know. How many women would put up with their man stepping out on them? Then to make matters worse getting their baby mama pregnant... Only a strong woman would raise another woman's child."

I nodded. My uncle had said the same thing. "You're right." The warmth from his fingertips penetrated through my skin.

"I'm all right...really." I swerved in my chair, removing his hands. "I better get back to work."

With his hands clasped behind his back, David was moving towards his seat when he stopped and swung around to face me again. "I want to help you find your mother," he volunteered.

I saw the pity in his eyes and shook my head. "No, I don't want your help," I argued softly.

His silence gave me a moment of hope. It was short-lived.

"You need my help," David finally said as he lowered back onto the chair. His voice held a ring of command and his smile came slowly as if an afterthought to soften his order. "That way you can talk to my mom. I'm sure she knows how to find the others."

"No, really, I can do this on my own," I assured him with cool poise intended to mask my own uncertainty.

"No, you can't." David locked firmly into the argument.

I sighed and rubbed the tension at the base of my neck. Common sense told me to refuse his offer, but my strong desire to uncover my past prevailed. "Let me think about it."

David gave me a triumphant smile. "Good."

The phone rang. Before reaching for it, I managed a smile as I said, "I really do appreciate your offer. Now, if you'd excuse me, I need to get back to work."

He didn't look at all fazed as he surged to his feet. "I'll be in touch." With that, he winked and left my office.

Chapter 5

ON THE WAY HOME, I stopped for Chinese take-out. Setting the sack on the counter, I quickly went to my bedroom to change into a pair of sweatpants and an oversized t-shirt before returning to the kitchen. I grabbed a shrimp egg roll, then moved to the living room and sat in front of the television. While channel surfing, I found myself drawn to a movie on *Lifetime* about a mother who was looking for her daughter.

Sighing, I curled my feet beneath me as questions swirled through my thoughts. What woman in her right mind could abandon her own child? Why did she leave me? Why had she never tried to get in touch with me?

I reached for a pillow and hugged it close to my middle. It was just too lonely of an evening. It was on nights like these that I missed having someone special in my life.

I hated to admit that seeing David had brought flutters to my stomach again. He was as charming and convincing as ever. There was no way I could have said no to his offer to help if I had wanted to. I'll never admit it, but I was glad and looking forward to his assistance. There were other reasons, but I wasn't about to go there.

Using all my energy, I forced thoughts of David from my mind. I channel surfed until I spotted an episode of *Martin*. I lay back on the sofa, and before I even realized it, I had drifted off to sleep.

I heard someone knocking. I opened my eyes to find the sun had just begun to set. Rolling off the couch, I rose and walked to the door. I looked through the peephole. Whoever was on the other side had the audacity to put their hand over the glass.

"Who is it?" I snapped. Somebody had some nerve.

"It's David."

I yanked open the door and stared up at the beautiful man, breathlessly. "David? What are you doing here?" Self-consciously I quickly ran my slender fingers through my tussled hair. I tilted my chin. "How did you find out where I lived?"

He chuckled as if he knew a deep secret. "This is Columbia. Everyone knows where everyone lives."

David did have a point. Of Columbia's population of ninety-five thousand, only about thirty percent were black. Everyone either worked together, were college students, or were related in one way or another.

He lounged casually against the doorframe still dressed in a suit and tie. His cocky grin was sexier than ever. I wore a t-shirt with no bra that I was certain left the outline of my nipples clearly visible through the delicate fabric.

"Well, what is it you want?" My tone was not as polite or as composed as his.

"Why don't you invite me in and find out.'" He looked me up and down and there was no mistaking the pleasure in his eyes.

"I was trying to take a nap," I swallowed, hoping he would just go away.

"I can tell," he commented and laughed as he ruffled my hair. Not giving me a chance to retort he brushed past me and entered the house. "Nice place."

"You arrogant son-of-a..." I muttered under my breath. Who did he think he was walking in my house? I had half a mind to demand that he leave right now. However, as much as I wanted to give him a piece of my mind, I reminded myself of his offer to help me find my mother. "I'm not in the mood for company." I wrinkled my nose and shook my head. This was much too personal.

David gave me a soft relaxed smile. "You need to shake off your gloomy mood," he suggested as he moved to my couch and took a seat.

I ran a frustrated hand through my hair as I stepped further into the living room. "You have no idea what I've been going through."

There was a prolonged silence before David replied in an apologetic tone, "You're right, I don't know, but I want to help."

"Why?" I asked suspiciously.

"Because I want to," he replied and patted the spot beside him. "Now come and have a seat."

"But I don't want your help," I mumbled. What if what I found out was so embarrassing, I would never be able to hold my head up in this city again?

"Please, sit down," he tried again. At my hesitation he continued, "I spoke to my mother tonight and asked her about the photo."

"You did?" Immediately, I moved and took a seat on the loveseat across from him. It was safer. "Does she know who my mother was?" I knew it was too much to hope for, but I had to ask and wasn't at all surprised when he shook his head. "Well, what did she say?"

David leaned back comfortably and draped his arm across the cushions. "She identified one of the women. Let me see the photo."

I scrambled to the dining room, grabbed my purse, dug out the snapshot and handed it to him. This time without even realizing it, I dropped beside him on the couch.

David looked at the photograph and started to chuckle. "Yep, that's her."

"That's who?"

"Aunt Wanda."

I looked down at the woman he was pointing at. "*That's* your aunt?" This was getting weirder by the minute.

He turned his head to look at me. "She isn't really my aunt. We just call her that. She's more like my godmother. I've known her all my life."

I looked at the nutty-brown-colored woman with long curly hair who had an arm draped across his mother's shoulder. Could she be my mother?

David read my mind. "I doubt it. Wanda never had children. Not because she couldn't, she just never wanted any. She worked as a nurse for the Department of Defense, and always had a thing for soldiers," he chuckled. "At least that's what my mother used to say."

So much for that possibility.

"Aunt Wanda enjoyed traveling and the excitement of living in different countries. Children would have altered her lifestyle. Don't get me wrong. She loves children. She just never wanted any of her own. You would enjoy talking to her."

I nodded absently. My mind was twirling with different possibilities. However, I wasn't about to scratch Aunt Wanda off my list just yet. Grown women do have secrets.

"Mama said if she and Aunt Wanda could get a closer look at the photograph, they might be able to remember something about who the other four women are."

My heart thumped with anticipation. I looked at him, trying to decide if I was going to give him the photo. "I can go by Walgreens on my way home tomorrow and print a copy."

"I got a better idea," he began and as soon as I saw a slow, sexy smile curve his lips, I knew I wasn't going to like his suggestion. "I'm flying to Texas. My sister's graduating with a Master of Education next Friday. I'd like you to come with me."

I shook my head as the warning bells went off in my mind. There was no way I was going to travel with him to San Antonio. "I don't think so. I'll just make a copy of the photo."

David shrugged. "Suit yourself. We're having dinner at my parents' after the graduation. Aunt Wanda will be there too." He paused, noting the indecisiveness that had crept into my expression. "Don't worry about it. I'll just talk to them myself." With that, he reached for the remote control and flipped to the news. "I'm sure the two of them have a lot of stories to tell. I can't wait to hear them."

I frowned and felt like stumping my feet like a five-year-old having a temper tantrum. I didn't want him talking to them. I wanted to talk to them myself. How would David know what questions to ask?

"I'll think about it," I mumbled.

David searched my face a moment, lips twitching. "Is that your answer for everything?"

"What do you mean?"

"I offered you an opportunity to subcontract our secretary pool. 'I'll think about it.' I offer to help find your mother. 'I'll think about it,'" he said in a falsetto.

He was making fun of me!

"Why can't you for once just say yes?"

"Because, David Soul, I know that at some point you're going to want something in return," I stated firmly.

He slapped a hand to his chest. "Keke, you sure know how to break a man's heart."

My heart fluttered at the sound of my nickname sliding off his tongue again.

"Oh whatever," I muttered and shifted on the couch. I folded my arms across my chest. He probably thought I was being stubborn. I was hiding my aroused nipples from his view.

I turned and tried to concentrate on the news. Instead the air between us sizzled with sexual awareness. During a commercial break,

David spoke, breaking the silence. "I wonder if any of the women are working as a nurse at the university? If I knew their name, I could look them up in the personnel system."

"I've already thought about that. My uncle is looking into it for me." I took a few moments to explain to him Thaddeus' connection to the group of women. "If they're not still around, I'm hoping that maybe one of his colleagues at the nursing school might have their contact information."

David shifted on the couch and faced me. "Have you thought about visiting the nursing school to see what you could find?"

I nodded. "I thought about that today, but where would I begin?"

He snapped his fingers. "I bet they have old yearbooks we could look at."

"That's a wonderful idea!" In my excitement, I threw my arms around him and kissed him on the cheek before I realized what I had done. Hastily, I dropped my arms and slid away, pretending to watch television.

It took David several seconds to speak. I wondered if his body was also on fire. "Did you get a chance to speak to your sales staff about the contract?" he asked, changing the subject, and I was grateful.

I grinned, relieved that he hadn't made more of the kiss than it really was. "Yes and they're as excited as I am."

"Good."

I caught him looking at me.

"What?"

"Have I told you how good you look?"

Oh brother. "Don't even go there with me, okay? I'm a wreck and it shows."

"Beauty starts in here." Leaning forward, he tapped me lightly on the chest. The innocent contact—to my annoyance—caused my nipples to harden again. I crossed my arms over my breasts again.

Placing a hand to my knee, he commented, "We used to be close. I want that back."

That was before we had gotten drunk and shared a kiss.

David must have been thinking about the same thing because he looked at me and our eyes locked.

Despite myself, I liked looking at him. For just a heartbeat, I found that I hungered to have him touch me, bring his mouth to mine, feel his body pressed against mine. I was irritated that David could evoke such foolishness. *You enjoyed it before!* The thought made me blush. I hastily dropped my eyes and removed his hand.

"I've spoken to Donna."

David scowled. "How's she doing?"

"She'll be down at the end of the month for a visit. She just broke up with her fiancé, so she's single again." I was fumbling nervously with my words. "I told her you were back in town, and she's looking forward to seeing you."

"I'd like to see her again." He smiled absently.

I saw that far-off dazed look on his face. He was reminiscing. Maybe this time David might have a better shot. Good riddance!

I rose from the couch. "Would you like something to drink?"

"Yes, that would be great."

Nodding, I moved awkwardly towards the kitchen completely aware David's eyes were following me. "Coke, iced tea or water?" I called over my shoulder.

"Iced tea," he answered.

I released a sigh of relief when I rounded the corner entering the kitchen. The scent of him had attacked my senses. What had I been thinking throwing myself against him like that? Stroking David's ego was the last thing on my mind. The man was used to attracting women like flowers drew bees.

Shaking my head, I opened the refrigerator and removed a pitcher of iced tea. I tried to concentrate on finding a glass. My heart was pounding heavy and my thoughts were scattered. Feeling slightly off balance, I blamed it on my lack of an appetite. "Would you like some Chinese food?" I called into the living room. "I've got plenty left."

"That would be wonderful."

At the sound of his voice, I spun around and collided into David's hard chest, spilling iced tea on his shirt, down my arm and onto my feet. I slowly lifted my gaze to his. I hadn't heard him move from the couch. Dang, why did he have to be so handsome? He was so close I found it hard to draw a normal breath.

"Look at what you made me do!" I snapped, trying to mask my attraction.

"Here, let me take that from you."

He was standing so close I could feel his sweet breath on my forehead causing me to shiver. His large fingers brushed mine as he reached for the glass. I stepped away as if I had been burned by the contact. Quickly, I swung around and opened the refrigerator, then removed several cartons of food and placed them on the counter.

It had been over twenty-five years, and yet I still responded to him. In fact, it was worse. My heart was pounding heavily against my chest and my throat grew dry. I had never acted like this before. Maybe it was because I had been without a man in my bed for so long. Well, whatever it was, I needed to get myself in check, quick!

"Have a seat," I ordered. The words had come out sharper than I intended. Having him invading my space was driving me crazy. I moved over to the cabinet and removed two plates. Reaching into a drawer, I grabbed serving spoons and eating utensils.

I pointed to the counter. "Fix your plate so I can pop it in the microwave for you," I instructed.

I loaded my own plate, then moved to put it inside of the microwave.

David moved towards the counter. "Mmmm, you have all of my favorites." He glanced over at me with an irresistible smile as he spooned orange chicken and shrimp fried rice onto his plate.

I tried to steady my heartbeat. I didn't want to feel an attraction to him. David would be my downfall. He would only break my heart again. Besides, Donna was looking forward to seeing him again. If I kept reminding myself of that, then there was no chance of me forgetting.

"My staff is overly excited about subcontracting. I think it will work out for everyone. A lot of our temporary employees have been seeking employment at the university for years." I was rambling. I knew it, but what could I do?

"I think this will be a great opportunity for everyone," he said as I removed my plate. He brushed past me to put his in the microwave. The contact caused the hairs on my arms to stand.

"So do I." I tried to deny the contact and was pulling my t-shirt from inside my sweatpants when I realized my hardened nipples were evident. Why hadn't I left my bra on? I scowled as I crossed my arms over my chest. "I'll be right back."

I retreated to the bedroom where I slipped a sweatshirt over my t-shirt and dragged a brush through my hair. When I returned, David had already taken his plate out of the microwave and was seated at the table.

"I was feeling a little chilly," I lied. Dropping my eyes, I took a seat across from him. Before I could bring the fork to my mouth, David stopped me and reached for my hand. His large hand engulfed mine and I ignored the sensation as I lowered my head and listened as he said a prayer that sounded as natural as saying "good morning."

Religion had never been a major part of my upbringing. I had attended services with my aunt and uncle on numerous occasions, but there had never been any consistency. As an adult, I had visited several churches in the neighborhood, hoping to find a place where I felt right at home, and so far, I had come up empty.

We were silent as we ate. David watched me carefully out of the corner of his eyes. I was trying so hard to be in control as I stared out the window behind his head. I was determined to fight the attraction. Deny it to the end.

"Your house is..." Eyes traveling around the room over to a small microwave cart in the corner stocked with rows of romaine noodles, popcorn, and teas. If he could see inside my freezer, he would have discovered it was full of TV dinners and other ready-made meals. Next to a blender were several instant breakfast packets. If he had not known I was raised in a wealthy family, he would have never guessed it.

"Not at all what you had expected," I said as if I read his thoughts.

He looked across at me and smiled. "No, not at all. I'm curious why you haven't moved into your parents' house."

I frowned as I chewed. "That house reeks of my mother's taste." Now that I knew Olivia wasn't my mother, it felt so weird calling her that. "Besides, it never felt like home. As soon as I'm ready, I'm going to put it on the market."

David nodded. "I just bought my first home."

I looked up, startled.

"Why do you look so surprised?" he asked.

"Because I had never imagined you doing something as settling as buying a house."

"There are a lot of things about me that you haven't realized."

His statement was met by another pregnant silence.

"Are you still a big Lakers fan?" I blurted. My words sounded forced.

He smirked at my attempt to relieve some of the tension. "Of course. Are you still following the Bulls?"

I frowned. "Not since Derrick Rose left." I spooned food into my mouth and swallowed. "The Lakers, they're the team to watch."

"A woman after my own heart."

I choked on a grain of rice. Reaching for my napkin, I covered my mouth and coughed.

David reached over and patted me lightly on the back." I'm sorry. I'm not trying to make you uncomfortable."

"Then quit saying things that embarrass me," I retorted as I returned the napkin to my lap.

"What would you like for me to say?" A challenging glint lit his eyes.

I sat silently staring at his silly smirk for several seconds, then resumed eating my food. I wasn't even going to go there. Not today. He was trying to get the better of me.

"I want us to be able to talk without having to watch what we say. You're a beautiful woman. I have always enjoyed being around you. That has not changed. You used to be one of my favorite people."

I gaped. "I couldn't stand you."

"Quit fooling yourself. I never believed you disliked me. We had what is considered a love hate, sister brother type of relationship."

I snorted rudely. "I thought you were a dog." Then with a shrug I added, "You're a Q, so you can't help yourself." In my opinion, all Omega men were dogs.

He let out a shout of laughter. "Is that what you thought of me?"

"Don't act surprised. I told you that on several occasions. Why do you think I was so dead set against hooking you up with Donna?"

He tilted his head slightly to study me. "I thought maybe you wanted me for yourself."

"What! You must be mad!" Despite my protest, I could do nothing about the flush of heat to my face.

"Then why did you kiss me that night?" he challenged.

My blood warmed with intimate memories. "We had both had too much to drink. Donna had just dumped you and Joseph decided he was ready for something I obviously was not. We were both on the rebound and feeling a little lonely." I tilted my chin stubbornly. "Besides as I remember, it was *you* who had kissed me."

"Then why were you on top when Donna knocked on the door?"

He was right. I had been on top. After completing a pitcher of Jungle Juice, the two of us had played a few hands of UNO. Before I had realized what we were doing, he and I were entwined on the floor between me and Donna's beds. I wasn't sure how long it would have gone on if Donna hadn't knocked on the door. I remembered opening my eyes and staring down at David.

My cheeks warmed. I wasn't sure when I had ever been so aggressive. That night I had initiated the kiss, and being the horny teenager that he was, David responded to my advances.

I simply shrugged. "I was caught up in the moment."

"So was I, although, I enjoyed the kiss very much."

I was annoyed at my pulse for reacting to him, wild and uncontrollable. Sure, I'd had a crush on him back then, and when he started dating Donna, I tucked those emotions away. Well...at least I thought I had.

I had been too afraid to tell Donna and even more terrified of her finding out. As a result, whenever I saw David I ran in the other direction.

"Isn't there someone else you could be bothering this evening?" I dryly replied.

"If you're trying to find out if I am seeing anyone, the answer is no."

I didn't know why but his answer gave me an annoying sense of relief. Things were quickly getting out of hand. The longer I was around David, the more I starved for his company. There was no way I was going to get used to him being around again.

Anxious to end the evening, I rose from the table to scrape my plate, then turned on the faucet and began filling the sink with dishwater.

David rose from the table. While reaching around me to place the dish in the warm sudsy water, he pressed his body against my back.

"We are two consenting adults. There's nothing for either of us to be ashamed of." His breath was warm against the back of my neck, causing a stir at the pit of my stomach.

In a panic, I ducked under his arm and moved back to clear off the table.

"Still running," he said.

I glared up at him but said nothing.

David moved to help. We worked together quietly while I tried to get my emotions under control but knew that wouldn't happen until after he was gone. I left the dishes to soak in the sink and pushed him back into the living room.

"Thank you so much for your help, but I have an early day tomorrow."

He nodded knowingly. "You're still running from your feelings."

"Not at all. I just have more important things to worry about right now. The only thing I plan to focus my energy on is finding my mother. Everything else will have to come second." I hoped I had made my intentions clear.

David paused to look at me. "We're going to find your mother." He reached for his suit jacket and moved to the door with me close behind. When we reached it, he turned and faced me. One long arm shot out and pulled me snugly against his hard frame. As I stared up into the fire burning in his eyes, my pulse quickened.

"I enjoyed spending time with you this evening. Thank you for dinner. Now I need to taste you." With that, he lowered his head and kissed me.

He crushed me to him, claiming my mouth and when my lips parted in surprise, he took swift advantage. I tried to protest but found I could not. My hands rose to his chest to push him away but relented. There was no way I could fight the fury inside me because my heart wasn't in it. Instead, the tension in my body began to relax and I released a sigh.

His lips moved with gentle pressure at first, then the kiss deepened. The taste and scent of him enveloped me and the firmness of his mouth sent a quiver through mine. When had David slipped a mint in his mouth? The result was so clean tasting, demanding attention and shooting fire through my veins. I found myself succumbing to the passion. He moved his hand to hold the back of my head as a wave of intense pleasure swept deeply within me. With the skillful stroke of his tongue, I felt as if I was drowning, drowning in the desire that surged through my veins. Another sigh escaped my parted lips and I felt myself leaning into him, giving in to temptation as I met his strokes eagerly. I welcomed the possession of his lips and savored the feel of my breasts pressed against his chest. Heat surged through me and spread fast through my body. My world was spinning like a top and all that mattered was being right here, right now with David. My arms snaked around his torso and I clung tightly, afraid that if I let go, I would discover it had all been just a dream. I heard David groan and then his hold on me tightened, drawing me closer to his hard, male body. I caught myself tilting my hips toward him, pressing my kitty against him. I had never been so turned on in my life.

The need for air finally pulled us apart. We stared at each other, hearts thumping and breathing heavily.

David's eyes had darkened. "I knew the passion was still there."

"You shouldn't have done that," I replied in a shaky whisper.

"You could have stopped me at any point, but you didn't. You felt it too."

He was right. My body was humming with sexual awareness. I pushed him away. "I have no idea what you're talking about."

He pulled me back into his arms. "Don't you feel that? Listen to what your heart is telling you," he commanded in a husky whisper.

I could not deny the strong beats of our hearts. David's was beating just a rapidly as mine.

"That's lust, nothing more," I lied.

"So, what's wrong with lust?"

"Everything." I pushed away again, needing to put some space between us fast. "Now go!"

David chuckled. "Goodnight, Keke." He opened the front door. "Sweet dreams."

All I could do was nod as I watched him walk through the door because I knew my dreams were going to be far from sweet. Quickly, I turned the lock on the door, then pressed my back against the cool surface and slid onto the floor.

Oh my goodness!

The kiss that we had shared in college now seemed tame in comparison. With maturity, David's lips were now confident and skillful. He had given me a glimpse of his skills and had stirred my desire. I had always known his kisses would fill me with more intensity than any other man was capable. What I hadn't expected was the magnetic pull that came along with it. I was drawn to him like a fly to shit.

Damn!

I had underestimated David's power over me. His presence affected me deeply. His touch had aroused an almost frantic ache deep within me. I closed my eyes and realized I was in trouble.

Chapter 6

I WOKE UP THE NEXT morning feeling more tired than I had before I went to bed.

Damn you, David.

After a night of tossing and turning with memories of him disturbing my dreams, I arrived at the office an hour later than usual.

I entered through the side to avoid traveling through the maze of applicants normally in the lobby at this time of the day. Mornings were a busy time. My interviewer scheduled most of the interviews and typing tests early, allowing plenty of time in the afternoon to conduct reference checks.

Moving down the hallway, the sound of my pumps was muffled against the mauve carpeting. I stepped into the large office on the left to find each of my staff on the telephone. On the floor were my staffing supervisor, Sherrie Sneed, and two staffing specialists, Tracy Parks and Amber Boswell. They were responsible for taking job orders, screening candidates and filling them with the best person possible. My sales team consisted of my manager Debbie and two sales associates, Jean and Sandra. All three were already out in the field making sales calls. In the front office were my payroll specialist Allison Simmons; interviewer Tyla Gavin; and my longest employee, receptionist and part-time mother hen, Norma Brown.

I moved near the cubicle to the left just as Sherrie had completed a call.

"Good morning, team. How's it going?" I asked.

The very petite coffee-colored woman swiveled around in her chair with a deeply embedded frown at the center of her forehead. "We're having a bad morning. Five call-ins, three no-shows and Aisha showed up at work yesterday with a newly pierced tongue ring."

"She what! What's wrong with that girl?" I grumbled as I lowered my briefcase to the floor. "Where's she working?"

When Sherrie hesitated, my eyes widened with realization. "Please don't tell me she already started in the finance department."

My supervisor gave me a painful nod. "I'm afraid she started last Friday. Georgia is livid."

Damn! Georgia Jefferson was manager of the city's finance department and a hard woman to please. Over half the temporaries we had ever sent her way, she seemed to have had one problem or another. Aisha would be our third replacement in a month.

Before the city stepped in and began monitoring staffing expenditures, Georgia had the liberty of using any service of her choice. In the ten years that she'd overseen the finance department, Georgia built a relationship with the manager of Staffing Unlimited. When the city decided to cut employment costs, temporary agencies were forced to bid on yearly contracts with the city. Kelly Services had won the contract and Staffing Solutions was used to subcontract the large demand.

Georgia argued both agencies were incompetent; only capable of providing unqualified candidates. Even though she lost the battle, she made certain the two agencies knew they were second rate every chance she got.

Feeling a headache coming on, I dropped down onto the chair beside Sherrie and faced her. "What does Georgia want beside my head on a platter?" My bark of humor lacked laughter.

Sherrie leaned forward resting her chin in the palm of her hand. "She wants someone to come over this morning and ask Aisha to either remove the ring or leave."

I glanced down at my watch. It was almost nine o'clock. "Why didn't she call yesterday and complain? At least then we could have called Aisha at home and asked her not to wear the ring again."

"That's what I told her, but she said her supervisor just brought it to her attention this morning." Unable to sit still, Sherrie sat back in the chair with her thin fingers tensed in her lap.

I threw my hands up in the air and mumbled under my breath that it was going to be one hell of a great day. I could feel it already. Damn you, David! I scowled inward. My bad morning wasn't really his fault, although he was the reason why I hadn't gotten much sleep. Not that I had been getting much sleep lately. Nevertheless, I had to blame someone, and he was the only person who came to mind.

"Have you tried to call Aisha?" I asked.

Tracy who had been quiet up to this point, twirled around in her chair and replied, "I did. Her cell phone is disconnected."

"Great," I mumbled. I tapped my fingernails lightly on top of the desk as I pondered a solution, then settled back, disappointed. What would have possessed Aisha Winters to do something so stupid as to pierce her tongue? I sighed. I had done everything I could to help her. With very limited skills, I had advised her interviewer to train Aisha on Word and Excel, two very demanding software packages. I had even gone a step further. When Aisha informed me that she didn't have proper clothing, I started a clothing pantry so people in similar situations would not have to feel ashamed. My staff and I spent a Saturday afternoon converting a large room we weren't using in the rear of the suite to store the clothing. I had since received donations from organizations all around the city.

Staffing Solutions had been partnering with the Welfare to Work Program for almost two years. The program had a high success rate.

Several participants of the program went on to full-time positions, allowing them to finally get off public assistance.

Aisha was one of several participants who had been sent my way. Barely twenty-one and already with two children, she had come to us eager to find a full-time position. Sherrie had been hesitant about sending her out to do anything other than short-term assignments. However, because she'd received high marks while on three other assignments, I ignored the warning bells and insisted that Aisha be given a temp-to-hire position.

"I'll go," I finally said.

Sherrie looked surprised. "Calaine, you don't have to."

"Yes I do." I rose from the chair. "I'm the one who wanted to give her a chance." I sighed.

Sherrie had over ten years' experience in the industry and was good at what she did, but under the circumstances, she was ill-equipped to undertake the task of Georgia Jefferson. I wouldn't have forced that stress on my worst enemy. It was like sending Daniel in the lion's den. However, somebody had to do it and that person was me.

Reaching down, I picked up my briefcase and headed towards the break room. "I hope there's some coffee ready, because I'm going to need it."

I pulled my car into a thirty-minute parking space in front of the Municipal Building just before ten. Staring out at the building, I thought about how old the structure was. It had a gothic appearance. My grandmother had once told me the building had been around long before she was a child.

Climbing out of the car, I reached into my purse and fished out two quarters, then fed them into the meter. When a breeze ruffled my hair, I scowled. It was too beautiful a morning to have to deal with personnel issues. However, it wasn't the first time and wasn't going to be the last.

On an average of three times a month, Staffing Solutions was asked to replace an employee. Lately our replacement rate was at an all-time low, which was proof we were taking the extra time to fill the position with the most qualified individual, opposed to just filling it with anyone just to get the job done. Recently, however, personalities had begun to play a major part in the screening process. Companies were not only wanting qualifications but also an individual whose personality was a perfect match for their organization.

This appeared to be one of those situations.

I pushed through the revolving door, then moved across the marble lobby with purposeful strides. I smoothed down the front of a long white skirt that molded my hips and thighs. The blue linen jacket had short sleeves and one button across the front. The sound of my navy-blue pumps echoed in the hallway as I strolled to the last office on the right.

I entered the administration office where Georgia's receptionist was on the phone. Delaney acknowledged me with a smile and pointed a pink talon-length fingernail toward the rear of the office, signaling it was okay to go back.

Georgia was sitting behind her desk just finishing up a call when I walked in. She was an average-looking fifty plus woman with an olive complexion, silver gray hair and a rotund body. As she hung up the phone, she returned my smile with one that didn't quite reach her blue eyes.

"I'm so glad you're here. We have a problem."

She signaled me to sit. I took the seat across from her desk, dropping my purse strap from my shoulder. Reading Georgia's strained expression, I nodded knowingly. "Sherrie told me. I want to apologize. I will ask her to remove the ring at once."

Georgia was still. Her gaze intent as she replied, "I would like you to ask Asia not to return."

I frowned at the way she mispronounced her name. She'd probably done it on purpose. Vertical lines appeared around her eyes. "Why is that?"

Georgia looked surprised I would have even asked such a question. "I think that part should be obvious. Asia, well, she just isn't right for this department. I don't think she has the maturity this position requires, and the tongue ring proves that."

Pursing my lips, I tried to keep my tone light. "*Aisha* works in the mailroom. How much daily interaction with the public does the job require?"

Georgia met my direct stare. "Well, none. However, that's not the point."

"Then what is the point?" I asked around a tight smile.

"This department requires a very well-rounded individual with not only skills, but maturity."

My temperature flared, however I reminded myself that the customer was always right. "Very well. We will begin screening for someone else as soon as I return to the office." I rose, slipped the strap of my purse back over my shoulder, then forced a polite smile. "Where may I find *Aisha*?"

Georgia pointed. "The mailroom is down the stairs, first room on the left."

I nodded and spun around, heading towards the door.

"Calaine, um, just a moment," Georgia called over my shoulder.

I turned and glanced her way.

The older woman cleared her throat, then leaned forward with her fingers steepled. "I'm willing to wait as long as it takes until we find just the right person."

"I understand," I replied with a nod. "Since this will be our third replacement, we will take that into consideration."

Georgia cleared her throat. "I would like for you to also consider the individual's ethnicity."

My brow rose in surprise. "Excuse me?" I stood there shocked, shaking. There was no way I had heard her right.

Georgia smiled, trying to lighten the mood. "I think it is only fair you take into consideration the feelings of the individual as well. My staff is predominately white. I believe Aisha may have felt a little uncomfortable."

I dropped my arm, the strap falling from my shoulder again. "Are you sure it isn't *you* who feels uncomfortable?" I asked bluntly.

"Oh no, n-not at all," Georgia stuttered. "I just feel that if you could find a mature Caucasian woman, it would be to everyone's best interest."

I brought a hand to my hip. "As you know, Georgia, screening according to race, creed or color is against the law."

"Of course it is. All I'm asking is that you take it in consideration," she quickly corrected.

"And I'm telling you I won't do it," I retorted. "That's not that way I do business. I can screen for the best fit and that's where I draw the line. Color will not now or ever play a role in my company's screening process. I hope I've made myself clear." With that, I spun on my heels and departed the room. I didn't care if Georgia ever used my services again. Discrimination was one thing I would not tolerate.

Looking straight ahead, I walked through the office. I wanted to grab Aisha and depart the building as quickly as we possibly could. I hated dismissing employees; however, this was one time when I felt I was doing one a favor. As long as I was in business, none of my employees, black or white, would ever be subjected to that type of racial behavior.

Returning to the problem at hand, I descended the stairs and followed the signs that lead me to the mailroom. I nibbled on the inside of my jaw, hating to break the news to Aisha, even though I knew it was my responsibility to do so.

Aisha had come in the office only last week to thank my staff for providing her with steady employment and even went on to say how great it felt to have a purpose to wake up every morning. Now I had to burst her bubble.

Entering the mailroom, the floor supervisor, a fat bald man, met me at the door. Seeing the grin on his face when I introduced myself, I could almost bet he was the one who had called Georgia and complained.

He directed me to a cubicle at the back of the room. I moved through the maze and found Aisha in front of a sorter, humming while it tossed mail into several bins. Aisha turned when she saw me. She looked surprised and then delighted I had come to see her.

"Hi, Ms. Hart."

I returned the smile. Aisha's glowing youthful face had finally emerged. I remembered the sorrow that used to weigh her down. She seemed relaxed and happy about life, which made the task at hand even harder to digest.

"Hello, Aisha."

"Are you checking up on me?" she teased. When she smiled, I noticed the gold stud protruding from the center of her tongue and remembered it was the original reason for my visit.

"Can I speak to you privately for a moment?"

Aisha saw the sober expression on my face, and she stilled. "Is something wrong?"

I nodded. "I'm afraid so. I need you to grab your things and follow me."

"D-did I do something wrong?" she asked.

Noting the fear in her expression, I shook my head and gave a tender smile. "No, you didn't, but we'll talk about it when we get outside."

Quietly, Aisha put the mail down and moved to grab a beat-up leather purse and a brown sack that looked to contain her lunch. Together we walked past the others. The floor supervisor stood to the side, still grinning as we departed. I ignored him as I signaled Aisha to walk beside me, shuffling her feet.

"Are you sure you got everything?" I asked when we reached the lobby.

Aisha nodded.

"If not, call me and I will pick it up. You are not to return to the mailroom for anything," I informed her as we traveled through the revolving door.

As soon as we reached the sidewalk, Aisha swung around and faced me. "Will you please tell me what's going on? I mean just last Friday they was tellin' me I was doin' a good job?"

I could see that she was hurting, and it tugged at my insides. Shifting my weight to my other leg, I looked down at Aisha. "They didn't feel as if you were a good match. The position requires someone with several years of experience. They are also considering reclassifying the position to include a year of data entry experience."

"Oh," was all she could say. "You sure it wasn't cause I'm black. I see how all deem white folks be lookin' at me."

I noted the dejected look on her face. She knew I had lied, but she and I both knew that other than in-house training, she had no real hands on computer training. I hoped Aisha understood the reason because there was no way I could ever mention color. All I needed was for the local NAACP chapter to come knocking on my door. In a small city like ours, discrimination would cause quite a stir.

"No, not at all, however that piece of jewelry you stuck in your tongue didn't help matters at all. It is very unprofessional. That's like showing up at work dressed like a hoochie."

Aisha smirked at my choice of words. "My cousin dared me to do it."

"Well, it looks tacky. Stick out your tongue," I ordered.

Like an obedient child, Aisha obeyed. After a quick examination, I could tell the piercing had been done rather recently. The base of her tongue was red and swollen.

I sighed with frustration. "Aisha, I can't help you if you do stuff like this." I didn't normally talk to my employees on such a personal level, but I had known Aisha long enough to know what it would take to talk some sense into her.

Aisha nibbled on her lower lip like a scolded child. "I'm sorry. I promise not to wear it to work no mo'. Does this mean I'm fired?"

"No, not at all." I noticed her shoulders relax and was glad that some of the tension had dissipated. "It's not your fault. The finance department is a tough department to please. You are their third replacement in a month." I watched Aisha smile, pleased she wasn't the only one they had let go. "They require a certain caliber of person that I don't think we can provide them." I thought about the conversation I'd had with Georgia regarding *caliber.* "Call the office tomorrow, and I'll have Sherrie find you another assignment."

"Thanks, Ms. Hart."

I smiled. "You're welcome."

Glancing around, Aisha hesitated before asking, "You think you can give me a ride home?"

"Sure, come on." I signaled for her to follow me to the car.

By the time I had returned to the office, Sherrie was waiting for me in the hallway. "How did it go?"

"As well as expected. Aisha was hurt but she's a big girl. She'll get over it. I told her to give you a call in the morning so you can find her another assignment," I said over my shoulder as she stepped into my private office with Sherrie right behind me. "Be careful where you send her. Her tongue is pretty swollen, so it will probably be a while before she can remove that piercing." I dropped my purse and keys on the desk. "I guess you need to start finding a replacement for the mailroom."

There was a pregnant pause before Sherrie spoke. "Georgia called just before you arrived."

With an irritated sigh, I moved behind my desk. "What does she want now?" The woman was a pain in my ass.

"She decided to let Kelly Services refill the position."

I mumbled several four-letter words before deciding it was probably for the best. "I think that is probably a wise decision."

"Did something happen I need to know about?" Sherrie asked curiously.

"Nothing I can't handle." To me, Georgia was already water under the bridge.

I sat in my seat, then smiled up at Sherrie. "How are we doing screening the customer service positions for Verizon?"

Sherrie beamed with pride. "We have already filled ten."

"Good. That means we only have ten more to go."

When Sherrie departed and returned to the floor, I slipped off my shoes and leaned back in the chair. With my palm to my cheek, I sighed. It was going to be a long day.

I spent the rest of the morning returning phone calls and signing invoices that my secretary had prepared. The bonus checks looked quite well this billing cycle. My staff was going to be pleased.

The phone rang and I reached for the receiver by the second ring. "Staffing Solutions, this is Calaine."

I heard a faint voice on the line. "Yes, I would like to request fifty telemarketers for tomorrow."

"Excuse me?" Someone was out of their mind.

I heard chuckles. Someone was playing with me. "Who is this?" I insisted.

The laughter grew deeper before I realized it was David. "Very funny."

"I'm sorry, Keke, I couldn't resist."

"Still the jokester, I see."

"Life's too short. We're supposed to have fun."

"If you say so," I murmured, pretending to be annoyed. "What do you want?"

If David had registered the ice in my voice, he totally ignored it. "Can I come by? I have something I think you'll want to see."

"What is it?" I could not camouflage the curiosity in my voice.

"If you want to find out, you'll have to invite me over." After a prolonged pause he added, "I have a lead for you."

"Did you visit the School of Nursing?" I asked, hoping he'd at least give me a hint. I hated surprises.

"Yes," he finally said. "But I'm not telling you anything more. Can I come over or not?" he repeated.

The corner of my lips curled upward at his determination. I needed him more than I had realized. And for that reason I gave into my curiosity. "Why don't you drop by my place this evening."

"I thought you'd never ask."

"I'll see you at seven," I replied.

"I'll bring dinner." David hung up before I could protest.

Chapter 7

AFTER THE INCIDENT with Aisha, I had been so busy I hadn't had time to think, much less try to explore my past. However, by the time I was driving home, I had made the decision to call my mother's sister and try again for answers. There had to be a reason why she hadn't told me the truth and I was determined to find out what that was. In addition, I decided to accompany David to San Antonio.

Turning onto my street, I grinned. I lived in a comfortable family neighborhood a short distance from work. I waved at my neighbors, an elderly couple, who'd lived on the block longer than I had been in existence. Together they were outside tending to their yard.

I hurried into the house, dropped my mail on the table without looking at it and rushed to my bedroom to take a quick shower. After toweling off, I rubbed down in my favorite peach-scented lotion, then slipped into a pair of jeans and a white cotton shirt. I fingered mousse through my hair, vowing that tomorrow I would call my beautician. Looking in the mirror, I caught myself reaching for my make-up bag before I stopped myself. What was I doing? It was only David. Yet, I had bathed, brushed my teeth, rubbed on my favorite lotion and was now considering lipstick and eyeliner. What was the point? I tried to convince myself I wasn't interested in him as my fingers curled around my mascara brush. I was doing it for myself. *Just a little mascara nothing more.* I am a woman after all, and there is nothing wrong with keeping it cute.

By seven, I had washed a load of laundry and was folding clothes on the dining room table when I heard a knock at the door. Even though I had been listening out for the purr of his expensive car, my heart went off in a tailspin. I took a deep breath to maintain my composure before I walked through the foyer to greet him.

When I opened the door, I found it impossible to breath before I realized I had been holding my breath. A smile curved his lips, deepening the dimples on either side of his cheeks. There was no mistaking the magnetism that made David so attractive. I blinked trying to pull my eyes away but couldn't quite yet. Instead, I took in the blue polo-style short-sleeved shirt he was wearing that revealed strong dark forearms. His jeans were faded with wear, fitting his hips snugly. This was the first time I had seen him in jeans since college and he still looked just as good he had then. I suddenly had a yearning for him to turn around so I could see if he still had a scrumptious ass.

"Hey, beautiful." His voice was low, soft and intentionally seductive.

I raised my gaze back to his face and froze as I stared at him. David was the most masculine man I'd ever laid eyes on. Over the years, nothing had changed, only intensified. Sexy, irresistible, sensual, those words didn't begin to describe him. It went a lot deeper than that. No man should look that good. And it bothered me. It bothered me that I noticed, and my traitorous body chose to respond.

"Are you going to let me in?" David asked with a glint of humor in his eyes.

I stepped aside so he could enter. I had been so busy eyeing his physique, the bags he was carrying had gone unnoticed.

"What do you have?" I asked.

He waved a large bag in front of my nose. "Tony's Pizza and gyros."

"Yummy." Their Greek-style pizza was the best in town.

I followed him into the kitchen as if it were his house. While he set the bags on the table, I went to the pantry to find paper plates and napkins, then placed them on the table next to a large Greek salad.

As I walked over to the refrigerator, I called over my shoulder, "Iced tea or lemonade?"

"Iced tea would be great," he answered as he finished emptying the bags.

I removed an iced cold pitcher of freshly brewed sun tea from the top shelf, then looked in the dishwasher and removed two glasses.

While filling each glass with ice, I glanced out the corner of my eye as David unwrapped one of the gyros. The smell of lamb drifted under my nose. Watching his large hands, I thought about them touching me, and my body immediately responded. I jerked. *Stop it Calaine!* I had to pull myself together quickly.

David must have sensed me watching him because he paused from what he was doing and smiled over at me, a smile so charming the warning bells went off.

"Everything okay?" he asked as if he didn't know. Okay, maybe he didn't, or at least I hoped he didn't.

"Everything's fine." I took a deep breath. Why had I made the mistake of inviting him to my house again?

I carried the glasses over and sat them on the table, making certain not to rub against David. When he lifted the lid of the pizza box, my eyes widened. "Ham and pineapple! How'd you remember it was my favorite?"

Standing dangerously close, he looked at me—a smile as intimate as a kiss. "Some things you never forget."

My skin tingled by the innuendo of his words and all I could think about was how wonderful his lips had felt. I remembered clearly how my heart had leaped against my chest, and when he kissed me every cell in my soul had urged me to respond. Never had I felt anything remotely close to the fierce hunger that ripped my body as he held me in his arms. In fact, it came dangerously close to the intense feeling I was experiencing right about now. I shook my head and as swiftly as the thought had arisen, I shifted it.

"So what's the big surprise?" I asked and heard the irritation in my voice. David didn't seem to notice.

"I'll show you after we eat," David said as he sat in a chair and reached for a slice of pizza.

I nodded although the last thing I wanted was to feel like the two of us were spending quality time together. Dropping by with information was one thing, coming over to share a meal was another thing all together. I had been waiting since this afternoon for information I was certain David had gathered about my past.

"What if I don't want to wait?" I challenged.

He took a thirsty sip, then glanced up at me towering over him. "Too bad. I bet you skipped lunch."

He was right, I had.

"If this is the only way I can get you to eat, then so be it. Now sit down and eat," he ordered.

Without any further protest, I flopped down in the seat opposite him. This time, when he reached for my hand, I was prepared to bow my head, but not for the electric charge that zipped up my arm and then soared down to the space between my thighs.

A soft gasp escaped my parted lips. Damn him! By the time he said "amen" and I opened my eyes, I found David staring and watching me with interest. I rolled my eyes and reached for a slice of pizza.

"Have you made a decision yet about San Antonio?" he asked between chews.

"Yes, I'll go with you."

"Good," he replied and looked pleased. "How about we leave next Friday and return on Monday?"

I nodded, then reached for my glass. "How long a drive is that?" Twelve, fifteen hours? I couldn't imagine being in the car with him for that many hours. It would be completely unnerving.

David chuckled openly. "Too many to count. We're going to fly."

I sighed with relief, then raised the pizza to my lips. "Fine, just let me know what time so I can book my flight."

"I've already taken care of it," David mumbled with his mouth full.

I stopped chewing to glare at him. "If you had already taken care of the arrangements, then why did you even bother to ask me if I would be ready to leave on Friday?"

David shrugged a broad shoulder. "Out of courtesy."

"Courtesy!" I barked. He had a lot of balls and was still as arrogant as ever. "What if I had said no?"

"But you didn't," he challenged.

Heat flared at my cheeks. "No, but that's beside the point."

"No, I think that is the point. I know you're anxious to find your mother and nothing's going to stand in the way of that."

I chewed my pizza in silence while wishing I had a quick retort for his arrogance. Instead, I met the challenging glint in his eyes and said nothing.

David studied me a few seconds longer before I heard him say, "Would you like me to apologize?"

I made a sound halfway between a snort and a chuckle. "Do you even know what you're apologizing for?"

"No, not really," he admitted honestly.

"Then don't bother." I took one last bite of my pizza and rose from the table.

That was the problem with him. He had always taken it for granted that a woman would feel honored to have the Great David Soul taking control of the situation. Well, this was one time he had been sadly mistaken.

After wiping his mouth again with a napkin, he reached into a small bag on the table. "Here, I brought you something," he said.

I swung around and noticed the dark bound book in his hand. My breath caught in my throat, then there was a noticeable pause before I asked, "What is it?"

"It's a yearbook."

I didn't even have to ask to know the book was from the School of Nursing. I took it from his outstretched hand. Holding it like a newborn baby, I slowly moved into the living room and sat on the couch. My fingers shook as a multitude of emotions vibrated through my body. I felt as if the wind had been knocked from my lungs.

"Are you okay?" David asked.

I hadn't even heard him follow me into the room, nor had I realized he was caressing my cheek. Instead, I began to shake. I was scared. It was the fear of what I might discover in the pages of the book that made my blood cold in my veins.

David draped a comforting arm around my shoulders. My body heated, but I didn't shrug him away. Instead, I glanced up at him and could see that he was genuinely concerned about me. The look of those gold-green eyes was compassionate. The tenderness brought tears to my eyes. Resting my cheek against his chest, I squeezed my eyes shut as I took several seconds to feed off his strength. I was going to get through this. As hard as it seemed, I was going to manage no matter what I found out.

After a long silent moment, I finally raised my head and nodded. "Okay, I think I'm ready."

I flipped through the black and white photos until I came across the faces that had become familiar to me.

David's mom and godmother were in several shots together and then I found a group photo of the freshman class. It was easy to identify the six women since they were the only African Americans in the group.

I saw girl number three, Ursula Winters, with long brown hair that was pulled up in a loose ponytail. She had dark mahogany skin with enormous brown eyes and a generous smile. In the same photo, I found Dorlinda Meyers, raisin-brown, tall, with a wide nose and short hair. In the center was Coletta Ross, light-skinned, with tight slanted eyes. The third row from the left was the final woman, Eunice Roberts, the woman who had allegedly committed suicide. She had an average height and build with a cinnamon complexion, and large round topaz eyes. She had worn her shoulder length hair in a traditional seventies flip.

I could not pull my gaze away from the photos as I tried to catalog every feature from their hair to their lips.

"One of these women is my mother," I finally whispered. "I just know it."

David squeezed my hand. "We've got our work cut out," he said, breaking into my thoughts.

I had almost forgotten he was there. I eased back to look at him. "We?"

Leaning closer, the fragrance of his body lingered in my nostrils. "We're in this together."

Closing the book, I shifted from under his arm. My head came up slowly and I found David watching, waiting for me to speak.

"Why are you helping me?"

Eyes fused, he replied, "Do you have to ask?"

I swallowed. "Yes."

"Because I want to. I like being around you."

What is this really about? Helping an old friend or the challenge of melting my icy heart? I just hadn't quite figured it out yet.

I stared wordlessly at him for several seconds and suddenly felt self-conscious under his watchful eye. I smoothed down my hair and frowned. "Isn't there some woman you could be spending your time with?"

"This is the second time you've tried to find out if I'm seeing someone in a roundabout way," he replied with dangerous softness.

My voice was hesitant. "No. I just think there has to be something else you could be doing besides hanging out with me."

"You're right. There is something else I could be doing." David's eyes were fixed on my mouth. I drew in a sharp intake of my breath as he scooped me up into his arms and positioned me across his lap.

My heart galloped making mincemeat of my willpower. Was he about to kiss me again? I didn't want David to get the impression that he could kiss me whenever he felt the urge, however, despite my best effort my lips yearned to feel his again. Ever so slowly, I tilted my head and parted my lips.

It occurred to me that I might have lost my mind, but I didn't say a single word to stop David from settling his mouth against mine. After all, I had pretty much given him the green flag. Slanting my mouth, I met his lips eagerly. His soft mustache caused tingles of excitement to race through me like a raging river. This was what I had been wanting all day, no matter how much I tried to deny it. His kisses were sweet, hot and gentle. As he pulled me snuggly against him, I wrapped my arms around his neck and the kiss deepened.

It had been too long since I had been held by a man. When David traced my lips, I opened for him without a second thought and the feel of his tongue gently sliding into my mouth sent heat soaring through my veins. David explored, and I lost control giving into the need, meeting every sensual stroke as he tasted and teased. My toes curled and an empty ache pooled deep inside me until a feverous moan escaped my lips. Only David was capable of kissing me with such mind-shattering tenderness and mastery.

Somehow, his hand slipped under my blouse. He pushed my lacy bra aside and cupped the fullness of my breasts. It wasn't until I felt his fingers caress my rock-hard nipple that my brain zapped back to reality.

"Don't," I commanded as I was suddenly anxious to put some distance between us. I tried to scramble off his lap, but David held on firmly to my waist refusing to let go.

"Why?" he asked in a thick breathy voice.

"Because I'm not looking for that," I snapped, annoyed for letting things go as far as they had.

His lean dark fingers came up to caress my cheek. "Then what are you looking for?"

Seeing the smoldering desire in the depths of his hazel eyes, my heart pumped rapidly. I paused a moment longer, then admitted softly, "I-I'm not sure. But whatever it is, I know I don't want it from you."

"And why is that?"

I couldn't even look at him because if I did, I would be the one initiating the next kiss. "Because you and my best friend have a past, and I don't operate that way."

"It didn't stop you before?"

"T-that was a mistake. I was drunk. I didn't know what I was doing."

"Would it help if I say nothing ever happened between Donna and I?"

"No, it doesn't matter. Donna will be here in a few weeks, and I know for a fact she is anxious to see you," I added stubbornly.

"Keep fooling yourself. It was never about me and Donna. It was about me and you." Before I could find my voice, he added. "You are attracted to me. And I know I'm crazy about you."

He lowered my head to his chest. I didn't fight. I closed my eyes, confused about what I was doing. This was not what I wanted, I told myself. There was nothing going on between us besides a friend providing comfort when I needed it most.

David reached over for the remote and clicked on the television. While he watched the news, I closed my eyes again. In the comfort of his arms, I soon began to doze off. My lips curled into a smile as I allowed myself to dream that things were different in my life.

I FELT DAVID BRUSH back several strands of my hair. I marveled at the feel of his velvety smooth hand against my skin. "Sweetheart?"

"Uh?"

I snuggled my body closer to him.

"Are you falling asleep?"

"No," I denied.

"Then what would you call it?"

My lips dipped into a smile as I realized what I was doing. "I guess I am a little tired." My voice had a dreamy sound to it.

David dropped a kiss to my forehead, then the side of my face traveling down near my ear. With a soft sigh, I threw my head back giving him access to my neck. He moved to taste the hollow of my throat, and I realized that again it was growing almost impossible to stay in control. It appeared I wasn't the only one.

I pulled back, nibbling my lower lip. My eyes caught his gaze. David dipped his head, brushing his lips with mine. Damn! They were firm and full and when he parted them the warmth of his breath brushed over mine. Goodness. He smelled wonderful and his mouth was so intoxicating. I let him take control, closed my eyes and enjoyed the moment. David drew me closer to him. I felt the warmth of his body and tried to slow this moment down in my mind. But the evidence of his arousal was pressed against me and it was close to impossible.

His tongue danced with mine in a rhythm that had my mind swinging. All I could think about was what was happening right now. I thought instead of the way his flesh felt against mine. I thought of the way his lips parted my lips and his tongue was pushing past the barriers and tasting me deep.

The way he took control of the entire embrace. Control. It had always been something I prided myself on, but now it seemed unnecessary. I was willing for him to take over.

His arms were big and strong as he wrapped them around me and I felt the muscles of his upper arms, the strength in him. I put my hands on his shoulder and pushed back to look at his face.

"I'm going to go home and let you get some sleep. If I stay any longer, I might not be responsible for my actions," he said.

I looked up at him, eyelids heavy and saw the open invitation smoldering in the depths of his eyes. I made a noise that sounded like a moan, then closed my eyes again, snuggling closer. It would be so easy to just say yes.

"You're right. I do have an early day tomorrow."

With me still in his arms, David carried me to the front door where he lowered me gently to my feet. Holding me close, he whispered in my hair, "I borrowed that book from the alumni office."

I locked my arms around his waist and tilted my head up to meet his heated gaze. It would be so easy to give in to everything I was feeling. "I promise to take care of it."

"Good." With a groan, his hands came up to caress my face. He captured my lips in another passionate kiss for a long sensuous moment before he moved to my chin and then my throat. He could have swept me into his arms again and carried me to the bedroom and I wouldn't have protested. Instead, he lifted my face for one last, sweet kiss, then eased back to stare down at me. His grin was rueful. "Lock up. I'll call you tomorrow."

With a sleepy yawn, I nodded and closed the door behind him, securing the deadbolt.

I padded to my bedroom, pulled off my clothes and climbed under the covers. It was almost midnight before my mind settled and my eyelids shut only to dream of David. My mind and body were at war, and I had a feeling I was going to lose the battle.

Chapter 8

ON SUNDAY, I DECIDED to pay my uncle a visit.

Thaddeus and his wife, Alma, lived near the state capitol in Jefferson City, a thirty-minute drive from my driveway to theirs.

Shortly before five o'clock, I pulled my car in front of a beautifully maintained, two-story, red brick home in an established neighborhood where most of the residents were retired. The front garden had a large oak tree and the petunias on the side of the house had blossomed since my last visit.

I climbed out of the car to find my aunt in the yard tending to her flowers. She was a round petite woman who wore a short, tapered salt and pepper cut. The effect was dramatic with her round face and small pudgy nose.

Hearing the car door slam, Alma looked up. When she realized who it was, she raised from the kneeling position on the ground. "Hello, dear." Removing her garden gloves, she walked to me and gave a warm embrace. "How are you holding up?" she asked, as we pulled apart, her coal black eyes studying me.

I smiled at her lovely face. "I'm managing."

Alma's expression grew sober and concerned. "If you need any help with the house, please let me know."

"I promise." My eyes misted. My aunt had always managed to make me feel loved and welcomed. Hand in hand, we moved into the house where I found my uncle sitting in the sunroom sipping iced tea and reading the newspaper.

Thaddeus smiled when I entered the room. "There's my Keke. Come sit down and keep me company." He folded the paper and lowered it to the table.

I leaned over and planted a kiss on his cheek. "I didn't mean to disturb you. I won't be staying long," I said as I sat in the seat beside him.

He shook his head, dismissing the idea. "Nonsense, you're always welcome. Please stay for dinner."

I glanced from my uncle to my aunt. "Oh no, I don't want to impose. I can eat when I get back home."

Alma shook her head. "There's no imposition. I made a meal big enough for a football team."

I giggled knowingly. Alma liked to cook extra and freeze servings for future meals. "Well, in that case, dinner sounds wonderful."

Thaddeus patted my hand. "Good. You could use a little fattening up. You don't look like you've been eating much lately."

I understood their concern. I hadn't realized how much weight I had lost until I climbed on the scale the previous night. It was a shock to discover I had lost more than ten pounds. At one hundred and forty-two pounds and five-foot seven inches, I had always been a slim woman, so even a few pounds were quite a bit.

"I promise to clean my plate." I was teasing, however, my aunt and uncle both looked pleased. Alma left and returned with another glass and a pitcher of iced tea, then retreated to the kitchen to finish preparing dinner.

"What have you been doing?" Thaddeus asked, his eyes sparkling with interest.

I sighed. "I'm still trying to find my mother."

Thaddeus gave me a sympathetic smile. "Something will turn up eventually."

"Actually, I've been doing quite well. I ran into an old friend of mine and discovered that one of the women in the photograph is his mother." I explained how David discovered the photo in my office.

He studied me. "You're one determined young lady."

"I've learned from the best." I grinned. With my elbow on the table, I rested my chin in the palm of my hand. "I know it's going to take time, but I am certain she's still out there."

"Keke, baby, I—"

"Please, Uncle Tad, don't say it. My mind is already set. I have to find out the truth."

He took a sip of his tea and stared at me for the longest time before saying, "I hate to see you get hurt. Sometimes people just don't want to be found."

"And sometimes they do. I won't be able to rest until I know for sure."

Seeing the stubborn set of my jaw, he simply nodded. "I've passed the word around at the hospital. Hopefully, someone will remember something. Columbia's small. I'm sure someone is bound to know how to get in touch with at least one of them."

"I hope so." I poured myself a glass of tea. "David borrowed a copy of their yearbook from the nursing school, so I now have the names of each of the women. He's going to San Antonio on Friday to attend his sister's graduation, and I have agreed to go with him so I can speak to his mother and Wanda."

Thaddeus ran a hand over his face as he sighed. "Then that leaves four women."

Ursula, Coletta, Dorlinda, and Eunice.

I took a long drink before saying, "David is going to do a public search on the Internet and see what he can come up with. I tried but came up empty."

With his observant gaze, Thaddeus studied me quietly for several seconds before asking, "How well do you know this man?"

I set down my glass and deliberately looked out at the rose garden behind him. "What do you mean?"

"I mean is there something going on between the two of you?"

"N-no, nothing at all. He's j-just helping me," I stuttered.

Thaddeus raised a brow at my rapid response. Damn. He knows I only stuttered when I'm nervous. "You're not fooling anybody," he said with a smirk.

"I'm serious. I don't have time for a relationship right now."

He shook his head at my protest. "That's not what I'm saying. I just think you're fooling yourself. I saw the way your face lit up when you were talking about him."

Thaddeus captured my hand. "You have every right to get on with your life. No one will blame you if you do. You're a beautiful young woman with your entire life ahead of you. I don't want you to become so consumed with finding your mother that you put everything else on hold."

"How can I ever have a relationship with a man without knowing who I really am?"

"You're Calaine Hart. What else is there to know?"

My expression narrowed. "Uncle Tad, you know what I mean. I need to know where I came from. What if I want to adopt and finally start a family? I would want my children to know."

"I wish you would. Alma and I aren't getting any younger. We're depending on you to give us some great-nieces and nephews," he replied with a lopsided grin.

I smiled.

As he released my hand, his expression sobered again. "Keke, I want you to be happy."

"Happy or happily married?" I teased.

"Both would be nice," he admitted with another grin.

While tapping a fingernail lightly on the table, I said, "I would like to talk to Aunt Greta and see if she will shed a little light on my past."

Thaddeus frowned. He had never cared for the woman. "When was the last time you've talked to her?"

"It's been awhile. She hasn't taken my mother's death well. I thought about driving to Kansas City to see her."

"Maybe that would be a good idea."

Alma called for us to come and eat. We stood and my uncle draped an arm across my shoulders as we left the sun porch and stepped into the dining room. My aunt had fixed my favorites: pot roast and mashed potatoes with homegrown string beans and her special made-from-scratch biscuits. After eating fast food and microwave meals all week, I looked forward to a home-cooked meal for a change.

I turned to her; my brown eyes wide with surprise. "How did you know I was coming?"

"Call it an auntie's intuition." Alma leaned over and draped an arm around my waist. "We haven't seen you in a while. I figured you'd start feeling guilty and come by sooner or later. I was hoping it was today. If not, we'd have to eat all this pot roast by ourselves."

My eyes became misty at the love I received in their house. How could I have ever felt as if I was alone in the world? If I never found my mother, it was good to know at least there were two people in my life who adored me.

I stayed long enough for dessert and a game of chess with my uncle before I kissed them both goodbye. I promised to call before I left on Friday.

I pulled my car in the garage, then lowered the electric door. Shutting off the car, I was met with a wave of silence, the same sound I would hear when I get inside the house. I sighed, then reached across the seat to retrieve my purse before getting out. Entering through the side door, I put my keys and purse on the table. I reached for my cell phone and looked down, checking for a text message or a missed call only to find there were none. *Who were you expecting to call,* I asked myself. David? I didn't bother to answer; instead, I moved to my room and slid my feet out of my sneakers and into a pair of pink slippers.

Now what, I thought. Was I going to spend the rest of the evening staring at the photograph or spend another solitary night in front of the television, eagerly searching for something to occupy my mind?

Or someone?

"This is ridiculous," I mumbled under my breath before I rose. I refused to waste another minute thinking about David. He wasn't the type of man any woman in her right mind would trust her heart with. So why couldn't I get him out of my head?

I scowled. It was because of that kiss, or kisses, for that matter. I had made the mistake not once, but twice.

Angry with myself, I went into the kitchen and looked inside the refrigerator on the door for my last tropical wine cooler. I hoped it would help me sleep. I had no time to waste thinking about David. I already had enough on my mind and yet I found myself yearning for something I didn't have. A lover, a husband, a friend, someone to love me unconditionally. Someone to comfort me in my time of need. *Like now.* It just disturbed me that the only possibility I had was with David.

Chapter 9

"IDX EXPERIENCE SEEMS to be the most important qualifications," I informed my staff as my gaze swept around the table. We had spent the better part of the morning going over the contract with the university. After addressing every issue with a fine-tooth comb, we were able to identify that the teaching hospital's largest demand was finding qualified medical receptionists for more than two dozen clinics.

Sherrie sat back in her seat and relaxed. "Yes but finding people with IDX is going to be difficult because anybody who already has hands-on experience scheduling appointments is definitely not unemployed." Her professionally waxed eyebrows shifted slightly when I saw doubt register on her co-workers faces. "Calaine said so herself, the hospital's secretarial pool can't keep those employees. By the time the clinics have spent hours training them to use their system, they have already made the decision to keep them."

"So how about partnering with the hospital's training and development department? We could ask them to train our temporaries to use IDX," Amber suggested with the usual twinkle in her blue eyes.

Sherrie quickly agreed. "That isn't a bad idea. SOS sends their employees for training. I don't see why they won't let us send ours. After all the computer training is to benefit the hospital."

"I like that idea. I'll have to run that by Human Resources." I had been making notes of all their suggestions on my tablet. All changes and additions would be drafted tomorrow and sent by carrier on Friday. "Okay, anything else?" I asked looking around the table. When they each shook their heads no, I nodded. "Good, then let's move on. What else do we need to talk about?"

Sherrie looked down at her notes. "We've nominated Janet Jones as our employee of the month."

My gaze widened with approval. "Wonderful choice." Janet was a long-time employee who had been assigned to the courthouse for almost six months.

I reached for my half empty coffee cup. The employee of the month program had been implemented a year ago and had thus far proven to be quite successful. Employees were given an engraved plaque, dinner for two, and their picture included in the monthly newsletter. "What kind of gift certificate are we giving out this month?" I asked as I took a sip.

"How about Olive Garden?" Amber suggested.

Tracy's lips thinned noticeably. "We did that last time. We haven't used Cheddar's in a while."

When the others agreed, Sherrie nodded. "Sounds good."

While I leaned back in my chair, I listened to Debbie as she went over the prospective businesses, she had solicited the prior week and the type of employees used in each department.

"Calaine," Norma intruded over the intercom. "You have a call on line three. He says it's important."

I set the cup on the table, then moved to answer the telephone sitting on a table in the corner. "Calaine Hart speaking."

"Hi, beautiful."

"Hello." I blushed despite my best intentions not to. I wanted to be mad that David was calling me when I was in the middle of a meeting, but I was in such a good mood today that not even David Soul could ruin it.

"Sorry I told your receptionist that little white lie, but I have something I know you'll want to see. Are you free for lunch?"

I closed my eyes briefly, pleased at his offer. The weekend had been a long one with David constantly on my mind. Even though I would never admit it, I had missed him.

Glancing down at the slender gold watch on my arm, I smiled. It was barely eleven o'clock. I still had plenty of time to go over rates for the next fiscal year and make any changes long before the day was over. "Lunch would be fabulous. I should be ready around one."

"I'll see you then."

As he said goodbye, the deep sensual tone of his voice caused me to tingle. When I turned to face my staff, there was no way to mask the effect his call had over me. And they noticed. The table had grown quiet and all eyes were on me.

"There's only one thing that can cause that kind of glow and *that's* a man," Sherrie joked.

I blushed openly but remained quiet. I wasn't in the habit of sharing my personal life with my coworkers. I did however grin and say, "Let's resume our meeting because I have a date."

DAVID PULLED IN FRONT of the building at one o'clock sharp to find me already standing outside. As I moved towards his car, I felt that ridiculous flutter at my stomach again and was thankful I had worn a new outfit that complemented my complexion. My slender frame was outlined in a beige rayon pants suit, which was accessorized with pink pumps and a matching purse. I averted my gaze to the concrete so he wouldn't see the excitement in my eyes while he put the car in Park and jumped out.

"Hello, beautiful." He greeted me with a wide genuine smile that made my heart flip-flop.

"Hi," I said shyly.

Bringing a hand to my waist, he leaned forward and brushed a light gentle kiss to my lips that sent my pulse soaring.

"I've been waiting all day to do that." He pressed his lips against mine once more, then released me to open the passenger's door. David placed a hand to my elbow and guided me as I slid into the car. As I reached for my seatbelt, David shut the door and moved around to the other side and then eased his long legs into the car.

"Where are we going?" I asked once he pulled away from the curb.

"How about G&D Steakhouse?"

"Good choice." Nothing beat the taste of their charbroiled steaks, melt-in-your-mouth baked potatoes with lots of butter and sour cream, and fabulous Texas toast.

I turned my head and stared out the side window. David had the air conditioner on, and the scent of his cologne was subtle and yet arousing enough to draw my attention. I closed my eyes briefly and inhaled.

David eased the car to a stop at the red light and drew my attention when he reached onto the back seat for a manila folder and handed it to me.

I glanced down at it, then over at him. "What's this?" I was afraid to open it.

The light turned green and David put his foot on the accelerator, pulling his eyes away from the road long enough to say, "I took each of the four women's names and ran a search."

My hands began to tremble. I opened the folder and tried to focus on the papers perched across my lap. My eyes scanned through each page and found several women named Ursula, Dorlinda, Eunice and Coletta.

"I can't believe there are so many people with those unusual names."

Turning the corner, David nodded. "I was surprised myself."

"How will I know which one's the right woman?"

"I don't know. I first ran a search using their maiden name, then I considered the possibility that they have probably gotten married. Since their names are so uncommon, I also ran a search using only the first name regardless of age. But it should be easy to narrow down. Let's just say your birth mother was twenty in nineteen-seventy-five... then she should be around sixty-four," he replied as he stared out the windshield.

"Wow." Was all I could manage.

"I even found an Ursula who was seven years old." He chuckled. "In this day and age who would name their daughter Eunice, Coletta or even Ursula?"

"They are pretty old school," I admitted.

David chuckled lightly. "Can you imagine saying, Ur-su-la, come here right this minute."

I turned to smile at him. "That sounds like you're saying Ur-kel."

"No, Ur-su-la sounds a lot like Dra-cu-la," he joked as he came to stop at another red light. Looking across at each other, we dissolved into laughter. I was happy I could still find humor at a moment like this.

I socked him playfully in the forearm. "Hey, that might be my mother we're talking about." My laughter slowly died, and my expression sobered as I thought about how true my words could be. What if Ursula was my mother? My heart sped with possibilities. Answers to my past could be right at my fingertips.

I looked down at the list and found ten women named Ursula. There were twenty Eunices, fourteen Dorlindas, and seven Colettas. It would take me weeks to contact all these people. Some of them didn't even have phone numbers, which meant I would have to send a postcard or a letter of some sort. What would I possibly say? Lost in my thoughts it took me a moment before I spoke again, "I've got my work cut out."

Pulling up to another traffic light, David took my hand, drawing my attention to his dark sincere expression. "*We* have our work cut out."

I was quiet as he continued to gaze at me with such intensity it astounded me.

"I told you we were in this together and I meant it," he assured me.

I hesitated, then nodded my head. When he squeezed my hand, I had to blink back the tears that clouded my vision. David's simple words touched me deeply. It pleased me more than I would have ever imagined that he was willing to hang in there until the very end. *Then what will happen?*

His hand on mine had sent a thrill so intense that I would have believed his fingers were magical. It was like he had cast a spell over me. Had he felt it too? When he looked at me, I thought I saw in them a reflection of what I was feeling. I was struck by their gentleness as he continued to caress my skin. I didn't pull my hand back. Instead, my fingers tightened around his, enjoying the feel of his calloused palm as we pulled into the shopping center parking lot.

David dropped my hand only long enough to climb out the car and open the door for me. As soon as the door shut, he reached out and caught my fingers in his, tugging me in tightly against him.

David stroked his finger over my lower lip until I drew back. My lips parted and my breath brushed against his finger.

"I can't think when you do that."

"Then don't think," he replied. He tightened his arm along my shoulders and drew me closer to him. I licked my lips and my eyelids started to close as he lowered his head.

And I exhaled.

Temptation was an understatement. David tempted me on so many levels, and I wasn't sure how to deal with someone who'd had that kind of effect on me. I wanted to believe this was just a moment, and curiosity was all this was about. But I knew better. This wasn't the first time we had kissed, only this time it was far more tantalizing and arousing. In fact this kiss came with years of experience and then there was that arrogant confidence he had perfected. His lips were dangerously delicious. I heard myself moan and then I was leaning in close, deepening the kiss. And that was a double dose of aphrodisiac. Easing back I shook my head trying to shake it off, reminding myself that I wasn't looking or wanting anything from him.

David draped his arm around my waist and steered me towards the restaurant.

We ordered KC strip steaks medium-well, baked potatoes and Texas toast. Trays in hand, David gave me the honor of leading us to a booth in the corner. Once we settled in our seats, I opened the folder again. I stared down at the names of dozens of women from all areas of the country.

"Maybe we need to narrow our list down to just the three women and investigate Eunice at a later date," I suggested.

David sat back against the cushioned seat and crossed his feet underneath the table. "I think we still need to investigate her. Just because she's dead doesn't mean she wasn't your mother."

Glancing up from the pages, I ran nervous fingers through my hair. "How would we research someone who is dead?"

David shrugged matter-of-factly. "It's public record. For a minimal fee, we can get the information off the computer. There's also the possibility that we might locate a family member."

I nodded unable to speak, so full of emotion. To my relief, a server arrived with our plates.

After he left, then returned carrying a bottle of A-1 sauce, David reached for my hand from across the table. "Hey, everything is going to be all right, just wait and see. We're going to find your mother." His gaze was full of promises.

I smiled at him, then carved into my steak and found it tender and mouthwatering as ever. While I ate, I discretely studied his handsome features. My eyes lingered on the length of his lashes, then perused the strong bones of his jaw. I wanted him to pull me in his arms again.

David caught me staring, and when our gazes locked, the air snapped, crackled, and popped. Regarding me over his glass, he asked, "Have you started packing?"

I shook my head. "Not yet."

"My mother says the weather has been pretty hot lately, so dress comfortably."

"I'll keep that in mind," I replied quietly between bites.

David was dressed in black slacks and a gray button-down shirt and matching tie. His left his jacket lying across the back seat of his car. The shirt outlined his broad shoulders and forearms. His lean muscled body made me tingle thinking about how good it had felt to be held against every inch of his fabulous frame. I was grateful for everything David had done for me, but was it only gratitude I was feeling? I tried to tell myself I would probably feel just as attracted to any handsome man. After all, I hadn't been sexually involved for quite awhile. It just happened to be David I was around, so it was only natural to be affected by him. Only I was beginning to think that those emotions ran deeper than that.

Glancing up, I found his eyes fixed intently on my face. It was so hard to concentrate with him sitting so close. His every movement, his every breath was a distraction.

I raised an eyebrow and swallowed a mouthful of potatoes. "What are you looking at?"

"Nothing." His eyes danced and I could see mischievous humor playing at their depths.

I set my fork down and folded my arms across my chest. "Are you going to tell me or not?"

"The real question is do you really want to know?" A seductive teasing smile made my nerve endings tingle.

"I wouldn't be asking if I didn't."

David leaned back and clasped his hands behind his head. The muscles of his arms bunched under the fabric of his shirt. "You're so pretty."

The smile that overtook his features made my insides tremor, but I laughed it off. The compliment was more intoxicating than fine wine. I peered up at him from lowered lashes. "Pretty? What happened to beautiful?" I grinned playfully at him.

David laughed aloud.

For the rest of our lunch, I allowed myself to relax and enjoy my time with David. I felt myself being drawn to the intense pull of his energy, his security. He didn't have to do or say anything special, nothing but just be himself and that frightened me.

On the drive back, I was quiet as we listened to soft jazz. A warm pleasant feeling passed through me, and I exhaled a deep breath. I clutched my purse in one hand and the folder in the other. When we pulled up in front of my building, I said nothing for a long moment. "So where do I begin?" I finally said.

David reached for the folder and removed several pages, then handed the rest to me. "How about we split the list in half?"

My eyes misted and I blinked rapidly as I agreed, "Okay."

David climbed out the car and came around to open the door for me. I rose and our eyes fused. I found his eyes on my lips and froze. David stepped forward. His face was so close I could feel the heat of his body and inhaled the spicy scent of him. He could have leaned forward, kissed me if he wanted to...and he did.

David drew me near him and kissed me with a ferocity that made me feel I was drowning. My hand rose and rested lightly on his chest. Parting my lips, I allowed myself to react. Fire swept through me, feeling my soul, commanding me to erase my apprehensions and succumb to the attraction. I tilted my head back further, giving him total access to my mouth. Somehow my arms wound around his neck urging him to deepen the kiss. David's tongue slipped inside. A groan rumbled in his throat, and I kissed him back answering his longing. I savored the sweet sensuous taste as our tongues merged in a passionate dance. However, remembering we were outside in a public parking lot, I eased back from him, breathing heavily and met the dazed look in his eyes. A look so intense I suddenly felt weak to my knees.

"Thanks again." Was the only thing I could think to say.

David pulled me closer and buried his face in my hair. "You don't have to keep thanking me," he whispered.

"Yes I do," I insisted.

Loosening his hold, he looked down, studying my face. "All right then, how about doing me a favor?" he asked, pinning me with a gaze so intense it made my head spin.

"Sure, anything."

He was still staring deeply into my eyes when he said, "See a movie with me tomorrow tonight."

"A movie?" I laughed. I had thought he was going to ask me to go home with him so he could make wild passionate love to me. *Stop it!*

David pulled me closer. "Yes. When was the last time you'd seen a movie?"

I took a moment to think, then shook my head. "It's been a long time."

"Then it's settled." He released me. "I'll pick you up at eight."

I giggled. "You haven't even given me a chance to say yes."

His lips met mine, warm, and persuasive, receiving my unspoken answer. "You need to start finding time for yourself, and I am just the man to make sure that happens." His tone left little room for argument.

And I didn't waste my time.

Chapter 10

THE NEXT MORNING I walked out of the hair salon under the warm May sunshine feeling like a new woman. I felt vibrant and more alive than I'd felt in...how long? Weeks? Months? Nevertheless, it was a good feeling. If this was what happened after spending a few days with David, then I was going to enjoy it and accept our relationship for what it was. But what was that exactly? I smiled and closed my eyes. I wasn't sure, and yet David had given me a gift—a few precious moments of lighthearted fun amid dark reality. His patience and words of encouragement had lifted my spirits and had made me feel like a woman.

Stopping at Panera Bread, I lingered over lunch, enjoying the broccoli cheese soup while thinking about him. When David was around, I somehow forgot about my problems and thought only about what was happening between us. Maybe my uncle was right. Maybe it was time for me to live my own life. One thing was for certain; I was attracted to David, no matter how much I tried to deny it. I groaned. What would Donna say?

WE HAD A WONDERFUL time at the movie. David arrived promptly at eight dressed comfortably in another pair of blue jeans that framed his muscular legs. This time, however, he was wearing white Air Force One sneakers. I also wore jeans and sneakers that

I paired with a blue blouse. Knowing that the theatre tended to be cold, I slipped a white button-down sweater over it.

David drove south of town to the Hollywood Theatre where we decided to see the new Spiderman movie. David loaded down our arms with popcorn, sodas and candy. During the movie, he held my hand and I did not object. In fact, I embraced it.

When the movie was over, we drove to Texas Roadhouse. After gorging on popcorn and candy neither of us had much of an appetite, so we ordered frozen margaritas and Buffalo wings. We talked about everything from life after college to where we planned to be in five years.

"Church's Chicken?" I gaped with the drinking straw between my lips. "I can't believe you want to buy a chicken franchise."

David nodded and reached for another wing. "Why not. We have just about every other restaurant in Columbia. Why not another chicken house? The only competition I would have is Kentucky Fried." He swallowed down a bite with a glass of water.

I reached for my napkin. "Why not Popeyes?"

He shook his head. "Don't you remember? We already had one and it didn't last, although I strongly believe the location was the problem."

"But their wings look as if they'd been injected with steroids," I implied while sipping my drink.

David chuckled and nodded his head. "That's true, but they are definitely delicious."

I pushed my plate aside and crossed my arms on top of the table as I watched him devour another wing. "I can tell you love chicken."

We shared a laugh. "I love chicken, but not as much as I love looking at you."

I peered at him through narrowed eyes. His compliment made my insides quiver. "Always the charmer."

"That's me. Charming, sexy and a wonderful lover. How about we go back to your house and I show you?"

I launched a chicken bone at his head, but he ducked just in time.

"Hey, you can't blame a brotha for trying," he chuckled.

We would have sat there all night if our server hadn't pointed to her watch, indicating closing time.

It was obvious David wasn't ready to end the evening. Good, because neither was I. He suggested we take a stroll. Holding hands, we walked across campus while I talked about my parents' death and the void I had felt ever since.

We strolled through the Francis Quadrangle, the symbolic center of Mizzou campus. It was located behind Jesse Hall, a large administrative building constructed of red brick. It featured a dome that was one of the most recognizable landmarks in Missouri. Deciding to take a moment to rest, we stopped and took a seat on a bench near a set of six tall columns. The columns were the most prominent feature of the quadrangle. There was also an art and archeology museum, which had been my mother's favorite.

"I guess if my life had been different, I wouldn't be so interested in finding my biological mother. Sometimes I feel so guilty as if I'm betraying my parents."

David caressed the back of my fingers with his thumb. "It's only natural to be curious. If it were me, I would do the same. Besides, your mother wouldn't have told you if she hadn't wanted you to find out the truth."

I simply nodded.

We were silent as we stared up at the star-studded sky, both lost in our own thoughts. David moved closer and draped an arm across my shoulders. I rested my head against him, inhaling his scent. To my amazement, David began to sing Mint Condition's "Someone to Love." As the words to the song poured out with rich clarity, my head raised in amazement. I had forgotten about his beautiful tenor voice.

David had once sung Jodeci's "U&I" at a talent show in college and had every woman in attendance dropping to her knees.

I gasped and could not ignore the effect the sound had on my insides. "Oh, my God! I love their music."

"I know. I remember when you used to play their album over and over again on your stereo."

I shook my head, still in awe. "You still have such an amazing voice."

"Thank you." David stopped walking, we turned, facing each other. Leaning forward, he kissed my forehead, then continued to stare at me. His gaze lingered taking in the shape of my eyes and the curve of my face. His fingers spread and grazed my cheek. I was ready when our lips met. The kiss was brief but just long enough to cause my pulse to race.

"I want to show you something," David whispered against my nose.

I nodded.

We walked back to his car with his arm around my waist and mine around his. I was curious where he was taking me, but I waited as we made the fifteen-minute drive. He stopped in front of a beautiful two-story brick Colonial house.

"It's beautiful," I cooed as we climbed out the car.

As he led me through the house, I took the time to appreciate the elegance of the rooms. I moved through a large two-story foyer to the living room on the right, which lead into a formal dining room. Most of the house was empty, however the parts that weren't, reflected his personality—rich dark woods, and shades of black, gray and white. David led me to the family room, which featured a fireplace and a nineteen-foot ceiling. Columns framed the wide entryway. The room was warm and inviting, as well as dramatic. To my right, French doors opened to the kitchen and breakfast area.

Taking my hand, David led me upstairs to the master suite. It had the ambience of a luxurious hotel suite—very large and private—with a sitting room and a large bathroom with a separate shower as well as his and hers sinks. The large Jacuzzi tub was big enough to bathe a baby elephant.

However, it was where he slept that had all my attention. The large king size bed had a massive mahogany headboard and was fit for a king. Chairs covered with thick paisley upholstery were found on either side and an antique cherry desk and chair were in the far corner. An image of David stretched out on the bed wrapped in nothing but a silk sheet made my mouth grow dry and my palms sweaty.

I wasn't sure how long I stared at the bed before David came up behind me and wrapped his arms around my middle. Fingers gentle but firm tugged me around until I faced him. His hands circled the back of my neck, his thumb stroked the delicate lines of my face. The light caresses sent waves to tingle clear down to my toes. Gazing up at him I saw the fire burning in their depths.

"You're the most intriguing woman I have ever met," he murmured, before his gold-green eyes fell to my mouth.

I couldn't find the words to speak or to resist when David covered my mouth with his.

The kiss was gentle yet powerful, his lips warm and inviting. Abandoning myself to the whirl of sensations, I followed his mouth. Mind-boggling. My arms snaked around his neck, my fingers gliding in between the locs of his hair. From a long way off, I heard David moan as he pulled me snuggly against him. I felt the tightening muscles of his chest under the crisp fabric of his shirt and registered as his maleness hardened and throbbed against my stomach. I parted my lips and his tongue slid into my mouth. I found myself lost with overwhelming passion meeting each of his thrusts with a stroke of my own.

Somewhere during the drugging kisses, we had somehow made our way over to his bed and I found my body stretched out beneath his. I could feel him against every cell of my body and his hardness pressed against my inner thigh. I had no desire for him to move. My body was burning with fire as David's mouth moved from my lips, searing a path down to the sensitive place at my throat. Hearing the moans escape my lips, he loosened the buttons of my blouse, exposing my chest. His fingers slipped beneath a satin bra to caress my breasts. I was shocked by my own eager response to him as I arched my body up to meet his touch. He stroked my nipples until he brought them to throbbing fullness.

Just when the world was spiraling away out of control his cell phone rang. Holding me tightly, David buried his face at my neck and breathed a kiss, making no effort to move.

Weak and lightheaded I clung to him. "Aren't you going to answer the phone?" I asked with deep uneven breaths.

"They'll have to leave a message. I'm busy," he murmured as his lips traveled to my neck. But instead of leaving a message, the phone continued to ring and then the calls were followed by a chime.

Someone had sent him a text message.

I stiffened, suddenly realized where I was, what I was doing and who I was doing it with. For all I knew, the caller was a woman.

David sensed the change in me. "What's wrong?" he asked as he stared down at me.

"Nothing," I squirmed. "Can I please get up?"

David rose and reached for his phone on the nightstand and glanced down at the screen. "That was my real estate agent."

I sat up and commenced to re-buttoning my blouse. "You don't have to explain. It's really none of my business."

He stood over me. "Then what's the problem?"

"I just think things were getting a little out of hand," I murmured, unable to look at him.

David took my hand and pulled me up from his bed, then placed a hand under my chin forcing me to look at him. "I'm sorry you feel that way. I was enjoying you."

I didn't respond.

"You liked my lips on you, didn't you?" he asked, his fingers caressing my skin.

My nipples tingled. I cleared my throat and said, "This was a mistake."

David gave a ragged sigh and lowered his hand. "I would never do anything to you unless it was mutual. No pressures, no demands, nothing."

My eyes met his and I nodded. "I know."

On the ride back, I was quiet. I wanted him with a hunger that had exceeded any he had ever encountered.

Then why did you stop?

I'd probably be asking myself that question the rest of the night.

David pulled in front of my house, helped me out of the car and escorted me to the door. He leaned down and kissed me gently on the lips, then drew back and our eyes locked as he replied, "I'm officially putting the ball in your court." Without waiting for my response, he turned and walked away.

Chapter 11

AUNT GRETA FINALLY contacted me.

I left work at five-thirty and steered my car onto I-70 towards Kansas City. Instead of her calling my cell phone, she had left a message on my voicemail at work, saying she needed to see me tonight around seven. Her tone had been so emotionless it had sent a chill through my spine. *What did she suddenly want to talk about?* The question tore at my insides. Maybe, just maybe, she was ready to talk to me about my past.

I caught myself driving well over the speed limit. I couldn't help myself. My mind was a crazy mixture of frightened anticipation. I was confident my aunt knew something that I did not, and yet I was afraid of what she was about to reveal.

At exactly seven o'clock, I pulled onto the driveway that curved in a semi-circle in front of the house...well, a baby mansion would be a better choice of words. The large French-style house was fabulous, the grounds country club impeccable.

Besides inheriting money from her father, Greta had married a computer genius who had designed a financial database that was being used by corporations all around the country. Her dearly departed husband had believed Aunt Greta deserved only the finest things in life and had a massive stroke at fifty-five trying to give it to her. She never remarried; instead, she had spent the last eighteen years keeping her husband's memory alive. I shut the car door and climbed the steps to a pair of huge mahogany doors. Before I raised my hand to ring the bell, the right door swung open. A round ebony woman with gentle brown eyes greeted me.

"Hi, Katherine." I returned her smile, wrapping an arm around the housekeeper's waist as I hugged her.

"Calaine, dear, it's so good to see you again," she said as we parted.

"Thank you. How's my aunt doing?"

Her expression turned solemn. "She's been having a hard time since your mother's death. How have you been?"

"I'm taking it one day at a time." I was touched by her concern.

Katherine nodded, understanding. She had lost her husband of thirty years almost two years ago. "She's in the parlor waiting for you." She moved aside and I stepped into the white marble foyer. I glanced around at the twenty-foot ceiling and the familiar antiques that were prominently displayed along both sides of the long hallway.

I hated the house, as much if not more than the home I had grown up in. I remembered when I was a child my aunt had made it clear that her home was not meant for nosey little people. Being the curious person that I was, I had always been fascinated by the array of artifacts. As a result, I remembered having my hands spanked on several occasions.

I walked towards a closed door at the far right of the foyer. I paused and took a deep breath before I pushed the door open.

The room was like a large library with mahogany paneled walls and shelves after shelves of books I had never been allowed to touch. My uncle had been a collector of rare edition books. Just two hardbound copies would have covered Staffing Solutions payroll for a month.

The furniture was all drab shades of brown and burgundy. A large picture window was the only thing that brightened up the room, providing a view of the colorful garden beyond. To the far left, a birch fireplace held a carefully arranged stack of logs. Above it hung a large portrait of Aunt Greta and Uncle Bernard on their wedding day.

Stepping further into the room, I found my aunt sitting in the corner sipping a cup of tea.

"Well don't just stand there! Come on in," Greta fussed.

I moved across the gleaming wood floor to the Queen Ann chair where my aunt was sitting. Greta offered a wrinkled cheek where I kissed her lightly, then my aunt signaled me to take a seat across from her.

Greta was a short, plump woman with silver gray hair, deep dark skin and round amber eyes. She had high cheekbones and a wide nose. She wasn't a beautiful woman, but her well-bred qualities, not to mention wealth, were her greatest assets. As usual, she was dressed tastefully in an outdated, nevertheless, expensive gray suit. A long string of pearls hung from her neck and gems graced each of her fingers. She smiled at me, but the smile was trifling thin.

"Aunt Greta, how have you been?" I asked pleasantly.

"I've been better. I just wish my dear Bernard was still here. My arthritis has been acting up something terrible. He always knew how to make things better."

That explained the strong scent of Ben Gay. "Have you talked to your doctor about it?"

"What do they know," she said, frowning. "They're just a bunch of quacks trying to take rich folks' money."

I watched as her chin set in a stubborn line and drew her lips in thoughtfully. My aunt believed she had never been ill a day in her life because she had stayed away from doctors. Bernard had been the only one able to convince her to see one when her arthritis had begun.

"Aunt Greta, I would like to talk to you," I said, hoping to get right to the point and make my visit as short as possible.

My aunt raised a hand signaling me to remain quiet as a man stepped into the room and approached us. He was an older gentleman with olive-toned skin, dressed in an expensive black suit and carrying a briefcase. There was something familiar about him. I couldn't place it, but I'd seen him before. I just couldn't remember where.

Greta lowered her cup to a silver-serving tray. "Anthony, thank you for coming." She gave him a genuine smile. "This is Calaine."

He turned to me and put me at ease with a friendly smile. His eyes were a light brown, warm and inviting. His dark ebony hair was graying at his temples. "A pleasure to see you again, Ms. Hart," he said, holding out his hand. "I'm Anthony Conley. I've been your family's attorney for a very long time. I'm so sorry for your loss."

"Thank you." I shook his hand and forced a smile until he released my hand. Then I looked to my aunt for an explanation. "What is this all about? I've already met with my parents' lawyer months ago."

"Please, Anthony take a seat," Greta said before turning a hard stare in my direction. "Anthony has been representing the Graves family for years. This involves *my* family's money, not yours."

I sat quietly with my hands in my lap, waiting for my aunt to enlighten me.

"As you know I've been mourning my sister's death for several months, but I know some things can't be put off any longer." She looked to Anthony and nodded, giving him permission to speak.

Clearing his throat, he reached into his briefcase before he finally spoke. "I'm here to read your mother's last will and testament."

I sat there, blank, surprised and very shaken. How...why hadn't my aunt prepared me for such a visit?

As if Greta could read my mind, she replied, "Dear, I know this comes as a shock, but there's no way to put this off any longer."

I was too surprised to do more than nod and while in a daze I listened to the lawyer read my mother's will.

It seemed like something out of a fairytale. My mother had been richer than I had ever known. I knew the Graves had family money, but never at the multitude that the lawyer disclosed. A summer home in Jamaica, land on the eastern shore, a winter home on the west coast, stocks, bonds, and cash all totaling over five million dollars. It was too much to absorb.

With a jerk, I came back to the present, to my aunt asking crossly, "Calaine, are you listening?"

"I'm sorry." Flabbergasted, the words lodged in my throat.

Mr. Conley lowered the papers and gave me a sympathetic smile. "I'm sure it's a lot to digest in one day. I'm aware you knew nothing about your mother's wealth."

I nodded, meeting his kind gaze. "You're right, I didn't."

Aunt Greta rudely cleared her throat. "Very well. Now that we have gotten that out of the way, we need to discuss another matter."

The lawyer looked uncomfortable. "Would you like me to leave the two of you alone?"

"No, you need to hear this too," she drawled.

As she spoke, Aunt Greta leaned over and poured herself another cup of tea. "You asked me months ago about your mother and at the time my mind was in a turmoil. I couldn't bear to speak ill of my sister, not while her grave was still warm. Unfortunately, now I have no choice." Meeting the fear in my eyes, a shadow of annoyance crossed her face. "You indeed are not my sister's child. Your father forced her to either take you or shame the family with a scandal. She had no choice but to become your mother."

I flinched at her harsh words. Watching her spoon sugar in her cup, I asked, "Did she tell you who my birth mother was?"

Greta looked appalled. "Of course not. She tried to pretend you were her own child. Since I was her sister, I knew better. I thought you were adopted until I noticed how much you looked like your father." She paused and gave a harsh laugh. "When I tried to confront her for the truth, she tried to pretend that what your father had done was all in my head."

I was stunned by the harsh reality. My aunt's stare was brutal and unfriendly.

Greta took several sips of her tea before setting the cup back on the saucer. "I have asked Anthony here today because I think we need to do what my sister never had a chance to do."

I turned to Mr. Conley; sympathy mingled in his glance. "And what is that?" I asked.

Aunt Greta intervened. "Relinquish her estate to the family."

My aunt's tone aroused and infuriated me. "You *mean* to you."

"I have to admit that I'm the last of our generation, however I have three children and several grandchildren who are entitled to Olivia's estate."

Just thinking about my three spoiled cousins, who never had to lift a finger in their lives, and who could never do any wrong, caused me to raise my chin defensively. "She was still my mother."

"Not by blood," she said with unwelcome frankness. "And *that's* what we are talking about today. Our family line has been pure for generations, and it's my duty to continue that. My sister would have wanted it that way."

"Then why did she leave everything to me?" I challenged.

She gave a dismissive wave. "She wasn't thinking straight at the time. However, she told me she'd had every intention of leaving everything to the family estate."

I looked to Mr. Conley. He tried to speak, but Aunt Greta held up a hand silencing him.

"I had Anthony draw up papers that would relinquish all your rights to the Graves' fortune. All that is required is your signature. I think it's the honorable thing to do, considering... My sister would have wanted it this way," Aunt Greta added with a twist of her thin raspberry lips.

"I don't agree." I glanced to my right. "May I have a copy of my mother's will, please?"

"That won't be necessary," Greta replied sharply. "I believe it's time for you to break the ties and move on with your life. For your generosity, I'm willing to give you a sizable amount for your honorable gesture." She mentioned an amount that wasn't even a fourth of my mother's total worth.

My shock had yielded quickly to fury. "I think I need to get my own lawyer."

"What!" Greta sputtered as she fell back against her chair.

I rose, ignoring my aunt's distraught face. I bid Anthony a goodbye and walked out the room ignoring my aunt's cries for me to come back that instant.

I climbed into my car, feeling a mixture of anger and sorrow. To make matters worse, it started to rain just as I pulled onto the interstate. I didn't know which was streaming harder, my tears or the rain beating down on my windshield. How could my aunt have been so cruel? It just wasn't fair! In her own stuffy way, Aunt Greta had always been pleasant. Now because of money, she had shown her true colors.

I wasn't sure how I had made the drive back to the city. When I finally pulled off the highway, I considered going to my uncle and crying on his shoulder, but I could not. I couldn't bear for him to know how my aunt had treated me. Not now, maybe, not ever. I knew he had never cared for Greta and would probably commit murder. Instead I headed south and went to the only person I knew would understand. The only other person who cared.

David.

I was surprised I even remembered where he lived. After all, I had only been to his house once. I turned onto the driveway, barely able to see as the rain increased. As I parked the car I hesitated, not sure if I had made the right move. *What if he already has company?* When the tears began to fall again, I decided to take my chances. I turned off the car and ran out into the pouring rain. In my blind state, I tripped over a garden statue and fell flat on the soaking wet lawn. Slowly, I scraped myself off the grass and after fishing my left shoe from out of the mud, I climbed up the stairs and rang the doorbell. It wasn't long before the door swung open.

"Calaine, what..." David's voice trailed off as he noticed my appearance. I was wet, dirty and not to mention holding a muddy shoe in my hand. "Come in."

He stepped aside so I could enter, but instead I dropped the shoe, fell into his arms and burst into tears. "Oh, David!" I wailed.

Not caring about getting wet in the process, David scooped me into his arms, kicked the door shut and carried me up to his room where he sat me gently on the end of his bed. My head was bowed, my body slumped with despair. I was crying and sneezing at the same time, my feelings too raw to discuss. My suit was plastered to my body and I was covered in mud.

David moved beside me and tenderly caressed my cheek. "You're soaked. We need to get you out of those clothes before you catch pneumonia," he commented softly.

Looking up I met his gaze, then lowered my lids and nodded. I didn't object when David reached down and removed my other shoe. He peeled my jacket from my shoulders and discarded it. After he instructed me to stand, he unzipped my skirt, which dropped in a heap around my feet. He helped remove my blouse. When I was down to my bra and underwear, I heard him draw in a long breath. I looked up at him and saw the lust brimming in his gaze. I swallowed. I felt so exposed and yet I was too miserable to care. David reached for a blanket and wrapped it around me. Taking my hand, he moved over to one of the side chairs and settled me down onto his lap.

I was shivering as he clutched me tightly to his chest. The crying had quieted, but tears continued to stream down my cheeks, spilling onto his shirt. David didn't ask any questions. Instead, he held me in his arms and rocked me back and forth until I quieted.

I tried to tell him what happened, but started crying.

David's arms were wrapped protectively around me. His tender hold and the light strokes of his fingers stroking the center of my back were comforting.

"Take your time. Talk to me when you're ready."

Resting my left arm over his middle, I pressed my nose against his shoulder, feeding on his strength. I didn't want to appear vulnerable or weak, but the blow I received had rocked me to the core.

"It's horrible! So very horrible!" I cried.

In less than six months, I had lost both of my parents, found out my mother wasn't really my mother, and one of the last connections I had to my roots had knocked me to the ground and spit in my face. Closing my eyes, I told myself that it couldn't possibly get any worse. Only I wasn't so sure. No matter how I looked at it, all I had left was hope, Uncle Thaddeus and Aunt Alma.

When my breathing had returned to normal, David leaned down and kissed me lightly on the forehead. "Let me run you a bath."

Shivering, teeth chattering, I nodded.

David slid out from underneath me and disappeared into the master bathroom. When he returned to his room, he found me curled up in the blanket. He knelt beside the chair and reached for my hand.

"Baby, are you going to tell me what happened?"

I took a deep breath before my eyes came down to rest on him. The look in his told me his concern was genuine. "I don't know where to begin."

He leaned forward and kissed my lips. "Take all the time you need."

Tears swelled within my eyes again at his patience and understanding. My arms came up and wrapped around his neck. "Please hold me," I replied quietly, feeding on his strength. David pulled me down onto his outstretched legs as I began to weep again.

"Baby, it's going to be all right," he cooed as he attempted to comfort me. He held me while one hand made circular motions on my back. "I got you." Closing his eyes, he tightened his hold and allowed me to surrender to the protectiveness of his embrace. For several minutes, I yielded to the compulsive sobs that racked my body while David rocked me in his arms. He whispered words of assurance in my ears.

I swallowed hard, fighting back tears. "She was so mean to me. What had I ever done to be treated that way?" Eventually I got my sobs under enough control to pull away. I slid from his lap onto the floor beside him, then took a deep breath and glanced up at him. A light coming from the bathroom cast shadows on his face and emphasized a strong nose, his wide firm mouth and somber eyes. Deep concern was written all over his face. I wanted to avoid relating the entire humiliating incident with my aunt to him but somehow, I believed that if I talked about my problems, I would feel better.

David didn't comment. Instead, he just listened as I told him about what had happened. The dam burst as I expressed my feelings and emotions—past and present—only stopping long enough for him to turn off the bath water, then return to his seat.

Afterwards he pushed his fingers through my damp hair and said, "Don't let her ignorance kill your spirit. It would be exactly what she wants. Don't give her your power." David's tone was firm and deep.

"I-I can't help it." I felt my throat tighten with emotion and then I began to sneeze uncontrollably. David lifted my shivering body effortlessly in his arms and carried me into the bathroom where he placed me gently on my feet. After he tested the temperature, with me still wearing my undergarments, he placed me into the tub of water. Then he kneeled on the rug beside the tub and planted a kiss to my cheek. "I'm going to make you a drink. Try to relax until I get back."

Once I was alone, I stepped out the tub and moved to stand in front of the mirror behind the door. I gasped when I found my hair plastered to my head and dirt smeared across my cheeks. Hastily, I removed my bra and panties, climbed back in the tub and commenced to lather my washcloth. I had dried dirt under my fingernails and plastered to the backs of my arms.

I lathered a second time, then leaned back in the tub and groaned. I had made a total fool of myself. Not only had I come crying to David, but I had fallen in the puddle of mud and almost lost my shoe. I gave a choked, desperate laugh. If I hadn't felt so pathetic, I might have even found humor in the situation. Unfortunately, it did nothing to lessen the blow. Aunt Greta had made it clear I was no longer considered family. It hurt. It hurt like hell. Now Aunt Greta wanted me to hand over everything that had belonged to my mother.

I shook my head as if to clear my jumbled thoughts. Maybe Aunt Greta was right. Maybe I should relinquish my rights to the family. After all, the Graves family fortune wasn't really mine to claim.

I heard a light knock at the door. I reached for a large bath towel and draped it over my body before telling David it was okay to come in.

David walked in carrying two martinis. He took a seat on the edge of the tub and handed me one.

"Thanks," I said, feeling only slightly embarrassed.

Glancing down, David noticed the pair of pink panties on the floor.

He cleared his throat. "How are you feeling?" he asked.

"Much better. I...um...thanks." Self-consciously I pulled the towel up to my neck.

"I've told you; you don't have to keep thanking me." He bent over and brushed his lips across my forehead.

I closed my eyes, savoring the sweet taste of apple on his breath. Being with David always made me forget about my problems. I knew I leaned on him maybe more than I needed, however, right now David's presence was one of a few comforting things in my life.

"Calaine," I heard him call, breaking into my thoughts.

"Yes?"

"What can I do to make it all better?"

Tears I couldn't control spilled from the corners of my eyes and onto my cheeks at his question. "Just allowing me to be me with you is more than enough."

"Please don't cry," he pleaded. "*Mi casa es su casa.*"

Wiping my eyes with the back of my hand, I nodded.

"You hungry?" he asked.

"Maybe a little."

"How's a ham sandwich sound?"

I managed a smile. "Sounds wonderful."

He rose and looked down at me. "Take as long as you want. I'm going to lay a t-shirt and a pair of boxers on the bed. Just come downstairs when you are ready." With that, he reclaimed my lips for a sweet sensual kiss, then departed.

I found myself smiling long after he was gone.

By the time I emerged, the clock at the end of the hallway read midnight. I found David in the family room in an overstuffed recliner. Soft music was playing from the stereo and candles lit the room. My heart lurched. It was so romantic.

"Come in, Calaine," he said, startling me.

"I thought you were asleep."

"Nope. Just waiting for you. C'mere." The shirt hung down almost to my knees. His long thick socks covering my legs all the way up to my thighs.

Throwing caution to the wind, I sauntered over to him. On a napkin, on the TV tray beside him was my sandwich. "Thanks." Eager for something to eat, I reached for the sandwich at the same time David reached out for my waist and lowered me onto his lap. I felt every nerve in my body quiver as David pressed his chest to my back. The heat from his body seeped into me and I shivered noticeably.

He pulled me closer to him. "Are you cold?"

"No, just hungry."

One hand continued to rest at my waist while the other one took the sandwich from my hand and brought it to my lips.

"Eat."

I never had a man feed me before. Overwhelmed by feelings, I opened my mouth, accepting each bite until it was gone. I declined his offer to make another.

"Would you like another drink?" he asked as I lowered my head to his chest.

I shook my head not wanting to leave the comfort of his lap. "How about I share yours?"

He handed me the glass and I took a sip. Some spilled from the glass and onto my hand.

"Look what I did." I giggled.

David reached down and took my hand in his. Turning my palm upward, he kissed it, looking straight into my eyes as he did so. I found the gesture quite erotic and when his tongue slipped between my fingers, I moaned softly.

He lowered my hand to his heart. "Feel that?" he asked. "That is what you do to me, Calaine Hart."

I closed my eyes a moment savoring the feelings. His nearness kindled fire and desire in my soul. There was a bond between us and we both felt it.

To the sounds of a piano melody pouring from the speakers I relaxed in his arms. "I can't believe you like this type of music." I needed to change the subject.

"There are a lot of things you don't know about me. If you'd just give me half a chance you just might find out."

Laughter burned in the depths of my eyes. "Just shut up and hold me."

He pulled me tightly in his arms and nuzzled my neck causing me to giggle. As the laughter died, he planted light kisses across my cheek down to my chin and finally to my lips. And I gave in, savoring the wonderful taste of him and hated when it ended. Taking the glass from my hands, he sat it down on the table next to him and captured my lips once again. "You feel any better?"

"Quite a bit."

"Good. Let's go to bed."

He rose and lifted me weightlessly over his shoulder and up the stairs to his room. Pulling back the covers, he laid me down on the bed and moved beside me. When he saw the hesitation in my eyes, he stopped. "I told you nothing is going to happen between us until you make it happen. Now roll over so I can give you a massage."

"You don't have to."

"But I want to."

I obeyed and rolled over onto my stomach. David moved to the center of the bed and straddled me. He placed his hands lightly to my neck and began kneading the muscles between my neck and shoulders. I closed my eyes and bit on my bottom lip. I had the taste of warm blood on my tongue and knew I had bitten harder than intended.

"How does that feel?"

His words seemed to come from far away. David's fingers seemed to strip away all the tension from the past several weeks and the devastation of earlier in the evening. I felt his thumb digging into the muscles at the base of my neck and though it was painful, a few seconds later the relief was so significant.

"You're so tense. I think I have already smoothed out three knots," he informed me.

"It feels wonderful," I moaned as I folded both arms beneath my head.

"Good, I aim to please."

Oh, he was doing a lot more than pleasing me. I inhaled deeply, trying to ignore the fact that my nipples, pressed against the mattress, were now hard as pebbles. I felt so relaxed, so...very sleepy.

Only a piece of thin material separating us.

As my breathing became easier, he slid down past my buttocks and began kneading the backs of my legs. I couldn't hold on. I was so relaxed that I eventually fell asleep.

Chapter 12

I RACED AROUND THE room as I tried to find my other black sandal. Mumbling under my breath, I looked underneath the bed again and luckily found it in the corner of my comforter. Rising from the floor, I tossed it into the side pocket of my suitcase along with the mate.

I had a bad habit of always waiting until the last minute to pack, no matter how many times I told myself to start early. Unconsciously my brow furrowed. Once again, I was paying for my procrastination.

While retrieving a bottle of cocoa butter from the top of the chest of drawers, my eyes traveled over to a small digital clock on the nightstand. A soft gasp escaped my lips. I had less than thirty minutes to get ready. I raced into the bathroom, and in two minutes I was under the stream of hot relaxing water with memories of the days before dancing through my mind.

I had risen Wednesday morning to find it still pouring raining outside and David's body enveloped against mine. Without waking him, I had slipped out of the bed and out the door without making a sound. Lying next to someone as sexy as David had been almost impossible. He had held me through the night and his arousal was evident against my thigh. All I knew was with a long weekend ahead of us I had to pull myself together quickly. Otherwise, I was going to be in trouble.

A few moments later, I was dressed in a pair of sweatpants and a t-shirt. I took a seat on the end of the bed and was slipping on a pair of socks, when my cell phone rang.

I glanced down at the caller ID before picking up the receiver, smiling.

"Hello, Uncle Tad," I sang merrily.

"Hi, Calaine. Are you all packed?"

"Just about," I answered as I reached down and slipped on a pair of Nike tennis shoes.

"Well, I just wanted to catch you before you left and let you know that a colleague of mine knows Coletta."

"Really!" I gasped. "Have you talked to her?"

"No, not yet. She used to work for Boone Hospital but retired last year. I'm hoping to get some more information on Monday."

"That's wonderful! Thanks, Uncle Tad."

He paused shortly. "You don't ever have to thank me. You know there isn't anything I wouldn't do for you."

"I know and I love you for it," I replied, voice filled with emotion.

"Calaine, I...we—"

"Don't worry. Everything is going to be just fine." I had heard the worry in his voice. "Well, I better go. David will be here any minute."

"Good luck in San Antonio. I hope you find some answers."

"Thanks. I love you."

"I love you too."

After hanging up the phone, I found my heart sang with delight. Every discovery brought me that much closer to finding my birth mother. What if she had been right under my nose all this time? My pulse jumped with anticipation, and I had to take a deep breath. I was getting ahead of myself and maybe setting myself up for disappointment in the process. Then...maybe not. I pondered the possibility. Now all I had to do was find the other three. Hopefully, David's mother or godmother Wanda had answers.

The doorbell rang startling me. Quickly, I gathered the last of my things that were spread all over my bed and dumped them in my suitcase. I knew it was only for three nights but with uncertainty as to what to wear, I had overpacked.

By the time the bell rang a second time, I had finally gotten my suitcase to close. I sighed with relief and was just about ready to scramble down the hallway when the phone rang. Groaning, I fumbled around inside my purse for my phone as I made my way towards the door.

"Hello?" I barked into the phone.

"Are you ready?"

"David, why are you calling me? I-I thought you were at..." my voice trailed off as I opened the door and found David standing on the porch with his cell phone to his ear. "Very funny."

"I thought maybe you were trying to bail out on me." David stared at me intensely and my anger suddenly flared into desire, hot and consuming as I found myself connected to his sexy-ass grin.

"I knew we had a lot in common, but I never thought it would include clothes," he replied.

My eyes traveled down to his attire and noticed David was wearing Mizzou Tiger memorabilia. Black and gold jersey, black sweats with tiger paws on the right leg, and a gold fitted hat with black lettering. He wore them well.

I raised a hand to my forehead and shook my head. We were going to look like a couple. Not only was I wearing a black t-shirt with gold lettering. I had matched it with gold sweatpants with black letters and black tiger paws across my ass.

"Great, just great," I mumbled under my breath. David threw back his head with abrupt laughter. Annoyed at him, I rolled my eyes.

While David made himself at home, I went back to my bedroom to retrieve my suitcase. As soon as I walked through the door, I tossed the phone on the bed and took a deep breath. I had to pull myself together. David looked so good I wanted to fall in his arms and have him smother me with his mouthwatering kisses. I raised my hand to my racing heart. I had to pull myself together, quickly.

When I came out lugging a large suitcase, his brow rose.

"Don't you think that's a little much for a weekend?"

I pouted my lips and shrugged. "I was undecided, and it is always better to be safe than sorry."

"That's your answer, and you're sticking with it?" he asked with a smirk.

"Exactly."

David reached out and took my suitcase. He made a joke of pretending the bag was so heavy he couldn't stand up straight. I couldn't help laughing.

After I locked up, we started on the hour-long drive to the airport.

My heart was beating a mile a minute, and I wasn't sure how I was going to be able to survive the journey with the scent of his cologne penetrating my senses with memories of the other evening.

However, it was easier than I thought. David as usual made me feel at ease. He told me he had sent postcards to each of the women on his list he thought might possibly have been Dorlinda Meyers. Every time his gaze met mine, my heart turned in response. I remembered my discussion with my uncle of his potential lead and shared the information with David.

Happiness filled me as we talked. I relaxed in my seat as the situation switched from my heritage to David's. He told me stories about his family while growing up and the way his parents still behaved as if they were still newlyweds.

"You wouldn't believe those two," he was saying as we pulled into the airport parking lot. "They are always slobbering and touching one another. I've gotten used to it, but as a kid, it used to be quite embarrassing."

I smiled, not missing the deep affection in his voice. "It sounds like you grew up in a very loving household." David simply nodded.

Staring out the window I couldn't help thinking about my own life. It was nice to know there were still couples out there who truly loved one another and were not ashamed to show their feelings. My parents had never been that way. I had faith that I had enough love in my heart that I would someday have the same as the Souls. As David searched for a parking spot, I found my imagination running wild as I envisioned spending a life with David. A warm feeling flowed through me at the image that I shook away.

The next couple of hours went by quickly and it was almost six o'clock when our plane landed in San Antonio. I was so exhausted I slept most of the trip in the air. Once we boarded the hotel shuttle, I settled back on the seat next to David.

David draped an arm around my shoulders and pulled me closer to him. "How are you feeling?"

"Rested." Tilting my chin, I smiled up at him sheepishly. "I can't believe I slept the entire trip."

"I can. You've had a long exhausting week," he replied. Lowering his head, David pressed a light kiss to my temple.

"You're right," I nodded and settled comfortably against his chest, enjoying the feel of his arm around me. I didn't want to think of anything else right now except David and the way he made me feel. I didn't open my eyes again until we pulled in front of the hotel.

I loved the Embassy Suites. I tried to stay at one every time I traveled. Even though they were all structured the same, each hotel had its own unique style. This one had a red Spanish style roof and terra cotta ceramic flooring that started outside and traveled into the hotel lobby.

David retrieved both of our bags and I followed him to the registration desk to find he had reserved separate rooms for us. I was a tad bit disappointed that he had. When David had told me the next move would have to be mine, he meant it.

Keys in hands, we took the glass elevator to the fourth floor and found our rooms were right next to each other.

David walked over and opened my door before handing over the key. "Are you hungry?" he asked.

Nodding, I took my suitcase from his outstretched hand. "A little, but I'd like to settle in my room and freshen up a bit first."

David agreed. "How about I meet you near the bar in an hour?"

My full lips softened with a smile. "Sounds good."

Lowering his head, he kissed my waiting lips. As he moved away, our eyes met, and I discovered our passion mirrored. After one final glance, I moved into my room and closed the door.

He was right next door. I smiled, thinking that a door was the only thing separating us for the next three nights. The mere thought was delightful.

I WAS SEATED AT A SMALL table near the bar when I saw David coming off the elevator. My mouth went dry as my eyes slid rapidly from a white cotton t-shirt to a pair of comfortably fitted navy walking shorts. I had forgotten how gorgeous his legs were. David had never played football, but his calves and thighs were as large and defined as a running back.

I waved him over in my direction and he greeted me with a pearly white smile that sent my pulse racing.

"Have you ordered yet?" he asked.

I shook my head and answered in a low sultry voice, "I was waiting for you."

He couldn't pull his eyes away from me. A simple pink sundress flattered my coloring while hugging the swell of my breasts. I left my hair damp, loose, and wavy. "You look incredible."

I blushed. "Thank you."

"What are you having?"

I hadn't missed the hungry look in his eyes before David dropped his head. Fighting urges of my own, I reached for a menu and studied it. There were several precious seconds of silence before I replied, "I'm not sure." I couldn't think straight, but then how could I with David's clean scent traveling over to my side of the small intimate table.

"I think I'll have salmon and rice with a spinach cream sauce," he announced as he dropped the menu and gave another heart-stopping smile.

I felt the menu slip from between my fingers. Nodding my head, I looked down, then replied, "I think I'll have the same."

David leaned forward and rested his chin in his palm. "How about a bottle of wine to celebrate?"

"What are we celebrating?"

"Finding your mother."

I was touched by his confidence that we would uncover the truth. I just wished I could feel so sure. With that in mind, I was able to put my relationship with David in perspective. As long as I didn't have a clue about my past, my future would forever be uncertain.

Forcing a weak smile, I agreed to a bottle of Chardonnay and was relatively quiet until our waiter returned.

I found my eyes traveling out to the garden through a pair of double doors where an indoor pool was visible. The blue green water gleamed beneath the sun that had begun to set on the horizon. The patio was crowded with guests eager for a drink or in need of a bite to eat before the kitchen closed for the night.

David was the first to break the silence. "After I got out the shower, I called my mom. The graduation ceremony should begin tomorrow around two. That should give us plenty of time to get up, have brunch, and meet the rest of my family."

"That will be great."

Our food arrived and while I dived into my meal, David observed me. Yes, I was noticeably quiet.

"We can go and visit with my mother this evening if you'd like?"

My fork froze in midair as I looked up at him. The thought was tempting but I shook my head. Part of me was anxious to find out the truth but the other half was still scared to death. I shook my head and returned to my food. "No. Tomorrow will be soon enough."

David nodded, then attended to his plate.

"What's wrong?" I asked after noticing the change in his expression.

"Nothing. I was just thinking about something at work."

There was silence again.

"What's on your mind?" he asked.

"Nothing," I lied.

"Yes, it is. I know you."

"You don't know me," I argued.

"Yes I do. I always have," he replied as he reached for his wine glass. "Now I can't seem to get enough of you."

His words caused a stir down low between my thighs causing me to shift slightly in my chair. The weekend was going to be quite a challenge. How was I going to make it through Monday?

"I spoke to Donna. She should be here the end of next week," I replied, trying to keep our relationship in perspective.

David smiled. "I can't wait to see her. Maybe the three of us can have dinner."

I stirred my glass. "Donna was thinking maybe just the two of you. I wouldn't want to impose."

"No imposition." He reached across the table and cupped my hand with his. "I don't want to spend time with Donna. I want to spend my time with you."

I averted my gaze to my plate and tried to ignore the twinge I felt at his response. I scolded myself for having more than a few sips of wine. Now I felt my resistance was low.

After another hour of conversation and three glasses of wine, David finally asked for the check. As we rose from the table, he placed a large hand to my waist and drew me near him.

We boarded the elevator, and I could feel the full effects of the alcohol leaving me feeling loose and very relaxed. I had to fight the temptation to lean over and kiss his smooth cheek.

The doors closed and the car rose. The quick jerk sent me stumbling into David's arms. My breasts brushed against his chest. David's fingers slipped up my arms bringing me closer to him. One hand rose to trace my cheekbone, then captured my chin and lifted my gaze to meet his. "You're something else, you know that?" His warm uneven breath against my cheek washed away any hope of resisting him. Instead, he left me feeling vulnerable and exposed. There was no way I could have pulled back not with his arm warm and heavy against my hips. There was no way to deny his lips against mine. Not when his warm breath was only mere inches away.

I blamed my behavior on the effects of alcohol, and I would scold myself later. Now was not the time.

I raised my hand and placed it against his cotton shirt. Heat seeped through, warming the blood in my veins. The heat, tautness of muscles and bone, and the hard pounding of his heart made me lightheaded. I lost all control of my common sense. Instead, I found myself lost in the deep pools of his eyes. My heart was beating so heavily against my ribcage that it further disoriented me, and I found my head tilting upward and my lips parting. Trying once more to extricate myself I pushed back slightly against his encircling arms and moaned, "David, please!"

"Please what?" he asked as he brushed against my lips. "Please kiss you?" he chuckled. "I plan to do just that."

He found my mouth shutting off any further protest. At the first touch, I was lost. My head was spinning, and I wasn't sure any longer what I wanted or didn't want. All I could think about was the warmth of his mouth sealed to my own, seeking a response and demanding it. His tongue invaded my mouth and I welcomed it. Blind with need I dug my fingers into his back pulling him even closer and felt the hardness of his erection against my belly.

"Calaine." He groaned my name in between a storm of brief fierce kisses.

I was ready to pull off my clothes and allow David to take me right there in the elevator. And I probably would have if I hadn't heard childish giggles.

I felt David stiffen and together we turned to find the elevator doors opened and two teenaged girls dressed in bathing suits standing there with hands cupping their mouths.

Clearing my throat, I followed David off the elevator, and quietly, we walked hand-in-hand toward our rooms. Once there, I turned and stared up at him. Desire still burned in the depths of his eyes. The yearning in my soul had simmered just enough for that voice of reason to scream, *I hope you know what you're doing because with actions there are consequences!*

"Well... uhhh, I've had a great evening," I stammered. "But I'm feeling tired and ready to call it a night. It's been an exhausting few days."

David's brow quirked. "You're running again."

I shook my head. "No, I'm not." I just needed time to think.

"Okay." David nodded. "We'll talk in the morning." He leaned forward and pressed his lips to mine once more, then stepped aside.

I swiped my keycard and scrambled into my room before I changed my mind.

The moment I was alone, I fell back on the bed, eyes closed.

I had fallen in love with David. I couldn't believe it. No matter how much I had tried to keep our relationship about finding my mother, it had gone in a different direction. I was now in love with him. I thought the distraction would have prevented that from happening, but I guess love wants what love wants. But why David?

I rolled over onto my side and groaned.

Although I had known love would strike me like this, I hadn't expected it to strike me here and not with him! A man who loved women and did not believe in the kind of love that I wanted in my life. But it was David I wanted. Heart and soul, I wanted his tenderness, his love, his heart. That indefinable something that put what I felt beyond the scope of any attraction I had experienced before. That something was the magic ingredient that told me I was head over heels in love.

Unfortunately, love wasn't part of David's equation. As far as he was concerned, what he offered was a little harmless affair to pass the time. Now that my heart was ruling my emotions, we were no longer playing the same game. There was a lot more at stake. To have a brief affair with a man you were physically attracted to was one thing. To have an affair with a man you had fallen in love with was a different story all together.

Chapter 13

I HADN'T SLEPT WELL, instead my mind was consumed by the fact that David was on the other side of the wall. Some time between one and two o'clock I found myself clicking the television on, hoping to drown out my erotic thoughts.

Tossing the pillow over my face to muffle the sound, I screamed with frustration. I was torturing myself when all I had to do was open the door and run back to him, but I couldn't. I had too much pride for that. David wanted an affair and even though that was all I could offer, I just wasn't strong enough to go down that road with him. I knew my heart would yearn for more.

Around nine, my stomach began to growl, and I knew there was no way I could hide in my room any longer without dying from starvation. I contemplated calling room services, but decided against it, remembering the fabulous breakfast buffet the hotel provided.

Boarding the elevator, nervousness swept through me. How was I going to feel when I saw him again?

Through the glass, I quickly scanned the dining area hoping David had already eaten and was back in his room. I sighed with relief when I didn't see him. However, once I exited the elevator and rounded the corner, I saw him. He was seated with his sister Caress and her children at a round table in the corner. Although my heart lurched at the sight of him, I was grateful he wasn't alone.

I ignored the fluttering of my heart, plastered on a warm smile and walked over to greet the group. "Good morning."

David lifted his head at the sound of my voice.

"Good morning," he returned warmly. "How did you sleep?" Our eyes met briefly, too brief for him to read what I was thinking.

"Like a baby," I lied before moving to the end of the table and gave his sister a friendly hug.

"I haven't seen you in quite a while," Caress said as we parted. We had often served on the same social event and planning committees. She was ten years younger than David.

I took the seat beside her. "I've been really busy since my parents' death."

"I'm so sorry for your loss," she said, offering condolences.

"Thanks," I replied, then my eyes traveled around the table. "Who are these adorable children?"

Caress beamed with pride. "These are my children Kyree, Latasha, and Lashawn."

They looked between the ages of four and eight with eyes identical to their mother's. Each of them waved, then returned to their waffles that were swimming in syrup.

Meeting Caress' gaze, I smiled. I wasn't sure how she managed to look so flawless. Even after having three children, she had managed to hold onto her naturally youthful glow. Her thin, toned body was draped in a flattering racerback peach cotton dress.

While we talked, I could feel the heat of David's gaze on the right side of my face.

"Excuse me," I said and stood. "I'm going to get something to eat."

I headed straight for the made-to-order omelets, then found a cheese danish and fresh fruit.

"Where'd everyone go?" I returned to my seat.

Caress tilted her head to the left. "They're standing over there. David has a thing for homemade waffles."

I nodded as I opened a package of sugar and poured it in my coffee. "I'll have to remember that."

"David is spoiled. If he had come alone, he would have stayed with our parents. Mom has been making my brother monstrous breakfasts for as long as I can remember, so he has grown to expect it. My kids have picked up that nasty habit. Now every Sunday morning I get up early and make a breakfast big enough for a king. My husband even looks forward to it."

"That sounds like a nice tradition," I commented in between bites.

Caress curled her fingers around her mug. "It is. I was lucky enough to have a mom who's a wonderful cook. She has plenty of room at her house for all of us, but I knew she had enough to do with my sister's graduation party."

"Where's your husband?"

Caress smiled affectionately. "He couldn't make it. He has a major case on Monday and was still preparing his defense." She shrugged her shoulder. "I could complain, but his law firm gives me the luxury of staying home and being a housewife and mother."

I could tell she was pleased with the choices she had made. While chewing my omelet, I wondered if I would ever consider giving up my career for the man I loved? My stomach quivered as I looked over at David and his niece and nephews as they came back to the table. For someone who looked like that, I just might be willing to give up a lot more than I'd ever dreamed.

"I hope my sister hasn't embarrassed you," David said as he returned to his seat.

I locked eyes with Caress, and we giggled. "No, not at all."

I dug into my eggs while Caress cut Kyree's cantaloupe into small pieces. The kids began to all talk at once, fighting for the spotlight and their uncle's attention. I watched the way he patiently answered all their questions and felt my heart flutter at his compassion. David would make a wonderful father someday.

I tried again to ignore him but found myself watching the way he shoveled his food in his mouth between questions and the sexy way his right brow quirked when he smiled. And before I could react, he looked up and his eyes met mine.

My body responded under his watchful gaze. Visions of him gazing down at me with my legs wrapped around his waist filtered my mind.

Don't even go there.

"Calaine," I heard Caress say. She glanced over at David who had one eyebrow lifted in silent query.

"I'm sorry, did you say something?" I asked, turning my attention to Caress.

Caress appeared amused by something or someone. "David was telling me that he's helping you find your mother."

"Yes," I replied as I sipped my coffee. "I'm hoping your mother and godmother can shed some light on my past."

Caress glanced over at her brother before continuing. "My mother and Aunt Wanda have a tendency to start talking without knowing when to stop. I hope you can make heads or tails out of whatever they tell you."

I grinned. "I hope so."

The children began to get restless. Caress excused herself and the four of them left, leaving me and David alone. I stared off at the growing crowd as I sipped my coffee.

"Are you going to ignore me all day?"

David was completely unnerving. There was no way to pretend that he wasn't there. The masculine scent of him assailed my nostrils so much so that if I had to, I could have found him in the dark.

I glanced across at him reluctantly and replied, "I'm not ignoring you. I'm drinking my coffee. As a matter of fact I'm finished," I declared as I lowered my mug and rose to my feet.

"Stay, keep me company," he insisted.

I tried to ignore his heart-pounding smile. It was so difficult to think let alone speak when he smiled at me that way. Nevertheless, I was determined to maintain my composure. "Can't. I need to call and let my uncle know we made it safely. Ring me when it's time to go." Before he could get a word in, I retreated towards the elevators. Once I was there, I turned and found myself disappointed that he had not followed me. *It is for the best.* If David had followed, there was no way I would have been able to resist again.

An hour later, with a towel draped around my neck, I headed down to the pool. A convention was in progress and the lobby was flooded with middle-aged men in suits. I was conscious of the appreciative glances as I sauntered confidently through the area.

Reaching the pool, I laid my towel on a lounge chair and slipped out of my shoes. There were a few senior citizens doing water aerobics at the other end but otherwise it was empty.

"The water must have been calling both of our names."

I turned to find David climbing out of the pool. I swallowed as my eyes followed a trail of water that had fallen from a lock of his hair and traveled down his chest. He was wearing navy blue trunks that emphasized long strong legs. Water-slicked hairs covered his legs and arms while his chest was as smooth as a newborn baby's bottom.

Tearing my eyes away, I murmured, "I thought I'd try to burn off breakfast."

"So did I."

Ignoring the attraction as he stood beside me, I turned away, slipped out of my coverup and moved to the edge of the pool. Bracing myself, I dove in, glad for the shock.

I moved to the top knowing David was watching me. The black two-piece revealed more than it was meant to hide. My stomach was firm and tight as well as my ass and legs. Oh, he was checking me out.

However when I surged to the surface he was no longer standing where I had left him. I was disappointed, but then seconds later, he emerged from the water and appeared before me.

David wiped the water away from his eyes and smiled. "The water is wonderful."

I nodded then swallowed watching a trickle hanging onto his left nipple. I felt the overwhelming desire to dart out my tongue and capture it before it dripped back into the pool.

"What's wrong?" he asked, obviously noting the play of emotion on my face.

"N-nothing," I lied.

Water trickled down his chest.

"Nothing?" he paused to laugh. "I don't believe you."

I lowered my eyes to the water, but David moved in closer and cupping my chin raised my eyes to meet his again.

"You feel it, too, don't you?" he whispered against my face.

That wasn't all I felt pressed up close against his body. I shook my head trying to deny the attraction, but it was useless. I wanted him.

"Ever since you slept in my bed while I held you in my arms, I can't stop thinking about making love to you." He stared at me with an intensity that made my pulse race.

"All you want is an affair." There. I said it.

His fingers grazed my cheeks. "Why don't you just give us a chance and see what happens." Lowering my hand, he reached out and encircled my waist. "Will you do that for me?"

Looking up at him, my gaze was as intense. "Do what?" I asked, stalling. I couldn't think straight when he was this close, looking that good. He started planting small kisses to my cheek and neck that was making matters worse. I collapsed weakly against him and my entire body shuddered in his arms.

"Give us a chance?" His lips brushed my ear in a whispery caress.

"Yes," I answered with a long sigh. "I'll give us a chance."

He kissed my lips gently, parting them with his tongue. The slow flow of desire was intoxicating. My tongue greeted him and as I tasted him all restraints fled. David slid his arms tightly around my waist. With our bodies pressed together, I was aware of his cock, thick, hard and aroused. Everything about him was so masculine and tempting.

Just as he pulled me even closer, I heard giggling. I opened my eyes and found the teenagers again. Shifting my head, I buried my face against his shoulder. "Oh, God, not again."

David turned and gave them a sheepish smile, then shrugged his shoulders apologetically.

"We are being a bad influence," I groaned.

Easing back, he smiled down at me. "You're right, let's go," he murmured as he escorted me from the water. We had reached for our towels and were heading through the lounge when he said, "We can resume this in my room."

I stared wordlessly at him. The offer was tempting. "We have two hours before graduation."

"I guess that means I'll have to cut it short." David smiled and a quiver slivered slowly though my body. I took his hand and allowed him to lead the way.

AS SOON AS HE CLOSED the door, David cursed and hauled me against his hard frame. "You frustrate the hell out of me."

God, his chest against my breasts had my nipples hardening on contact. I had a feeling his hand at my waist was the only thing steadying me on my feet.

"Dave," I barely managed before his fingers were cupping my chin. "I—" A shiver silenced me.

His hand slid to my cheek, then he dragged a thumb soothingly across my lower lip. "I tried to wait for you, but I don't want to wait any longer." His voice was a hypnotic whisper just before he swooped in, gently taking my mouth. I was instantly floating, lost in the warmth of his taste and his touch.

"Admit it, Keke. Tell me you want me as much as I want you." he added with sensual appeal, then slipped his tongue inside of my mouth, flickering and arousing my senses. I brought my hands around his waist. David's hand slid up to my breasts, touching and igniting firm heat. I rose on my toes, leaned forward, pressing my body against his in surrender. A soft sigh escaped me while I lost myself in his touch and his mouth. Was this really happening? I thought I would faint before he finished kissing me. David was a dark, delicious and dangerously desirable man. A rush of pleasure swept through my veins. I no longer wanted to wait. Not anymore. I had craved him for far too long.

"Take me," I murmured against his lips.

David drew back. The tender warmth in his eyes searching mine. I barely nodded before he swept me up into his strong arms and carried me across the suite and lowered me down on the bed. I faced him, my eyes never leaving his as he slipped the bathing suit off my shoulder. I lowered the wet material down over my hips and thighs. My eyes never left his. It wasn't until I kicked it away that his eyes left mine to travel slowly down my naked body, heating it along the path.

"Fuck, you're beautiful," he muttered under his breath.

I didn't respond. There was no need. My body responded for me. I was on fire ready for him to take me and had to wait several pain-aching seconds for him to remove his wet swim shorts. As soon as he was naked, I swallowed.

Damn.

David was beautiful.

Wide football shoulders, Sculptured pecs, and tight abdominal muscles. His muscles rolled. My eyes followed the trail of hair that lead me to his penis. My eyes widened as I took in his length and girth. Oh damn.

He noticed my reaction and smiled cockily. "Too much?" he asked.

I licked my lips nervously. "No." I was certain once my body adjusted to accommodate, he would fit quite nicely.

"C'mere," he whispered.

I took a step toward him and his hands captured my hips dragging me closer. I met his gaze and there was no mistaking the hunger burning there.

"I can't wait to be deep inside you," he said.

I tilted my head back and his mouth descended on my throat while his hand caressed me from shoulder to thigh.

"Make love to me." I clutched at his shoulders to keep from sinking to my knees.

"Get on the bed," he demanded.

I smiled, stepped away and complied.

David lay beside me. "Your breasts are so beautiful. I've been dying to taste them." His hand rested on my breast, palm against my nipple. I moaned softly. I opened my mouth to speak and instead I drew a long hard breath when he lowered his mouth, warm wet lips captured a nipple and slipped it inside his mouth and just like he promised, he sucked. *Ahhh.* His lips felt amazing!

"You like that?"

"Mmm-hmm," I breathed and my eyes fluttered closed. Shit, how long had it been since I'd had a man touch me this way? I was already aching to feel him inside me. David behaved liked a starved man and yet I was the one who was hungry. I just had no idea that I'd been starving for a man's touch. But not just any man. David.

For the first time in months, I felt free. My problems and worries faded. Nothing else mattered than right here, right now.

"Do you know how much I want you?" he breathed as he took his time. With two fingers he held my nipple, rolling the peak back and forth, while his mouth sucked and feasted at the other. "Babe, you feel that? That's your body responding to my touch." While he loved both of my breasts, I squirmed and withered on the bed anxious for him to take me. Intense pleasure tightened every muscle in my body. I was aching and growing crazy aroused. David worked his tongue around my areola and then over to the other and my body responded, pulsed, and shook like crazy. And when he sank his teeth into the flesh just below my nipple, my entire body jerked, and I cursed under my breath.

"I knew you'd taste sweet," he growled against my skin as he began to lick the area soothingly.

He lowered his hand, skimming along my flesh causing me to flinch beneath him and I sighed as he gently stroked my clit. A few moments more and his lips slid from my breasts and he was separating my thighs and was down there tasting me. Oh God! I swallowed and tried to breath, tried to catch my breath, but my lungs felt restricted. His tongue was swiping along the slit of my pussy and driving me crazy.

I panted, "Oh, David."

"You taste so good," he said, his warm breath blew against my clit and caused me to arch off the mattresses toward him, moaning.

He drove in again, sliding his teeth against the quivering flesh, nibbling and teasing. My stomach rolled. He was driving me insane and when he pushed a finger inside, I tightened around him and shifted restlessly toward him. Next thing I knew I was spiraling out of control. Driving into his fingers, I rolled my hips, matching the rhythm and then I was moving faster. .

"That's it, baby. Come for me," he coaxed.

After several breathless moments, I managed, "What... I..." I couldn't even get my words or thoughts together. And then I shattered into a million pieces. I was spasming and crying out his name.

"Babe, that's it." David repeated those words until I was spent and collapsed onto the bed.

Before I could catch my breath, David had reached for a condom, rolled it on, and was spreading my thighs. "Babe, I need to be inside you. I've waiting too long," he grounded and then my eyes fluttered open at his sudden entrance.

"Shit," I heard him hiss and then he took what I offered. "Babe, you're so tight."

Goodness, he was big, fitting me just like I had hoped, stretching me just right until my body adjusted and tightened around his cock as if he was meant to be there. He was fucking me in slow, deep thrusts that were driving me so crazy I couldn't think. I wrapped my hands around his forearms. My breath hitched as he began increasing the speed until he was fucking me with a rhythm that was mind-boggling. David pulled out and then sank deeper. I whimpered. His thrusts and the pumps increased. Within moments my body was soaring and on fire.

"Please, don't stop," I moaned, arching my back, trying to drive him deeper. "I need this."

David drew back, then plunged forward, spreading my legs even wider. We were both pumping at a frantic rhythm that had me breathing so hard as I was trying to catch my breath and enjoy the moment at the same time. David pumped, driving me deeper into the bed. Harder. Faster. He showed no mercy in his assault of my senses. Reaching between us, he stroked my clit.

"David!" I cried as he rode me harder. How was I supposed to think when he was touching and fucking me? This experience was like nothing I had ever experienced and within moments, I was coming again. Thrashing on the bed, screaming his name. My arms were around him, fingernails digging into his flesh. David slammed into me and then the rhythm changed, intensifying. His thrusts, harder and deeper, bringing me to the brink of insanity. I could not speak in coherent sentences. He rose, cupped my ass cheeks off the mattresses, dragging me so I was where he wanted me. And then he was pumping hard and fierce and I was whimpering because I had never had anything feel so good before. Within moments, I was soaring into ecstasy so wild and intense that it sent the breath out of my lungs in a loud cry.

"You make me crazy," he muttered and then with one last thrust, a growl slipped from his lips and he was spilling inside me. David went rigid for a long intense moment and released a hard grunt. When I opened my eyes, I saw him staring down at me. Tenderness. Arousal. Desire. It was all there, and my heart lurched.

Completely spent, David slumped over me, his warm body covering mine. He held me close, kissing me. I wrapped my arms around him and drifted off to sleep.

Chapter 14

IT WAS CLOSE TO FIVE when we pulled up in front of the Souls' Spanish-style home located in a quiet upscale neighborhood with tree-lined streets and old-world architectural charm. The private neighborhood invited sidewalk strolls and promised the shortest commute into downtown. There were quite a few cars in the driveway that indicated that most of their family and friends had already arrived at the residence.

After we made love, I fussed over what to wear. David told me the weather was expected to be well over ninety degrees, so I had decided on a pair of pink Capri pants and a cool white cotton blouse.

I'm nervous, I thought as I stared out the windshield at their red tin roof. My feelings were a mixture of uneasiness about speaking to his mother and anxiety about finding out about my own.

The graduation ceremony had been long, but surprisingly interesting. The female guest speaker, who was from one of the state departments responsible for the tobacco lawsuit, was both interesting and delightful. I was grateful the ceremony had been held in the convention center away from the scorching heat and humidity.

There were close to two hundred students in the graduating class. By the time we arrived at the ceremony, the auditorium was already filled, and we were unsuccessful in locating the rest of the Soul family. As a result, David suggested we sit near the rear and we would wait to see his parents later at their home.

David shut off the rented Jeep Cherokee and looked over at the passenger's seat. "You ready?"

I removed the sunglasses from my eyes, folded them and put them in my purse. "As ready as I'll ever be," I murmured as I retrieved a small compact from my purse. While David came around to my side, I buffed the shine from my nose and applied a fresh coat of lipstick. He helped me out of the air-conditioned SUV. Climbing out it was hard to ignore the hot San Antonio breeze as it swept across my face.

"You're going to be fine," he said and kissed me on the lips. Holding my hand, he led me up the driveway and into the house.

We stepped into the foyer and my gaze traveled around as David toured me through the house. My lips curled into an unconscious smile as I found the house warm and inviting. Each room displayed proud photographs of several generations. There were also handmade crafts, crochet afghans, and an unlimited amount of personal comfort. It was the kind of house I dreamed of someday having of my own.

We moved into a large spacious kitchen where a beautiful young woman was tossing a salad.

"Lil Sis," David greeted.

His sister's startled gaze shifted in the direction of his voice. "Hey!" she shrieked with delight as she rushed around the island and threw her arms around his neck. "I was wondering when you'd get here."

David twirled her around in his arms and kissed her playfully on the cheeks, lips and forehead. She giggled like a teenager until he lowered her to the ground.

Turning to his right he said, "Calaine, this is my annoying sister, Daphne."

"It's a pleasure to meet you."

"The same here." Daphne's voice was low and soft.

She was a feminine version of her brother, probably in late twenties, considering she was younger than Caress. Her dark brown hair was pulled back and secured in a French braid that hung to the center of her back. She had also inherited hazel eyes and a wide nose, which was striking against her tawny brown skin. She was short and heavy around the hips.

"When Mom told me you arrived last night, I was planning to surprise you at the hotel." Her face brightened with animation. "That's before I found out you brought a friend along," Daphne smirked as she glanced over at me. "I didn't want to intrude."

"We're just friends," I blurted although the look on Daphne's face told me she didn't believe a word I said.

David's eyes met mine. The corners of his mouth twitched making my skin tingle. I should have known his family would think we were an item especially since David did nothing to convince them otherwise.

"Where's everybody?" David asked.

"Dad's out on the patio, Mom's upstairs changing into something more comfortable. Everyone else is in the family room."

He tugged his sister's braid, then reached for my hand again.

"C'mon. Let me introduce you to my dad." David led me out onto the deck where his father was in front of the grill with an apron tied around his body.

"Dad."

The elder Mr. Soul swung around holding a pair of tongs in his hands. "Son, you made it." His father moved forward and embraced him.

When they moved apart, David motioned his head in my direction. "Dad, I'd like you to meet, Calaine Hart."

He set the tongs on the table and wiped the grime from his hands onto his apron before he extended a friendly handshake. "Robert Soul, it's a pleasure to have you."

His brown eyes crinkled when he presented me with an irresistible smile that was so much like David. It was as if I was looking at David through a looking glass twenty years in the future. He was a tall, medium-built man with the same dark skin. His salt and pepper hair was collar length and his mustache was full, covering his upper lip.

"I'm pleased to be here, Mr. Soul."

"Please, call me Robert. We're all family here." He brought my hand to his lips and kissed me lightly on the knuckles before releasing it. "I don't remember my son ever bringing a lady friend home, so that means you must be someone special."

David must have sensed my discomfort because he placed his hand lightly to my elbow and said, "Why don't we go find my mom?"

As if on cue, a beautiful woman stepped out onto the deck. I knew immediately she was his mother. Not only because she resembled the woman in the photograph, but she and Caress looked so much alike. Her dark brown hair had generous strands of gray and was stylishly cut, complementing a smooth wrinkle-free face.

She handed a platter of raw seasoned meat to her husband, then kissed her son on the cheek before she turned toward me. "So this is the lady who's searching for her mother," she said with a warm smile. "Welcome, sweetheart," she caught me off guard when she opened her arms and hugged me.

"Thanks," I replied, feeling instantly at ease. I squeezed her tight before releasing her.

"Come on, you two, it's too hot out here. David, go on inside and introduce Calaine to the rest of the gang."

I followed David into the family room where the others had gathered. I smiled and shook hands as David introduced me to several friends of the family. It was an intimate group of family and friends, no more than twenty-five. Finding Caress smiling across the room at me, I waved, and hugged each of her children when they ran over to me to say hello. Taking my hand, David then led me over near the fireplace where a tall attractive man was holding a little girl.

"Calaine, I'd like you to meet my brother, Carlos."

At the sound of David's voice, his brother swung around and lowered the little girl to the floor. He turned to embrace his baby brother.

He was also handsome. Carlos was the same height and build as David, but that was where the similarity ended. He had a smooth tawny complexion and long black locs secured by a rubber band at the nape of his neck. With my head tilted I stared into chocolate-colored eyes that were surrounded by lashes long enough to make any woman envious.

"It's a pleasure to meet you." He greeted me with a warm smile that revealed dazzling white teeth.

"The same here." I accepted his proffered hand. "Your daughter is so pretty."

"Daughter?" He frowned while David chuckled heartily.

"Keke, Tiffany is our little cousin."

Carlos' eyes narrowed at his brother's humor before his smile returned. "I don't have any kids or a wife. Neither are in my DNA."

I was surprised. "But you looked like a natural."

"That's cause I had to take care of this big head brother of mine." He punched David lightly in the chest, then the two passed several playful punches back and forth before their mother stepped into the room and told the two to knock off the nonsense.

I grinned, admiring the closeness between the two. I'd always wanted a brother.

I asked David for directions to the bathroom, then excused myself and moved to the powder room at the end of the hallway. The small room had hardwood floors, embroidered towels and a pedestal sink. After washing my hands, I took a moment to look in the mirror, and finger-combed my hair before exiting the room. As I walked down the hall, I found a woman about David's mother's age standing near the living room watching me.

"You must be Calaine," she said as I stepped into the room.

I looked at a face that only took a few seconds to identify. "And you must be Aunt Wanda."

"In the flesh," she acknowledged with her hands clasped in a prayerful gesture.

I stood admiring the nutty-brown colored woman with fine chestnut hair and realized that she wasn't the only one staring.

"You look so familiar," Wanda commented with a quizzical stare.

Probably because you know my mother.

I nodded. "My uncle, Dr. Hart, was your instructor."

Her brow rose. "You're related to Dr. Hart?"

I nodded. Before I could ask questions, David and his mother stepped into the hall.

Wanda immediately called their attention. "Ruby, did you know Calaine was Dr. Thaddeus Hart's niece?"

Her eyes darted over to me, wide with surprise. "Oh my! I used to have a huge crush on him. We all did." She moved over to the couch, upholstered in rich gold fabric and took a seat.

"He was so handsome. I think I spent more time drooling over him than paying attention to his lectures." Wanda chuckled.

I smiled. I had heard countless stories of how handsome my uncle had been back in the day.

"And he had a younger brother who was also handsome." Ruby then added as an afterthought. "That was your father?"

I nodded.

Wanda snapped her fingers. "Oh yes! He was popular with the ladies."

"How so?" I asked.

"The girls and I used to sneak off to this hole-in-the-wall jazz club and he and Dr. Hart would show up looking as handsome as the devil! They'd take turns dancing with all of us." Wanda smiled at the memories.

My heart was pounding hard. She was talking about my father!

"Yes, those brothers had a way of making us all feel so special."

I swallowed because I had finally found my father's connection to the students. "All? Anyone in particular?" I had to know.

Wanda gave me a pointed look, then shrugged. "The brothers had a way with the women. You know the type... they'd say the right things, make you feel blessed to have been born a woman, but at the end of the night you look around and they're gone."

"Gone home to their wives," Ruby said knowingly and then the two women cackled.

My shoulders sagged.

David moved beside me and placed a hand lightly at my waist. "Calaine, did you bring the photo?"

Glancing up at his handsome face, I was barely able to contain my disappointment. "It's in my purse."

Wanda took a seat beside David's mother and crossed one leg over the other. "Why don't you go get it and we'll take a look at it."

I went into the front room where I had left my purse and within minutes I returned with the photograph.

Wanda reached for the photo first. Shaking her head, she chuckled. "Weren't we something else back then."

Ruby leaned over to get a closer look and smiled, eyes twinkling with mischief. "Yes we were."

"I wrote the names of each woman on the back if that helps." I offered as I took a seat across from them on a matching loveseat.

Wanda smiled. "Hmmm, let's see. Ursula was the silly one. She always had a joke. I don't think she ever took anything serious. I remember our dorm mother used to be pretty angry with her." She gave David's mom a sidelong look. "Ruby, remember that time she played a joke on her?"

She chuckled openly. "Oh yes, how could I have forgotten."

Wanda related the time that Ursula had put a diaphragm under the poor woman's pillow. "She was too embarrassed to accuse any of us."

Ruby took the photo from Wanda and studied it for several seconds before saying, "I don't remember much more about Ursula except she was smart as a whip and rarely needed to study." She paused to smile. "Now Coletta, she and I were close, but we lost contact over the years. These other two...they were strange."

"How so?" David asked. He had moved and taken a seat beside me. My skin tingled at the close proximity.

Ruby looked up and saw the gleam of interest burning in her son's eyes. "Eunice used to act like she was Dorlinda's mother. I don't think the poor girl was ever able to make a decision on her own. They had come from a small southern town. I can't remember the name."

Wanda chimed in. "Yes, but they didn't stay in the program."

"How long were they there?" I asked.

"Not long enough. Wanda and I were the only two to complete the program. Coletta went on to finish somewhere else. Ursula's mother got ill, and she had to go home and run the family business. And the other two had left long before that."

"My uncle said he heard Eunice committed suicide."

Wanda glanced over at Ruby with a puzzled expression that soon turned to a knowing expression. "I think I do remember Coletta telling me something like that."

"Do you remember why?" I asked, hoping for an answer.

Wanda frowned. "No, I don't."

"I don't remember hearing anything about that," Ruby added. "I never really got involved in the campus gossip. I was already married with a two-year-old son. As soon as my classes were done for the day, I had to hurry to pick up Carlos from the sitter."

"Do you think any of them could have been my mother?"

Ruby leaned back against the cushion. "Anything is possible. During the early seventies things like that were hush hush."

Wanda shifted slightly, crossing then uncrossing her leg before glancing across at the two of us. Something in her eyes told me I wasn't going to like what she was about to hear. "Calaine, you have to understand that times were hard for black women back then. We had to work even harder to compete with the white nurses. Even though it was the seventies, having a child out of wedlock was unacceptable for anybody, no matter what color you were. It wasn't like today when a teenager is allowed to finish high school while walking around with her stomach sticking way out. Back then... no way, no how."

Waving a hand in the air, Ruby nodded. "Amen to that. People were quick to point the finger if you weren't wearing a ring."

I nibbled slightly on my lower lips as I tried to absorb what my mother had probably gone through. She would have been scared. "Do you think that's why she gave me away?"

Wanda was the first to speak. "Yes. We didn't have options like y'all have today. Having a baby would not have been acceptable. If she gave you up, then chances were she had no other choice."

I had an uneasy feeling that Wanda was trying to convince me of something. I just wasn't sure yet what it was.

David reached for my hand and laced our fingers together, causing my body to heat with awareness.

"Do you know how to find any of these women or know of anyone who would?" I asked.

Wanda frowned. "No, but it would be nice if we could find our dorm mom, Ms. Butler. She would probably tell you anything you wanted to hear. By now, she should be in her eighties. If there had been a baby, then she would have known. We couldn't get anything past her."

Ruby slapped her knee and chuckled. "Ain't that the truth. I wished I had stayed in the women's dorm just so I wouldn't have missed all the fun. The girls used to come to class the next morning with all kinds of stories. Wanda used to stay in trouble."

Wanda smiled proudly. "Oh, yes. I was a risk taker. I remember when I had a date with this medical student and tried to sneak in after curfew. Ms. Butler was standing behind the door waiting for me." She chuckled with fond memories.

The two then began to talk nonstop about the parties they had attended and how great a dancer Wanda had been. Neither of us could get a word in.

Leaning over, David whispered in my ear, "Caress warned you." He laughed, a low sexy laugh that caused my heart to flutter.

Eventually the two stopped talking about the fancy dresses they had worn as if they had suddenly remembered we were still there.

"I'm sorry. Wanda and I like to travel down memory lane. I really wish we could have been more helpful," Ruby said sympathetically as she reached over and handed me back the photo.

I shook my head. "No, in fact you were quite helpful." They had helped to paint a picture of an era of hard times for a single and pregnant black woman.

The kids came running in from outside. We turned towards the door as Christie appeared wearing her cap and gown.

"There's my girl," Wanda said as she rose to embrace her. "I'm so proud of you!"

She was grinning from ear to ear. "Thanks, Auntie Wanda."

As soon as they moved apart, David lifted his youngest sister off her feet and kissed her soundly on the cheek.

"Hey, brother," she cooed as he released her.

Christie turned to me, her bottomless golden-brown eyes sparkling with excitement. "You must be David's friend. It's so nice to meet you." Christie stepped forward and gave me a warm hug, then whispered near my ear, "He's never brought anyone home before, so you must be special."

All I could do was smile.

Caress appeared at the door. "Now that our guest of honor is here, we should be eating shortly," she said with an affectionate smile.

"Do you need some help?" I asked as I watched Ruby and Wanda retreat towards the kitchen.

Caress shook her head. "I think we've got everything under control, but thanks for asking. I'm sure Dad could use David's help outside."

"I guess that's my cue," David murmured. Looking down at me, he planted a quick kiss to my cheek. "I'll be back."

"I saw that," Christie teased causing me to blush profusely.

"You just behave while I'm gone and don't fill Calaine's head with a bunch of lies," he warned his sister.

Christie pressed a hand to her breast. "You couldn't possibly mean little ole me?"

I giggled. David ruffled his sister's spiral curls before he left the room.

Christie shrugged out of her graduation gown and laid it on the couch, then signaled me to follow her into the dining room. We cut through the kitchen where the countertops were covered with platters of side dishes, grilled meats and desserts. Mr. Soul came in carrying another tray of meats. I could not ignore the mesquite aroma.

Christie reached down and scooped up a deviled egg. "You need me to do something?" she asked while she chewed.

Caress was pulling a pan of baked macaroni from the oven when she said, "Yes, why don't you two help Daphne set the table."

I followed Christie into the dining room where Daphne was removing the fine china from the cabinet and placing it on a large table. She glanced up in time to witness me arch an eyebrow.

"I know what you're thinking, who uses good china for a barbecue." She rolled her eyes heavenward and reached up for the last plate. "My mother won't have it any other way. To her, graduation means pulling out the china."

Christie groaned. "It also means that we can't use the dishwasher tonight."

I moved around the table and retrieved the silverware from the drawer. "My mother was the same way." Only I didn't bother to say that my mother would have never dreamed of serving barbecue in her house in fear of sauce getting on her expensive rugs.

"Well, at least you're the last Soul to graduate," Daphne groaned.

I glanced over at Christie's smiling face. She had inherited her father's eyes and dimpled chin. She also had dramatic high cheekbones, small bone structure and thick sandy brown hair. The overall result had made her a beautiful woman.

"So how did you meet my brother?" she asked curiously.

I took a moment to answer. I knew the questions were coming, I just hadn't expected them quite so soon. "We went to college together."

Daphne looked up from folding linen napkins. "Do you live in Columbia?"

I nodded. "All my life."

Christie frowned. "I was so young when we left and moved down to Texas that I don't remember ever living anywhere but here."

"Are you teaching in San Antonio?" I asked, hoping to steer the conversation away from me.

Smiling, she shook her head. "Yes, middle school, but now that I have my master's I'm going to be working in education administration in Dallas."

"Her boyfriend lives there," Daphne offered.

Christie flushed at the mention. "I can't wait! He had to work today otherwise he would be here. Tavis is a wonderful man. He's building a home and we're going to live together until we decide we're ready for marriage. I'm in no rush. I want to take my time and make sure I'm doing this right."

I nodded impressed. "Sounds like you got a plan."

"Yes, I don't ever want to get a divorce. I want to be like my parents and be married forever."

We spread out a lace tablecloth, then wiped each piece of china off with a cloth before setting the table. I was envious by the closeness of their family. It was something I had always wanted. A father barbecuing out on the deck and a mother cooking in the kitchen, not at all afraid of getting her hands dirty. We hadn't owned a barbecue grill, and Olivia refused to boil water. I could only hope to have the same someday.

"Why don't we let this thing between us play out and see where it leads."

David's words came back to me. Memories of my legs draped over his shoulders while he stroked in out of my wet core came rushing back. Quickly, I brushed the erotic thoughts from my mind and focused on setting the table.

As the time passed, I found myself growing relaxed around his sisters as we joked and laughed as if we'd been lifelong friends. Daphne had majored in journalism and worked for a small local magazine. She hoped to move to New York City and work for a major publication. After two failed relationships, she was in no rush to meet number three.

When the table was completely set, we returned to the kitchen to retrieve covered dishes and brought them out to the large table. Besides barbecue, there was grilled corn on the cob, spaghetti, macaroni and cheese, baked beans, five different kinds of salads and a large variety of desserts.

I stepped into the kitchen a third time to find David sitting in a chair talking to his father. As I passed, I found him watching me. My breath caught in my throat as my body stirred to life again. A voice in my head shouted, "Look away!" but for the life of me, I couldn't resist the smile that curled on my lips at the sight of his sensual smile. He was gorgeous in every way, and I was feeling things for him that I never guessed I would feel for any man, especially not him.

Christie must have seen her brother eyeing me because as we moved into the dining room again, she asked, "So what's the deal with you and my brother?"

I gasped as I tried to think of an answer.

Daphne clicked her tongue. "Don't embarrass her, Christie. They are just friends."

"Friends, huh?" Christie dropped a hand to her slim waist and frowned. "You don't think my brother is handsome?"

I didn't hesitate with my answer. "I think your brother is quite handsome. I also think he's very arrogant."

Christie and Daphne laughed in agreement.

I placed a bowl of potato salad on the table, trying to make room for more. "Your brother is helping me find my mother."

"Your mother?" Christie gasped.

I explained the photograph and the questions I had about my past.

Daphne's eyes grew large as saucers. "Wow! I don't know what I would do if I found out I was adopted."

Christie shrugged. "It wouldn't matter to me. I have wonderful parents. Nothing could ever change that."

If mine had been different, then maybe I wouldn't be looking so hard. Then again, I probably would still be seeking answers.

Ruby announced it was time for dinner and the rest of the family moved into the dining room. Everyone joined hands. David stood beside me. He covered my hand with his and we shared a tender smile before bowing for grace.

The younger kids moved into the kitchen to eat while the rest of us sat around the table. I listened to the sound of laughter as everyone tried to talk at once. They were an engaging bunch that made me yearn for what I had missed. I quickly found myself caught up in the family charm as they included me in several conversations. However, each time I spoke, I found Wanda watching me intensely. There was something about the woman that disturbed me. I wasn't sure what it was, but I had every intention of finding out.

Chapter 15

IT WAS CLOSE TO MIDNIGHT when we finally left and re-turned to the hotel.

"Are you okay?"

I exhaled, relaxing against the leather seat of the Jeep, then shift-ed my gaze to David. "I'm fine, why do you ask?"

He continued to study me. "Because you have been quiet since we left my parents' house."

He was right. I had been quiet.

Turning away to stare out my window, I recounted my evening. I'd had a wonderful time with his family. They all had made me feel right at home. The only part of my evening that was puzzling was Aunt Wanda. Throughout the meal and even after we all moved to the family room to watch home movies, I had the strangest feeling Wanda was watching me. But why? Sighing, I slid across the seat and leaned against David. Perhaps it was simply my uneasiness.

"Are you disappointed?" David asked.

At the sound of his deep voice interrupting my thoughts, I gave him a sidelong glance. "What makes you think I'm disappointed?"

He shrugged his right shoulder. "Because you had hoped my mother would have been able to shed some light on who your birth mother was."

"No, not at all. I learned quite a bit listening to your mother and Wanda reminiscing about the good ole days." In fact, some of my resentment had vanished. The pain of being abandoned had lessened. When I closed my eyes, I imagined myself young, pregnant, and alone during a time when being unwed and pregnant was unacceptable. I would probably have done the same.

David blew his horn at a car that was bold enough to jump out in front of him, causing me to snap out of my trance.

I reached out linking my hand with his, needing to touch him. "I had a wonderful time today. Thanks for inviting me."

"I thank you for coming," David said with a dimpled smile. I returned the smile and while he drove, I found myself watching him again. I couldn't stop looking at him. I could have looked into his eyes forever. With him in my life, he was the calm to a terrible storm. With David by my side, deep feelings of peace evaded my heart.

David raised my hand to his lips and kissed me gently across the knuckles and an undeniable heat snaked its way down through my stomach. Holding hands, he rested them on my knee. Leaning over, I rested my head against his arm. Closing my eyes, I tried to calm my thoughts. David's smell, personality, support and the way he made me feel all added up to one thing.

I wanted him to make love to me again.

David pulled into the parking lot on the east side of the hotel, then walked around to the other side and opened the door. Holding my hand firmly in his, he led me through the double doors. We boarded the elevator, then walked down the hall without an exchange of words. When we reached my room, I stuck my keycard in the door, then turned the knob before facing David again. His arms came around me in a vice-like grip, cradling me close to his chest. He then pressed his lips to my forehead. The kiss, only a brush of the mouth, caused me to gasp, shocked by the electricity caused by the touch. David's eyes traveled to my mouth and up to meet the gaze of my brown eyes. When he looked at me a rush of heat swept my body, leaving me shaking with desire.

"Babe, I had a wonderful day with you. I'm not ready for it to end."

Babe... His use of the endearment seemed so intimate as though I truly belonged to him.

David lowered his mouth and we met in a powerful passionate kiss, scorching in its intensity. His lips were like fire, licking and burning my tender skin. He kissed my ear, nipping the lobe, then his tongue trailed across my jaw until he reached my mouth again. My lips opened and he kissed me, wrapping his tongue around mine, licking the edge of my teeth.

"David," I moaned only seconds before my knees gave out.

Without breaking the kiss, David swept me in his arms and made his way into my room. After kicking the door shut, he moved over to the king size bed, whipped back the covers and deposited me gently on the middle of the bed. Boldly, he followed me down and slid his hand to my buttocks, aligning my body firmly against his.

He darted his tongue inside my mouth, and he groaned with satisfaction when my strokes met his. His lips trailed away from my mouth and my head fell back, granting him greater access as he traveled down to my throat leaving a wet path.

David slid his hand down my spine along my buttocks and then across my side to my waist. Moving under my blouse, his hand stroked my hip, flat belly and finally cupped my breasts. I released small moaning sounds. Hungry for his touch, I arched towards him, pressing closer and encouraged him to do more.

David found the zipper of my Capri pants and slipped his hand inside, caressing my buttocks. Just touching me made my walls clench with anticipation.

Coaxing me to lift my hips, he tugged my pants followed by a pair of satin panties over my hips. At the sight of me, he took a sharp breath.

"You're beautiful," he groaned. His hand caressed my cheek and slid down my neck before stopping at my blouse. Deftly, he released the top button of my blouse followed by a second and third until he finally released the last one. He swallowed before parting my blouse and stared down at a dark green bra. He released the front clasp and stared at the untanned swell of my breasts.

"David," I whispered, and the sound was swallowed up by his mouth. His tongue delved deep, tangling with mine, drawing me into a hot fever of emotions and cries. His hands kneaded my breasts, his thumb making arousing circles over each nipple, drawing them into hard pebbled peaks.

David released me to move off the bed, and I cried out at his sudden absence. Propping myself up on one elbow, I found him removing his clothes. His body was hard and beautiful. He reached into his pants pocket and removed a condom. I watched as he rolled the latex covering over the length of his large rigid flesh and my body began to tremble. He moved back beside me, the weight of his torso resting between my legs, sending shivers of excitement through my limbs. Sliding down, his lips closed over one aching tip. His thumb grazed one breast while his lips caressed the other. I gasped in sweet agony. His mouth was so warm, his hands strong, tender. Traveling even further, his fingers brushed through the apex of dark curls, seeking the hidden nub of pleasure within. I arched my back as he gently teased, my breathing now heavy and out of control.

"Yes," I moaned. My chest rose and fell in shuddering gasps.

When David parted my feminine folds, I was slick and ready, my need so strong that I arched into his hand. The urge for him to drive into me and be swept away in a tide of pleasure was so great, I had to bite down on my lower lip to maintain a thin strand of composure.

"Oh, David."

"Tell me, baby." He stared down at me, watching as I whimpered and twisted beneath him. My ragged breathing indicated I was losing control as quickly as he was. "Tell me what you want," he crooned.

I was ready to scream, desperately needing more of him than his touch. "I want you now!" If I had to wait any longer, I was sure to come apart.

"As you wish." Without any further hesitation, David positioned himself between my legs, his shaft pulsing at my opening. When he slid inside me the joining of our bodies was explosive. He buried his face at the base of my neck as passion pounded the blood through my veins.

"Am I hurting you?" he breathed against my lips as he searched my eyes under the dim moonlit sky spilling through the corners of the curtain.

Not yet, I thought inwardly. The real pain wouldn't start until long after the memory of our time together was over and the feeling of him deep inside of me had faded. I wouldn't fool myself. We were both caught up in the moment. When we returned home, we would both return to our separate lives. All I had time to worry about was what was happening now. To answer his question I shook my head, then wrapped my legs tightly around his waist.

David began to move slow at first, giving my body time to adjust to his size—the welcoming invasion—until my nails dug into his back urging him to continue. He pumped in and out of my moist body increasing the rhythm and together we found the tempo that bound our bodies together. He wanted to give me fulfillment, wanted me to come before he did.

"I don't know how much more I can take," he said, groaning. He pushed harder and deeper.

I met each of his strokes with as much intensity as his own. Each stroke pushed me much further over the edge until I was ready to explode. "Now!" I cried.

And that was all it took for David to grant my wish. He clutched an arm around my waist burying himself deeper inside, at the same time locking his mouth to mine. I arched off the pillow and my hips rose to meet his thrusts.

"Yes-s-s!" I screamed loud with erotic ecstasy. My cries of delight echoed off the walls as I felt his spasm of release. Shortly after, he held me in his arms as we drifted off to sleep.

I WAS THE FIRST TO awaken and found my head on David's chest. Memories of the night before came flooding back. The last thing I remembered was David kissing me on the mouth, then pulling me snuggly in his arms.

Swallowing, I glanced at the face of the man who still had a protective arm draped across my waist. To be able to wake up beside such a considerate and patient man gave me a deep feeling of security.

While listening to the relaxing sound of his breathing, I found myself overcome by more memories.

I had become one of David's conquests.

I groaned inwardly. What had I been thinking? I had been thinking about David. The same way I was now. Nothing pleased me more than to lie beside him and stare at his handsome face as he slept. The smell of him consumed me. The sight of him mesmerized me, and his touch had cast a spell on me, making it virtually impossible to think or even breathe for that matter. I had experienced something I would never forget, and I would be forever grateful.

Unable to resist, I skimmed my fingers down his arm as I wondered what he would think after our heated weekend together. Women were a challenge to David and now he had succeeded in getting what he wanted.

Closing my eyes, I tried to think about something else. I refused to think about how fabulous it felt, with him inside me. Instead, I told myself that it had been too long since I had been with a man and it was only natural for me to have reacted the way I had. I couldn't allow myself to make any more of what had happened than what it was. He said he wanted more, but I couldn't bring myself to believe that. Instead, it was just sex with no strings attached. So why did I feel a painful ache inside my chest?

"What are you thinking about?" David asked, breaking into my thoughts.

Shit.

His eyelids fluttered open and his gaze held mine.

"I'm not thinking about anything. How did you even know I was awake?" I asked as I moved from his chest and onto my pillow.

David shifted slightly and propped his head, resting it in the palm of his hand. "I could tell by your breathing. Now I'm going to ask you again, what's on your mind?"

He continued to stare at me, his gold-green eyes fixed on my face. I could feel the caress of his gaze and tried to ignore the throbbing in my lower limbs.

"My parents," I lied. For once they weren't on my mind. All I could think about was David's beautiful pecs and his nipple that was only inches away from my mouth.

David raised his hand to stroke my hair. "You miss your parents, don't you?"

I paused. "Yes, I miss them." Rolling onto my back, I shifted my thoughts from him, allowing the memories of my parents to resurface. "I don't know why I miss them so much. When they were around, I rarely ever saw them. My dad and mom spent so much time trying to portray this perfect image. When he was mayor, I could understand, but once he served two terms and officially retired, I couldn't understand why they still behaved that way." I tried to pull my thoughts together before I continued. "Before they were killed, my parents spent a lot of time traveling. They had just returned from a cruise and Daddy called to tell me that they were back. Before he said goodbye, Mama asked to speak to me. She told me how wonderful Alaska had been. We chatted for a few minutes and before she hung up, she told me she loved me. She rarely *ever* said that to me, so I remember hanging up and having this strange feeling that something was going to happen. It was two days later I received the phone call that their car had been struck on the way back from dinner. The driver had just left a local bar where he'd had too much to drink. My father was killed instantly. My mother lived long enough to tell me I wasn't her daughter."

David pulled me closer to him, sensing that I needed his strength. "I'm sure they loved you in their own way."

"My uncle said the same thing."

I closed my eyes and found myself lost in the comfort of his embrace. His arm was resting on the curve of my hip and my head was cradled against his shoulder.

Desire like I had never known before began to boil inside me. Awkwardly, I rolled away from him and rose. "We better get going if we're going to have breakfast."

Gently, David pulled me back down onto the mattress and rolled on top of me. I felt him grow hard. My body began to respond. Before I knew it, I was parting my thighs and inviting him back inside.

"Stop trying to fight what you're feeling," David whispered against my cheek. "You want me as much as I want you, don't you?"

I moaned.

"Say it, Calaine!" he demanded. When I refused to answer, he stopped mid-stroke waiting for my response.

I couldn't bear it and screamed. "Yes!"

"Yes, what?"

"Yes, I wanted this. I want you." He pushed deeper and moved slowly at first before the rhythm intensified.

I found myself helpless with desire.

SUNDAY WAS SPENT IN the company of a man who made me laugh one minute and shudder with desire the next. David was the most thrilling ride I had ever taken.

After we made love again, we dressed and headed to the River Walk in the heart of downtown. Lush green foliage and towering trees lined the banks of the historic river. Holding hands, we strolled from one end to the other, enjoying the sights and sounds of the area. For lunch, we dropped into a restaurant and had what I believed to be the best fajitas in the state of Texas.

That evening, we returned to his parents' house for dinner. To my relief Wanda wasn't there. I found myself laughing and enjoying the evening and had a chance to meet Christie's boyfriend and found him to be a wonderful man. As sunset arrived, we stepped out onto the deck together. David moved up behind me and wrapped his arms around my waist as we bid the sun goodbye. I paused to appreciate the serenity of the night. With a satisfied sigh, David turned me around until I was facing him. We stared at each other for the longest time before his mouth captured mine. The kiss was demanding and passionate. Accepting the fact that I was in love was frightening and exciting. There was no escaping it. I had wanted him in college, and when I saw him at the job fair, I wanted him all over again.

We left his parents a little earlier this time and returned to the hotel to his room where David spent the evening teaching me things in bed that I would have been ashamed to talk about. However, with David it seemed to be the most natural thing. He had the ability to make me feel like the sexiest and most desirable woman on the planet. I couldn't put our lovemaking to words. Our coming together was explosive and tender. Afterwards, David held me in his arms while he drifted off to sleep.

If I hadn't known I was in love before I left for San Antonio, I knew now. What frightened me was what was going to happen when we returned home.

Exhausted, I shut my eyes and tried to block out the past several hours. Tomorrow everything would be back to normal, but deep down I knew my life would never be normal again. The past several days with David were enough to last me a lifetime.

We rose the following morning in time for the buffet. An hour later, after a repeat performance in the shower, we checked out of the hotel.

Feeling like lovers, we dropped by one of his favorite spots on the way to the airport. It was a small mom and pop restaurant that was famous for its enchiladas. Our waitress had just returned with our food when a willowy caramel-colored woman came to stand beside our table. We both looked up at her at the same time.

"David, I almost didn't recognize you," she replied, her gray eyes sparkling with excitement.

He gave her a polite smile. "Hello, Chanel."

"*Hello Chanel?* Is that all you have to say? Why didn't you tell me you were coming to town? I've been trying to reach you ever since you moved back to that little college town," she pouted.

"I'm here for my sister's graduation." He glanced across the table and me. "Chanel, I would like you to meet a good friend of mine, Calaine Hart."

She looked as if she had just realized he wasn't sitting alone. "Hello." She gave me a tight smile and before I could respond, Chanel looked back over at David. "Let's get together this evening. We can go to Maurice's for ole' time sakes."

He shook his head. "My flight leaves in three hours. I'll call you the next time I'm in town."

I could tell the beauty wasn't used to being rejected. "You do that," she purred and walked away.

I didn't know why but the fact that he referred to me as a "good friend" really bothered me. And that fact that he planned to reach out to her so they could hang out at Maurice's *for ole time sakes* irritated me.

When David excused himself and went to the men's room, I found myself wondering about our relationship. Although we had spent the weekend together, nothing had changed between us. Nevertheless, my mind was troubled as I stabbed my fork into my enchilada.

Remember, you were only interested in sex with no strings attached.

I looked over toward the restrooms to find David standing outside the door talking to Chanel who was flirting shamelessly. His back was to the table, but I knew they were standing close. Chanel brought a hand behind his head, lowered it towards her and kissed him, her long, sculptured fingernails caressing his neck. My fingers tightened around the iced cold glass. How well did they know each other? I thought I'd known what jealousy was when I had found McKinley with another woman, but that was mild in comparison. The pain that filled my heart was unlike anything I had ever experienced.

I SLEPT THE ENTIRE trip. Once in David's car, we made the drive home from the airport. I closed my eyes with Chanel still on my mind. After I caught them kissing, David had walked back to our table grinning like nothing had happened. Bastard!

Was he also seeing someone in Columbia? It surprised me at how bothered I was at seeing him with another woman. Then I reminded myself that just because I loved him, I had no business feeling that way. David was free to see whomever he liked. He had made no promises to me.

Let's just see where this thing leads us.

It was obvious it had led to nowhere.

"You want to get something to eat?" David asked, breaking into my thoughts.

I shook my head and declined. "No, I'm anxious to get home. I have a few things to do before I get back to work tomorrow."

We drove several more miles in silence before he said, "You're going to continue to act as nothing has changed between us." It wasn't a question, so I didn't bother to respond. "Let's talk about this weekend."

"What's there to talk about? We're just having sex."

"You don't believe that."

"Yes I do. I'm not looking for emotional attachment and neither are you."

His brow quirked. "How do you know what I want?"

"Because I know you," I challenged. Turning on the seat, I looked him directly in the eyes.

"Obviously you don't know me at all." His fingers clinched tightly around the steering wheel.

We were silent for the duration of the drive. Once in my driveway, David carried my bags to the door. Before I could step inside, he took my arm and swung me around. I gasped in surprise. "David, I..."

His hands framed my face, his thumb grazing my mouth.

"At some point you'll need to quit lying to yourself. Because what's happening between us isn't going away." His warm breath stroked my flushed face. David lowered his mouth to mine. The kiss was rough although passionate. David drew my lower lip into his mouth, sucked it gently. His tongue licked and sucked, then slipped inside and began tasting. There was so much frustration in the kiss my grip on reality slipped a fraction and I couldn't think, only feel. David was a dangerously desirable man, able to penetrate my resistance.

When his mouth finally lifted, he stared deep into my eyes. "You felt that. I'm not alone in this. And I'm staking my claim."

With that, he turned and walked away.

Chapter 16

I SAT IN FRONT OF MY laptop, staring at a blank screen. *How do you write a letter to someone asking if they're your mother?* What if she never called or wrote me back? I sighed, releasing a lung full of explosive air. Maybe my uncle was right, and my mother didn't want to be found.

Maybe I just needed to leave well enough alone.

Tired of staring at the blank screen, I slid my chair away from the desk and rose. I was frustrated and so ready to give up my search, but I knew if I did, the nagging ache of not knowing would never go away.

Padding barefoot into the kitchen, I decided to make a cup of herbal tea. I removed a clean mug from the dishwasher and reached in a canister next to a wooden breadbox for a tea bag. After putting the teakettle on the stove, I leaned against the counter with my arms folded across my chest. My eyes traveled to the end of the counter where I spotted a menu from Tony's Pizza. It had been attached to the pizza box David had brought to my house over a week ago.

It had been two days since we returned from San Antonio and I hadn't heard from him. I had expected David to have at least called or dropped by unannounced like I had grown accustomed to him doing. So far, he had done neither. My jaw clenched. I couldn't understand why I was surprised or even disappointed, especially with his track record with women.

Who are you trying to fool?

Okay, so maybe I was trying to convince myself of something different. David wanted more. He had said so. The only thing standing in the way of that happening was me. What was I waiting for? I loved him. That was no secret and the more time I spent away from him, the more I realized just how much I missed him. He was constantly in my thoughts, which was why I had been increasingly irritable and impatient at work. It had gotten so bad Norma pulled me aside and scolded me for my ill behavior. I later apologized to my staff and spent the remainder of my day in my office, still thinking about David. My body craved for his touch. I wanted him holding me, caressing me, kissing me with his full sexy lips. So why was I torturing myself if I didn't have to?

Because you saw him kissing Chanel!

Nope. Because I needed the truth. I needed to uncover my past before I could begin thinking about my future. Okay, so that may sound a bit lame, but that's my story and I was sticking to it.

Tired of thinking about David, I decided that enough was enough. I had to decide whether I would or wouldn't before I hopped in my car and sped to his house.

Turning off the kettle, I decided to do something I hadn't done in months. I rushed to my room and changed into an old t-shirt and a pair of spandex shorts. Slipping my Nike cross-trainers on my feet, I returned to the living room. I pulled back the coffee table, then moved to the television and popped a DVD into the machine.

Along with Jillian Michaels and the rest of her crew, I kicked and punched for the next half hour. With my hands balled into fists, I swung an uppercut for every year I lived a lie. I bobbed and weaved while thinking about how my uncle had lied to protect me. I roundhouse kicked my anger at my aunt for turning against me and treating me like an outsider. My uppercuts were directed at my father for having an affair with a nursing student and getting her pregnant. My sidekicks were for David coming into my life and making me fall in love with him.

Breathing hard and sweating I worked off my anger. I felt great punching an imaginary bag, releasing all my pent-up frustrations.

By the cool down, I felt relaxed. The tension had vanished, and my anger had lessened. I even realized that I had no real reason to be angry with David. Even though I had watched him and Chanel kiss, it was no business of mine. David and I weren't committed. There were never any words of love and marriage. David had never promised me anything other than his help and friendship. Despite everything I thought about him, he had been there for me every step of the way. It was no one's fault but mine that I had fallen in love with him. Now I just needed to be strong and get over it. With as much disappointment as I've had in my life, I should be a pro at handling difficult situations.

The phone rang, ending any further thoughts on the subject. I reached over and grabbed it before the call went to voicemail.

"Hello?"

"Calaine Hart, please."

The gruff voice was unfamiliar to me. "This is Calaine."

I heard the man clear his throat twice before speaking again. "Ms. Hart, this is Anthony Conley."

My lips pursed tightly at the mention of the lawyer. My aunt had asked him to call. "What do you want?"

He cleared his throat a third time. "I would like to first apologize for your aunt's behavior. It was uncalled for and truly out of line."

I felt guilty for my immediate attitude. "Thank you. I appreciate it."

"No need to thank me. I should have spoken up, but I did not. Greta has always had a way of intimidating people, even me I'm afraid."

I had to chuckle at that.

"I wanted to reassure you that your mother knew what she was doing when she left all of her assets to you. Olivia came and saw me before she and your father departed for their cruise."

My stomach churned. "She did?"

"Yes, she did. She wanted to make sure her will was iron tight. She told me that even though you weren't her biological daughter, she loved you very much. I had her sign an affidavit to that effect."

I was speechless. My mother had done that for me?

"Don't worry about Greta, your future is secure. But I do need your signature on a few documents. How about I overnight everything to your office tomorrow?"

"That would be just fine. Thank you so much for calling, Mr. Conley. You have no idea how much this means to me." Tears surfaced and caught in my throat.

"You take care and if you need anything in the future, please feel free to call my office."

"Mr. Conley?" I asked just as he was about to hang up.

"Yes, Ms. Hart?"

"Did Olivia ever say anything to you about my..." I paused to swallow the lump in my throat, allowing Mr. Conley to intervene.

"No, Calaine. I'm afraid she didn't. However, she did say she needed to make everything right."

I managed to thank him again, then hung up the phone. I lowered into a chair unable to move. All these years I had been led to believe my mother resented me when all along she had cared about me.

Maybe she just had a hard time expressing herself.

Taking a deep breath, I returned to the living room, switched off the television, then went to the bathroom and took a long hot shower. As soon as I was done, I made a cup of tea. I carried it back to my spare room and sat at my desk. This time the words flowed onto the paper.

Chapter 17

I HUNG UP THE PHONE and blew out a frustrated breath. Another dead end. I had been trying to find Ursula for two days and after a dozen calls, I still wasn't any closer to finding her. Tossing the list aside, I stepped out to the lobby.

My interviewer Tyla was busy giving a young woman a typing test while another was filling out an application.

"How's it going?" After promoting Jean to the sales floor, Tyla had only been with me a month, but she was quickly stamping her mark in my company. She made sure each employee had adequate training and even conducted mock interviews.

Tyla's eyes sparkled as she nodded appreciatively. "Everything is going great."

Smiling was always a good sign. "Good. Let me know if you need any help today."

After giving a warm greeting to the other women, I moved out to the foyer and found David standing there.

I tried to control the rapid beat of my heart. It had been three days since I'd seen him. I had done everything to get him off my mind but found that besides trying to find my mother, David was the center of my thoughts.

My eyes drank in his powerful presence and I realized my memory had not done him justice. The man was seductive as sin. He looked gorgeous dressed in an off-black double-breasted suit with black wingtip shoes. Only he could pull off the pale pink shirt with matching handkerchief. A huge smile tugged at his lips as he moved towards me, his stride easy and powerful.

I forced myself to stay composed as I glanced up at him. "David, what are you doing here?"

"Hello to you, too," he greeted in a deep sensuous tone. His gaze traveled down the entire length of my body appreciatively as he took in a two-piece almond pants suit.

Tearing my eyes away from his calculated stare, I turned to find Norma looking at us curiously.

"David, please follow me to my office."

I nodded to the group, ignoring their curious looks and led David down the hallway to my office. As soon as we entered the room, he pushed the door shut.

I twirled around ready to blast him for not calling me in days when he pressed me back against the door and locked my lips with his. Instead of giving him a piece of my mind, I wrapped my arms around his neck and met his kiss.

What a way to end a busy day.

The kiss would have gone on for hours if he hadn't stopped. David eased away and took the seat beside my desk, smiling confidently.

The tingle of his kiss quickly vanished by the sight of his smug face. I moved around my desk, reached for a Kleenex and wiped away what was left of my lipstick. Looking up at him, my expression had darkened. "I would appreciate it if you would call before you decide to drop by my office."

David ignored the comment and reached into his jacket pocket. Removing several folded sheets of paper, he slapped them on my desk. "I found Eunice."

The tongue-lashing dissipated from my tongue. "How...when?"

He chuckled softly at the change of my expression. "I found her on the Internet."

I moved around my desk and took a seat, reaching the papers. Eunice Roberts resided in Wilmington, Delaware, but I didn't want to get my hopes up. "I thought she was dead! How do you know this is the right person?"

"I found three Eunice Roberts who would have been between the ages of 18-21 in 1975. But only this woman worked as a registered nurse."

I stared down at the paper and read. Her addresses for the past ten years were public record. She had worked as an RN at Wilmington Hospital. "This information is five years old."

David nodded. "I know. Five years ago she appeared to have fallen from the face of the earth."

"What do you mean?"

"I mean there is no record of her after that. No credit checks, no new address or places of employment."

My shoulders sagged. "Do you think maybe she didn't die until then?"

David shook his head. "I don't think so. But it won't be too hard to find out. Her death would be public information."

I dropped down in my chair. Never married. No children. Why? Was it because of me?

I noticed David watching the play of emotions on my face. I was still left with lots of unanswered questions. We still weren't even sure if Eunice was my mother, but at least we were a few steps closer to finding out the truth.

I looked over at him. "Have you had any luck with the other woman?"

"Dorlinda?"

I nodded.

"Not yet, but I will," he stated confidently.

I stared at him, feeling almost as confident as he sounded. I had never liked an arrogant man but something about him drew me to his confidence. It was as if he had no boundaries when he wanted something bad enough. That was what I loved about him most. I wondered if he'd pursue me with the same determination?

David put a brown bag onto my desk. I hadn't noticed him holding anything in his hand. "What's that?"

"Lunch. You've never been one to pass up CJ's wings before."

I took a quick sniff and my mouth watered.

My private line rang, and I immediately picked it up. "Calaine Hart speaking."

"Calaine, this is your Uncle Tad. I've found Coletta Ross."

By the time I had ended the call, I was shaking.

"Is everything okay?"

"Uncle Thaddeus found Coletta," I replied in an emotional throaty voice I hardly recognized as my own.

"That's great isn't it?" he asked as he wiped his hands on a napkin.

"I think so."

"Oh course it is," he said trying to reassure me. David reached across the desk and grabbed the notepad I had scribbled on. "Sexton Road?" He gasped. "She still lives in Columbia?"

I nodded.

"Well, then let's go." He clapped his hands together as he stood.

"Go where?" There was no mistaking the panic in my voice.

His gaze came down to rest on my puzzled face. "To see Ms. Coletta Ross."

"*Now?*"

"There's no time better than the present. I'll drive while you eat your lunch." Before I could object, he put our food back in the bag. Moving around the desk he took me by the hand and led me out to his car.

David hadn't given me a chance to change my mind until he started the engine. "I-I can't do this."

He put the car in Park and turned to face me. "Why?"

I looked over and met his probing gaze. "I'm not ready," I admitted quietly.

"What's there to get ready for?"

I didn't answer.

David reached for my hand and squeezed. "Just be yourself. You're going to be fine."

I lowered my eyelids briefly and nodded. David shifted the car in gear and when he pulled out of the parking lot, terror sprinted through me. All I could think about was that I was not ready. For all I knew, this could be the woman who gave me life, who first held me tightly in her arms. Coletta could be my biological mother!

"I don't feel so good," I moaned as I lowered my window and proceeded to stick my head out.

David reached over, pulled me back down in my seat and pushed the button, raising the window. "Calaine, the air conditioning is on. Relax, everything is going to be just fine."

I looked down at my hands. They were trembling. "What if she's my mother?"

"Then our search is over." He captured my trembling hand in his. "You will no longer have to go around wondering, because you'll have your answers."

I nodded, knowing he was right. If Coletta was my mother, then the mystery was over. If she wasn't my mother, then maybe she might be able to shed some light on several unanswered questions.

"Thank you," I said.

He lifted an eyebrow at me. "I thought I asked you to quit thanking me?"

"I know, but I want to say it anyway." I admitted my need for his support. I didn't want to impose on him any further, but deep down

I depended on his strength to get me through this entire pursuit of finding my mother.

"What are friends for?"

As we pulled onto Sexton Road, a chill ran through me. I had driven on the street several times before, but this time it looked so different. I had never noticed how different each house was structured as if they had been designed by several different developers. The flow of traffic was constant and with parked cars on the narrow road, there was very little room left for two-way traffic.

I took a deep breath and tried to relax. I had come to find out answers about my birth and only had mere seconds left to turn around and change my mind. *The truth.* I was about to find out the truth.

David slowed his car in front of a quaint brick house on the corner. "This is it," he announced, causing my pulse to dash off in a high chase.

I stared out the window, thinking about all the years I had driven past this very house without knowing it potentially held answers to my past.

The house was old but in fair condition. Hanging pots filled with petunias were on the porch. Crabgrass grew freely along a lawn that was long overdue for a cut.

"You ready?" he asked.

I flipped the visor down and using the mirror as my guide, I combed through my hair with my fingers. After another long thoughtful look, I nodded and climbed out the car.

Insecurity rose when I discovered children playing in the backyard. Three small girls, one a little taller than the other, came to stand against the chain link fence. It was obvious they were sisters. Identical kohl eyes watched with curiosity as David and I moved towards the porch. The door was open and through the screen, I could hear *Family Feud* playing on the television.

Shaking off the melancholy, I pressed the bell.

"Grandma!" I heard one of the girls yell. "Someone's at the door."

Seconds later, I heard feet shuffling towards the front door.

My heart was now lodged in my throat and I was tempted to make a mad dash for the car.

Sensing my uneasiness, David leaned forward, placing a hand to the small of my back. "I'm right here beside you," he whispered, his warm breath ruffling against my ear.

A short, busty woman finally appeared. "Hello, may I help you?" she asked in a sweet voice as she opened the screen and stuck out her head.

I returned the woman's wide smile. "Sorry to bother you, but I am looking for Coletta Ross."

The woman chuckled, drawing attention to a tooth missing from the front of her mouth. "I haven't been Ross in years. I married a Coleman two decades ago."

I took in her ebony eyes, the oval shape of her face and the caramel-color of her skin. Was there any resemblance?

Placing a hand to her thickened waist, she asked, "What can I do for y'all this afternoon?"

"Uh...excuse me. I'm Calaine and this is my friend David. We...I'm looking..." my voice trailed off as I looked over my shoulder at David for help. He stepped forward.

"She's trying to find her mother, and we were hoping you could help us."

Coletta looked at us suspiciously. "What makes you think I can help?"

I reached into my purse, pulled out the photograph and handed it to her. Coletta took one look at it and the color in her face drained.

Chapter 18

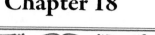

MY PULSE RACED. "YOU know something, don't you?"

Coletta shook her head and handed back the picture. "No, nothing at all. Now if you'd excuse me."

David stuck his foot out in time to keep the screen door from closing. "Ma'am, please, if you know something it would really help."

Her eyes shifted from side to side.

"Please," I pleaded. "I don't want to upset anyone, I just want the truth."

For a moment there I thought she was going to slam the door shut. Instead, she dropped her shoulders and said, "Come on in." She pushed open the door and showed us inside.

"Thank you," I whispered as I moved into the living room.

The room reminded me of my paternal grandmother's house. Plastic covered out-of-date furniture and different size pillows scattered around the living space and crowded with photographs of several generations of family.

"Please have a seat."

I moved to the couch and the plastic crackled beneath me as I took a seat. David sat beside me while Coletta lowered onto a blue recliner.

She held out her hand. "Let me see that photo again."

I handed her the photograph. I watched the older woman stare at it lost in her thoughts.

"Are you my mother?" I blurted.

"Your mother?" Coletta took a moment before she finally looked up and said, "No, I'm not."

The girls dashed in through the back door and into the living room. They stopped when they saw us sitting there and suddenly became shy. I smiled. They were well-groomed and dressed identically in jeans and red cotton shirts. Each had their hair in cornrows and decorated with red barrettes. The littlest one, who couldn't have been older than four, reached for her big sister's hand.

Coletta shifted in her seat and acknowledged the three. I could see the love in her eyes when she spoke. "Yes, girls, what is it?"

"Can you come push me in the swing?" the youngest asked in a soft voice.

"In a few minutes. I have company."

David cleared his throat. "If you don't mind, I can swing the girls while the two of you talk." We both noticed her slight hesitation before David added, "Don't worry. Ruby raised me well."

Her face lit up. "Ruby Soul is your mother?"

Nodding, he grinned. "Yes, she is."

"Well I'll be. How is she doing?"

"Quite well, Ma'am."

"Ain't it a small world? Your mom and I used to be real close. I lost touch with the others over the years. She and I kept in contact until we both got so caught up into our own families and just never seemed to have time to talk anymore." She asked David a few questions about his mother before she finally said, "All right. Tiana, Terry and Tabby, this nice man is going to swing you."

David rose and moved to stand in front of the three. They hesitated slightly, then he reached into his pocket and pulled out a roll of lifesavers. The candy was the perfect icebreaker. Within minutes, the girls were pulling him out the back door.

I smiled at the exchange, then looked over at Coletta who was watching them through the window.

I felt I needed to set the scene if I was going to get any answers. "I didn't find out until her death that Olivia Hart was not my mother. My father was James Hart."

She gasped. "Our former mayor?"

I folded my hands in my lap and nodded.

"He was a nice guy. I met him years before he was mayor at a small jazz club. It was back when all of us were in nursing school." She gave me a sweet sympathetic smile. "I'm so sorry. I read that he and his wife died in a car crash."

"Thank you. It's been hard but I'm taking it one step at a time. That's why I need to find out the truth. My mother confessed before she passed away that I was not her daughter. Now that my family is gone, I don't have anyone I can ask. I found that photo in her drawer and I think that one of those women gave birth to me in 1975."

Coletta rose from her chair and paced across the floor before looking at me again. "There was a baby."

I couldn't breath as I waited for her to continue.

"Eunice and Dorlinda were inseparable. They had both come up from some small country town in Mississippi with high expectations, and quickly got caught up into partying and hanging out. They were constantly breaking the rules and Ms. Butler was hard on them."

"She was the dorm mother, right?"

Icy contempt filled her eyes. "The mean old goat! She was so strict that if you were even a minute past your curfew, she would take away your privileges for a week."

I looked on with bewilderment. "But all of you were grown women."

Coletta sadly shook her head and shrugged. "That's just the way it was. The school had rules."

Folding her arms beneath her large breasts, she moved across the floor as she began again. "I remember one night hearing a baby cry. I know because the sound woke me up out of my sleep. I grabbed my robe and went down the hall to their room and there was this baby lying on the bed. Eunice and Dorlinda were sitting there looking scared while they tried to quiet the baby down before Ms. Butler heard her. Thank the Lord, she was a hard sleeper." Coletta stopped pacing and frowned. "Beautiful little thing, but she was colicky. After having six younger brothers and sisters, I learned a thing or two from my momma. One thing she had taught me was that rocking a baby across your knees helped to soothe the tummy. Sure enough, I had that little angel sleep in no time." Coletta moved and returned to her seat in the recliner.

"Whose baby was it?" I asked as I wrung my hands nervously.

"I asked them and they both said the baby was theirs." She gave a laugh of disbelief. "I never could figure out whose child it was. Neither of them had ever looked pregnant, so I thought they were lying. They were no bigger than a minute and so pretty." Coletta paused and stared off to her left, lost in her thoughts.

I cleared my throat trying to get her attention. "What happened to the baby?"

Coletta looked at me and blinked several times before she spoke. "One of them would go to class while the other stayed behind. They tried to keep that precious bundle quiet, but I knew it was just a matter of time before Ms. Butler found out." She stopped and took a deep breath. "I remember that night. Ruby was at home with her family, Wanda and Ursula were at a movie and I was in our room waiting for a phone call, when I heard shouting come from down the hall. I was too afraid to leave my room, but I heard a lot of screaming and crying. The next day the baby was gone. Eunice didn't leave her bed for almost a week. Dorlinda neither. I asked what happened to the baby, and they said she with her father."

I was momentarily speechless as I thought about the photo of my mother holding me, wrapped in a receiving blanket.

Did...did they ever mention the baby again?"

She shook her head. "No. The two became withdrawn and rarely spoke to any of us. I tried cheering them up, but nothing worked. I even found Eunice crying a few times. If I had to speculate on whose child it was I would say that baby had belonged to her."

"Do you know if she committed suicide?"

"Lord, no! Although, I wouldn't be surprised. Eunice was truly heartbroken, and I can understand why."

I searched her eyes. "Why didn't you want to talk to me?"

She hesitated. "Because I was paid to never talk about that baby to anyone."

"What?"

She shrugged. "I received a large envelope one day with cash inside and a note that I'd keep receiving money twice a year as long as I said nothing. That check stopped a couple of months ago."

"Did the checks stop after my parents were killed?"

She looked confused for several moments before her eyes widened. "I think they did."

This wasn't happening.

"I never asked questions. Was just glad to receive that cash. It helped me through some rough patches," she explained, combing fingers through her hair. "I never thought it was anything illegal. Although I often wondered why all the secrecy and whatever happened to that baby. That little girl was a beauty. I will never forget the distinct birthmark she had on her thigh."

"Birthmark?" I suddenly felt lightheaded.

She nodded. "Yes, it was shaped like a strawberry."

I stiffened just as David entered the room. Coletta rose and said she had to get dinner on the stove before her husband got home from work. I wasn't sure how I found the strength to stand. I thanked Coletta for all her help and hurried out to the car. I felt like I was suffocating and was thankful for the fresh air.

David came up behind me and reached for my arm. Turning me gently around to face him, he stepped closer and stared deeply in my eyes. "What happened. What did you find out?"

"Oh my God...that baby was me!" I could barely control my gasps.

His eyes lit with excitement. "That's wonderful, Calaine. You sound certain. How can you be so sure?"

"I had my doubts, but when she mentioned the strawberry birthmark on my leg, I knew it couldn't have been anyone but me. It was me, David! Oh my God, I can't believe this." Tears began to stream down my cheeks. It now felt so real. My mother was out there; I just needed to find her.

He stroked the back of my head trying to comfort me. "Are you going to be okay?"

I clung to his middle, absorbing his body heat and nodded. "I think so. It's just so much information to digest."

He held my hand on the ride back and listened as I recanted my conversation with Coletta. Afterwards I asked him to take me home. I was quiet and grateful that David allowed me time to digest the information.

When he pulled in front of my house, he parked the car but left the motor running. "You going to be all right?" he asked.

My lower lip trembled. "I will never be the same. Not until I find out which one of them was my mother and why she gave me up?" Feeling increasingly depressed I didn't want to be alone, brooding over what had happened today. "Can you stay awhile?"

He turned the car off and rushed around to open the door for me. He looked down at me, still sitting there lost in a daze.

"Calaine?"

I jumped. "Ooh! I'm sorry." I reached for my purse and climbed out the car. David placed a hand to the small of my back and assisted me to the front door. I fumbled around in my purse for my keys and made several ill attempts at opening the door. The set finally slipped from my hands and I began to cry.

David picked up the keys and opened the door. He swept me effortless into his arms and carried me over to the couch where he placed me upon his lap. I lowered my head against the warm curve of his throat and shoulder. I closed my eyes. I knew I needed to be strong and silently scolded myself for falling apart, but the truth was much more than I could handle. The nightmare surrounded me and at that moment, I didn't know how I could handle not being with David. There was no way I could leave his warm, strong embrace not when I so badly needed him. David pressed his face next to my hair and my body trembled. His hand opened and gathered me protectively against him.

"Sweetheart, it's going to be okay," he whispered shakily as he began to rock me.

I buried my face against his chest. "No, it isn't."

For a long time he simply rocked me in his arms and whispered words of encouragement. The tears increased with his kindness. He was truly concerned about my welfare. Never had I ever felt so safe and protected. David had the ability to make me forget my pain and fear about my uncertain future.

I shook my head vigorously as I tried to bring my lips to form words. "Why?"

His gaze came to rest on my tear-stained face. "Why what?"

"Why did my mother give me up?" I asked in a trembling, choked voice. "Was my father so mad that he refused to help her raise me? And why in the world was he paying Coletta to stay quiet?" I briefly told him about our conversation. It made no sense.

David held me tightly in his lap. "I don't know why, babe. But we're going to find out." Leaning forward, he kissed the tears away.

I searched his eyes. "Why are you helping me? Why would you want to be involved in this mess?"

"Do you have to keep asking me that? Can't you see I'm crazy about you?"

David pulled me in a close embrace. Relaxing in his arms, I felt a warm peace I hadn't felt in months. I had to believe that loving him wasn't wrong as long as I kept the extent of our relationship in perspective. With David, I felt safe.

I rested my head on his chest, feeling the vibrant beats of his heart. Everything about him was so male and comforting. "I need you," I whispered. My mind was in turmoil, and I needed to soothe it the only way I knew how.

"You're upset. I don't want to—"

"But I want you to," I interrupted as my hand moved to cup him between his thighs.

That was all the inviting David needed as he brought his mouth down on mine in possessive firm heat. With his hand, he gently lifted my head to give him easy access to my lips, parting them, seeking out the honeyed depths with his tongue. I welcomed him eagerly. I wanted this. Needed it. Regardless of what David might feel for me, I loved him and the only way I could ever show it was giving my body. Tonight we would make love and it would be precisely that for me.

I pressed my body deep against his and released a moan. David broke off the kiss long enough to lift me in his arms and carry me to my room.

I couldn't remove my clothes fast enough. I wanted to touch him, to feel his bare chest against me. With wild impatience, I took off my jacket. While he removed his suit, I unzipped my skirt and threw it across the room. David took off his shorts and tossed it in the pile with mine. We were two minds with a single thought.

Swiftly, he carried me over to the bed. I moaned softly when he laid me on my back, then straddled my hips. He pushed my hands above my head before trailing his fingers down the tender flesh of my arms and across my chest, finally hovering at the shadowy cleavage between my sensitive breasts. Instinctively my body arched, inviting him to release the clasp and touch me as I longed for him to do. I settled back with relief when at last he undid the fastening and eased the lacy cups aside. After what seemed ages, yet were mere seconds, his hand moved magically across my breasts, his thumb finding my nipples and caressing first one and then the other with tantalizing possessiveness until they were rock hard. I shifted beneath him needing more. A whimper of pleasure broke from me as I watched David lower his head and take a nipple and lavished it with his hot moist tongue, then move over to give my other equal attention. Unable to lie still, I lifted my hands to the back of his head and clung on as waves of ecstasy robbed me of my strength and caused spasms of desire at my wet throbbing core. Then he moved, his lips and hands tracing, scorching a path down my body meeting the barrier of my panties only momentarily as he tugged them down and they were gone, leaving me naked before him.

"Do you have any idea how beautiful you are?" he murmured. Not waiting for an answer, his tongue skimmed up the insides of my legs to the juncture of my thighs. He parted my trembling limbs and sought out the hot moist center of me. Suddenly I was overcome by an extraordinary rhythm of release.

"No. Wait," I protested faintly, wanting this to be a shared pleasure, but David had other ideas.

"Babe, it's all about you," he insisted throatily. "I want to make you forget everything except what I'm doing to you." He lowered his head again and began, working his magic on me until one last stroke of his tongue sent me tumbling over the edge.

Moans of ecstasy slipped through my lips as my whole body flooded with desire. I lay beneath him with my eyes closed, unable to control the outcry of delight as I exploded.

I was struggling to catch my breath when David came up beside me planting a kiss to my face.

"Brotha, you've got skills," I sighed, my desire momentarily appeased.

He smiled, his fingers tracing the contours of my cheekbones, his thighs rubbing against my hips. "No, I just love the way you taste," he replied, and that caused me to smile.

"Then it's my turn," I declared, sliding from underneath his leg, he was forced to fall back and, in an instant, I was straddling his body. Grinning mischievously, I met his gleaming gaze. "Scared? You should be, I'm going to make you feel even better," I promised as my fingers begun to explore the taut planes of his powerful chest.

David's teeth flashed. "Just being with you makes me feel good," he retorted. His breath hissed in through his teeth as I found his nipples and lightly teased them with my fingers.

Smiling with satisfaction now that I had his attention, I dropped my gaze to his chest after I saw his eyelids flutter weakly. I loved the way he responded to me, keeping nothing back. A groan escaped his lips and I felt my desire stir to life again as I set about tantalizing him as he had me. Dipping my head, I let my lips find his nipples and my teeth nipped him, bringing forth another moan of pleasure, then my tongue traced lazy circles before licking back and forth across the sensitive nubs.

I seared a moist pathway down over his firm stomach, feeling the tension grow inside him as I approached his waist. In all his naked glory there was no doubting his wanting me and I felt my own body start to throb with awakening desire.

It was no longer easy to keep my movements slow. My hands trembled faintly as I ran them over his thighs, getting closer but never quite reaching the place I instinctively knew he wanted me to touch. Finally, I gave in to my own need and my lips encircled him. Stroking the length of him with my tongue, I tasted and teased, laving him with my tongue.

It wasn't long before David moaned aloud and reached for me. "No more!" he gritted out through clenched teeth as my head came up. I looked at him meeting the fiery blaze in his eyes. Knowing he could take no more David clasped my hips, holding me to him as he sought to keep some measure of control.

"David." His name was an ache of longing on my lips and with it his immense control finally broke. He pulled me down and held me so that I stayed locked against him. Then he rolled over until I was beneath him. Spreading my thighs wide, and at last, he claimed me with one powerful thrust. The presence of him inside made me feel whole again.

"Hold me, Calaine. Move with me."

I clung on, matching his thrust, seeking an ending. Wrapping my legs around him, drawing him deeper inside me. I whimpered his name repeatedly as his body pumped in and out of mine. I sighed with relief when my body begin to climax beneath him. As the last ripple of passion overtook me, David joined me, climaxing with a groan that seemed to be drawn from the very depth of his being. Clinging together we rode out the stormy seas of passion until at last we washed up on the shore exhausted and fulfilled.

Chapter 19

I ROSE EARLY ON SATURDAY. After fixing a quick breakfast of toast and coffee, I dashed off to the grocery store. Donna was a country girl who believed in real down-home cooking, no microwave or canned meals.

On the way back, I grabbed my dry cleaning and made the short drive home. I changed into an old t-shirt and black stretch pants and set to cleaning my house from top to bottom. I went to the bathroom to take my allergy medication before the dust got the best of me.

I moved into the guest bedroom that I used as an office and put away the papers I had scattered across the sleeper sofa. Running my finger across my dresser drawer, my eyebrows drew together in a frown. Dusting was long overdue. I popped in my favorite CD and hummed along with Mary J. Blige as I cleaned the room. While reaching into the linen closet for a set of fresh sheets, thoughts of David slipped through my mind.

The rest of the week had been special. We had shared either lunch or dinner together each day and after work, David would make a mad dash to my house where we spent the evening lying in the bed in each other's arms, making love and talking until we dozed off. I wasn't sure *how* I was going to bear bringing the relationship to an end. I just wasn't ready yet to deal with my dilemma. All I knew was that the last several weeks would be forever imbedded in my mind and I wished things could continue as they were, but I knew deep down they could not. It was only a dream.

I needed to stay focused. Finding my birth mother was my priority. Whenever I was with David, everything else seemed to float away from my mind. I couldn't think straight. I couldn't even remember what time it was. All I could think about was how he made me feel. That was the problem, I thought with a scowl. I was in way over my head.

A year ago I would have jumped for joy to have found someone who made me feel the way David made me feel. But not now. Not when I was uncertain what the future held. I had no idea who my mother was. It could be Dorlinda or Eunice, although I didn't even know that for certain. There was still a chance my mother could be Wanda or Ursula. Even then how was I to know if maybe my mother had given me away due to some hereditary disease? I just didn't know and until I did, I couldn't make any promises.

I put the bottle of furniture polish away and dropped down on the couch. Last night after spending time listening to David share his dream of having a family, I realized that it was time to bring the relationship to a halt. It was unfair for me to continue to mislead him into thinking he had a chance at having a future with me. As far as I was concerned, my biological clock had stopped ticking, and until I knew who I was, I couldn't consider adoption. Instead, because I loved him as much as I did, I believed it was only fair that I put a halt to our relationship before it was too late. Brushing the thoughts from my mind, I turned on Pandora and got back to work.

Two hours later, I fell back in a chair in the kitchen quite satisfied. My house was spotless. I was exhausted, but the effort was well worth it.

While drinking a glass of water, I heard a horn blow out front. I moved down the hall to the door and opened it just as an airport express shuttle was pulling out my driveway and Donna was coming up the steps.

"Hey girl!" she exclaimed. Putting down her tote bag, she met me halfway.

"I'm so glad you're here," I said as we embraced.

"I'm glad to be here. I missed my girl."

I eased back and frowned. "I thought you were only here for three days?" I said, referring to the large suitcase the driver had left at the bottom of the steps. I lugged it up the stairs while Donna grabbed her other bags.

"A girl never knows for sure what she might need."

I chuckled as I suddenly remembered the oversized bag I had packed for Texas.

Donna sauntered into the hallway where she dropped her bags and turned to look at me. "I think a little shopping trip might be in order. You look... tired," she offered affectionately.

I realized that I probably looked a sight. Moving over to the hall mirror, I found cobwebs dangling from my hair and streaks of dust across both cheeks. Feeling increasingly self-conscious, I couldn't help noticing how gorgeous Donna looked. She was tall and graceful and the jeans she wore made her legs look a mile long. Her chemically relaxed auburn hair was an artful tumble of curls that fell to her shoulders. Her tawny oval face was delicate and as smooth and clear as ever. I had always admired her naturally long lashes that framed honey-colored eyes.

I removed the bandana from my hair and tried to finger my tendrils into place. Turning, I found that Donna had already moved into the living room. Kicking off four-inch pumps, she made herself at home.

I flopped down onto the couch beside her. "All right, Donna, what really happened between you and Bruce?"

She shrugged. "A little of this and a little of that. You got any food in this joint? 'Cause that airport food sucked."

It was obvious Donna didn't want to talk about it. "Sure, come on."

I went straight for the cabinet and made a pot of fresh coffee. Within minutes, I was whipping up a batch of pancakes while Donna volunteered to make scrambled eggs and bacon. She was a natural in the kitchen.

Her mother, Rita Davidson, had died of breast cancer when Donna was seven and after her death, she had become the woman of the house. Her father and little brothers depended on Donna so much that her life revolved around them. She never participated in any after-school activities and had no dreams of ever attending college. During her senior year, her father remarried and after a little resistance to losing her title as the woman of the house, Donna and her stepmother formed a strong bond. It was at her insistence that Donna enjoyed her last year of high school and with her family's support, left home to attend college.

I felt guilty that I hadn't shared with Donna my discovery, especially when I knew that she would be genuinely interested in knowing what I had been emotionally going through. While pouring batter onto the electric griddle, I decided I would talk to her after brunch.

"Breakfast was also Bruce's favorite meal of the day," Donna blurted, interrupting my thoughts.

Spatula in hand, I looked over to the stove where Donna was violently scrambling eggs. I gave her a long hard stare. "Do you want to talk about it?"

Donna sighed, dropping one hand to her hip. "All right, if you insist."

I chuckled inwardly. Donna had always had a way of wanting you to twist the truth out of her. I moved from the counter over to the stove and rescued the eggs while Donna took a seat at the table and explained their breakup.

I found myself only half listening as I remembered how much my mother had admired her. In fact, Olivia thought Donna was a positive influence and had even went as far as to say on several occasions I couldn't go wrong by being more like my roommate.

"Do you think I was wrong?" Donna asked, breaking into my thoughts.

"About what?" I asked as I reached for a plate and slid the eggs onto it.

Donna blew air between her front teeth. "For wanting to buy a Mercedes."

I blinked as it suddenly registered. Hand resting on my hip, I swung around. "You mean to tell me the two of you broke up over a car?"

Ignoring the implications of my soft voice, Donna whined, "I work hard for my money. If I want a Mercedes, I think I should be able to buy one."

"True, but if the two of you are trying to save up for a home, why can't it wait?"

She snorted a laugh. "You're beginning to sound like Bruce."

"Good," I said as I moved over to the table carrying two plates of hot food. "I thought you were tired of dating men who thought only of themselves?"

"I am."

"Then what's the problem?" I asked as I took the seat across from her.

"The problem is Bruce bought an Expedition last month and I didn't say anything, but when I decide it was time for me to buy a car that makes me feel good, he acted a fool!"

"Your priorities are screwed up, not to mention you sound like a spoiled brat."

"I do not!"

"I'm afraid that you do," I mumbled in between bites.

Donna looked down at her plate as she stirred her eggs. "Maybe I do, but I don't think it's fair that he can buy what he wants, and I can't."

I shrugged. "Double standards."

Donna chewed roughly on a strip of bacon. "Well I don't like it." Rising from her seat, she moved to refill her mug with coffee when the doorbell rang. "I'll get it," she offered. Setting her mug on the counter, she strolled into the other room before I could rise out of my seat.

A few seconds later I heard Donna scream with excitement. I knew it was David even before I heard his voice.

Donna returned to the kitchen with her hips swinging in slim-fitting jeans. David was behind her. "Look who's here?"

My eyes met his. His expression was intense. Standing in the door, David looked as handsome as ever. He was dressed in black jeans and a white polo shirt that stretched across his broad shoulders. A gold-faced watch hung on his wrist and a diamond stud was in his left lobe. His locs had been freshly twisted. Blood pounded at my temples and heat flowed through my veins. I had missed him.

"You look a mess," he joked, trying to break the tension.

"Who asked you?" I retorted even though I self-consciously combed through my hair with my fingers.

Donna chuckled as she returned to her seat at the table. "I see there's still no love lost between the two of you. You always did fight like brother and sister."

Brother and sister don't make love.

My eyes darted over to where David still stood, and I could see that he was also thinking the same thing. Heat rose to my cheeks as I thought about the things he had done to my body last night and the way he had made me feel. The thought caused heat to travel between my legs. Turning away, I rose and reached for another coffee cup in the cabinet above the stove.

"Take a load off your feet and stay awhile. Here, have some coffee." I slid a mug across the table.

David caught it before it fell off the edge. "Aren't you going to fix it for me?" he teased.

My lips curled upward despite myself. "Don't push your luck." With that, I escaped to my room. Sitting on the side of the bed, I tried to calm my racing heart. There was nothing I could do to change the way he made me feel as long as I was in love with him.

Brushing aside the thoughts, I moved to the bathroom to shower. Twenty minutes later, I was dressed in jeans and a lime green t-shirt.

I returned to the kitchen to find the two of their heads together having a serious conversation.

Donna sprung from her seat. "Keke, why didn't you tell me Olivia wasn't your mother?" She draped her arms around my neck and gave me a comforting hug.

I looked over at David and rolled my eyes. He had no right telling my business.

He sensed my anger and nodded apologetically. "I'm sorry. I had no idea you hadn't told Donna."

Donna pulled away. "I can't believe you didn't tell me!" she pouted.

"I was waiting until you got here so I could talk to you in person."

Donna threw her arms around me again. "Oh girl, I can't imagine what you're going through!"

"I'm fine, really," I said as we both moved to the table. "David has been a big help."

David looked up from his mug and I could tell that he was surprised by my admission.

"Well, David didn't tell me the details. So have a seat and spill your guts."

I refilled my mug before returning to my seat, then he and I took turns telling Donna about my discovery and how he had come into the picture.

By the time we were done, Donna was shaking her head with disbelief. "Unbelievable! Calaine, I would have never guessed."

"I have to thank David. I don't know what I would have done without him," I admitted, not trusting myself to look his way.

"It was my pleasure," he purred.

Donna gave him a curious look before she smiled. "I'm glad you were here for her."

Frowning, I reached for my mug and took a sip of the lukewarm drink. I wondered if Donna had picked up on the sexual energy between David and I. Damn, I hoped not. The last thing I needed was to have to share my feelings with Donna especially when I wasn't sure how she felt about David.

Donna squeezed my hand. "I hope you find her."

"I hope so too."

"Let's think positive. Give me the names and a computer and I'll try to track down the last three women before I leave on Thursday."

"Why don't you come by and check out my new place tonight? I have a brand-new MacBook you can use while I pop open a nice red wine," David suggested.

Donna batted her eyelashes flirtatiously. "Make it dinner and you've got yourself a deal."

David chuckled and nodded in agreement.

I felt a twinge of jealousy but forced a smile. "You guys have fun."

David glanced across the table at me. "That invitation is open to you also Calaine."

I shook my head. "No, you two have a lot of catching up to do. I'll just be a third wheel."

"Don't be silly," Donna protested. "It will be like ole times."

Still shaking my head, I declined again. "No, I think I am going to spend some time at my parents' house packing."

Donna's face warmed with concern. "You want me to help?"

"Yeah, me too," David offered.

"No, you go have fun." I rose and put my mug in the sink.

"All right. David, how about we go to Spanky's afterwards for a little dancing?"

David tore his eyes away from me to look at Donna and grinned. "Sounds like ole times."

DAVID AND DONNA LEFT shortly after we cleaned the kitchen to take a crack at surfing the net before they dressed for dinner. Remembering I was out of milk, I hopped in my car and drove to Walgreens. I didn't know if I could return to my lonely life before David. Not now. Not after I'd discovered what love truly felt like.

The love I felt for David was real. I would never be able to share my heart with any other. Not ever.

While moving to the cash register, I heard someone call out my name. I turned around to find Damien Martin moving into the line behind me.

"How have you been?" he asked with a wide and eager smile.

I returned the smile with not quite as much enthusiasm, but genuine nevertheless. "I'm doing fine, and you?"

"Great. Just great."

We had dated briefly before my involvement with McKinley. Damien was a minority recruiter for Mizzou's Veterinary School and because he traveled a great deal, our relationship never got off the ground. He was a nice person, always a gentleman, and always saying the right things. He was the type of guy a girl would love to bring home to meet her parents and of course, Olivia had loved him. Unfortunately, I never felt anything when I was with him.

"Thanks for the flowers," I said as I moved up in line.

"It was the least I could do. Your parents were wonderful people." He offered his condolences and we engaged in idle chitchat until I reached my place at the register.

"How about dinner?" he suggested.

Glancing over at him, I was about to decline, but before I could form the words, I changed my mind. "Dinner would be great."

His dark eyes sparkled with possibilities. "When would be a good night for you?"

I handed the cashier my money, then suggested, "How about tonight?"

Damien nodded eagerly. "Tonight would be perfect."

Chapter 20

DAVID

I PULLED UP IN FRONT of Calaine's house at exactly seven o'clock to pick up Donna. Shutting off the car, I paused, resting my elbows on the steering wheel and stared up at her bedroom window.

I planned to convince Calaine to spend the evening with us. It would be just like old times. In college, the three of us had attended several functions together and usually Donna saw someone she knew and ended up leaving Calaine and I alone. The last time we were at the Boone County Fair and Donna ditched us to hang out with some of her teammates on the track team. Calaine and I strolled around seeing the exhibits while enjoying the cotton candy and we had such a good time. How come I hadn't realized then how much she meant to me? I frowned. Things were getting way out of hand and if Calaine was going to be stubborn and not admit her feelings, then I was going to have to make her see reason.

Climbing out of the car, I moved up the stairs and rang the doorbell. It was only a few seconds before Calaine came to answer the door. As soon as I looked at her, I couldn't speak. I had expected her to answer dressed in her usual sweatpants and oversized shirt. Instead, she was wearing a short black dress that hugged every delicious curve. The dress was short—too damn short—exposing a pair of toned thighs and calves. She had oiled her legs until the velvety smoothness glimmered. Her painted toes were visible in a pair of black open-toe sandals.

"Where are you going?" I asked, not caring if my tone was sharp and brisk.

She rolled her eyes at me. "If you must know, I have a date."

"With who?" I needed to know.

"That's none of your business. Now are you going to come in or not?"

I stepped inside and brushed against her. The scent of her perfume traveled to my nose. She smelled like a bed of roses, and my stomach tightened with longing. I followed her into the living room, not missing the enticing sway of her hips as she moved.

"I thought you wanted to spend the evening going through your parents' belongings?"

She shrugged nonchalantly. "I changed my mind."

I tried to mask my jealousy, but knew I was doing a terrible job. The thought of her being with someone else annoyed the hell out of me. I had hoped if Calaine saw me with Donna maybe she would finally admit her feelings. Instead, she went and found a date of her own. *Dammit!*

"Don't you look nice," Donna complimented as she sauntered into the room.

Turning around Calaine met her radiant face. "Thanks, you don't look bad yourself."

Donna was wearing a blue two-piece outfit. The top had spaghetti straps and the skirt stopped several inches above her knees.

"Where are you guys going tonight?" Calaine asked,

"I don't know. David hasn't said." Donna turned to me looking curiously.

I moved and placed a hand to her shoulder. "We'll think of something. Ready to go?" I asked, not trusting myself to look at Calaine.

"Sure, let me just grab a sweater and I will be ready." Donna moved back to the guest room leaving the two of us alone again.

Calaine took a seat in the chair, leaned her head back and closed her eyes. I couldn't stop looking at her.

"You look nice."

She opened her eyes and met my smile. "Thank you." Giving my khakis and blue short-sleeve Polo a once over she replied, "You don't look half bad yourself."

"Where are you going tonight?" I asked.

She glanced down at the slender gold watch on her arm and rose as she said, "I'm not sure either, but I'm certain we'll think of something."

"I have a better idea." I met her direct gaze and before she could say it, I dragged her up against me, and my mouth descended over hers. The touch of her mouth was like nothing I'd ever felt with another woman. Soft and gentle. I used every ounce of expertise to coax a response from her. It was a low moan, but just enough to know she felt it too. I was surrounded by Calaine—her scent, her taste, her incredibly lush body locked against mine. Fire burned deep at the pit of my stomach. I backed her against the wall, my weight pressing her against the wall, my mouth never breaking contact with hers. Calaine placed a hand against my chest, as if intending to push me away but instead laid it lightly against me. With my mouth still on hers, I lifted a hand to her face, stroking her cheek gently while using my tongue to trace the seam of her lips and dip inside.

She gasped.

"You like that, don't you?" I breathed huskily against her lips, then lifted my eyes to hers. Her breathing was not so steady. I looked down at her mouth, now glossy and wet from my kiss. "When are you going to stop lying to yourself?" I murmured and she shivered just before my mouth descended over hers again. I subjected her lips to the same treatment, only this time my strokes were deeper, rougher and she gave me complete control. My hand slid up her back, teasing her body while mine ached. Desire raged with need. I wanted to carry her up to her room, part her thighs, and feel her warmth snuggly around my—

The doorbell rang. I ended the kiss. Calaine stared up at me, her breath coming in shallow pants.

"I wanted to give you something to think about," I said and winked.

Before she could move, I was already opening the door and found myself face-to-face with the competition. The man was a couple of inches shorter but dressed very stylish. The way I would have expected Calaine's date to look.

He looked surprised almost as if he thought that maybe he had knocked on the wrong door. "Is Calaine home?"

I was tempted to tell him no, but I knew with Calaine a few feet away, it wouldn't go over well.

"Yes," I said, sounding guarded and a lot less cordial than he had. Well, it was the best I could do, considering he was getting ready to go out with my woman. "Come on in." I stepped side.

"Damien, you're early." She smiled. I frowned.

"I'm sorry I wrapped up my business a little sooner than expected. Although, if I'd known you'd look this good, I would have arrived even sooner." He openly admired her outfit. I was ready to grab him by the collar and throw him out the front door.

She ignored the side-glances I was giving him and reached for her purse. "I'm ready."

"Where are you two going?" I asked.

"None of your business," she interrupted before Damien could even answer.

"We're going to CC's City Broiler," Damien offered.

I fumed. I knew that was Calaine's favorite steakhouse. I also knew it was childish to resent her date for knowing what she liked. Nevertheless, knowing did nothing to stop resenting him like hell.

THE LINE AT SALACIA'S Italian restaurant was long with an hour wait, so Donna and I decided to eat at Boone Tavern. We shared a plate of piping hot Buffalo wings while sipping on margaritas. We reminisced over old times and filled each other in on the last decade.

Donna was still a wonderful outgoing person who had blossomed over the years into a beautiful and confident woman. But she wasn't Calaine. I couldn't get her off my mind. I wondered how her dinner was going and wondered if they were going back to her house or going somewhere afterwards. Either way, I couldn't help but feel violated.

I tried to cool my anger as I slowly chewed on a wing. Hell, I hadn't even known she was seeing anyone besides me. I knew that sounded selfish, but I had dominated so much of her time over the past several weeks that I thought I was exclusive. Now the joke was on me.

Our meal arrived, and I tried to focus on Donna while carving into my medium rare steak.

"So when are you going to admit you're in love with Calaine?"

My brow rose at her observation. "Is it that obvious?"

Donna toyed with her potato as she spoke. "Yes. I also suspect she feels the same way. I don't know why the two of you won't stop playing games and just go for it."

"You're not mad?"

She snorted. "Why would I be mad? Now don't get me wrong. You're still one *fine* brotha, but you know as well as I do our relationship never made it past first base. I really liked you. I still do, but I never felt anything other than friendship." Lowering her fork, she placed her elbows on the table. "I always thought the two of you would make a cute couple."

"You did?"

Donna nodded. "Sure I did. I also know something was going on between the two of you even back in college. I'm not blind you know. I saw the way y'all looked at one another. Why you think I used to leave the two of you alone all the time? I saw it again today."

I sat back in my chair and chuckled heartily. "I guess you've got it all figured out."

"Yep." Donna's eyes narrowed suspiciously. "And if you break her heart, I'm gonna have to cut you."

Even though she was laughing, I heard the seriousness of her comment. "Don't worry, my intentions are all good. I just need to help her find her mother first." I took a bite of my steak, then asked between chews, "So what about you and what's his name?"

She was so surprised by my question that she blushed. "Bruce. I don't know. I love him so much, but he makes me mad."

My brow rose. "Isn't that what love's about?"

She was still for a moment before she met my gaze. Donna smiled as she responded, "Yeah, I guess it is."

AFTER SPENDING TWO hours listening to Damien talk about himself, I couldn't take anymore and asked him to take me home. I was out the car before he could shift it in Park.

Changing into my favorite two-piece cotton pajamas, I went into the kitchen and made myself a cup of chai tea. Sitting at the table, I sipped and felt sorry for myself.

Donna and David were probably out having a wonderful time and instead of joining them as David had suggested, I had gone out with motor-mouth. Now I would spend the rest of the evening tormenting myself with thoughts of them together reminiscing.

I brought the rim to my lips and took a cautious sip as I stared up at the clock on the wall. It was a quarter past ten. The night was too young for Donna to return. She probably wouldn't get in until well after midnight.

Irritated, I rose and moved into the living room, hoping to catch an interesting movie on *Lifetime*. I turned on the television only to find they were showing a rerun. Dropping the remote, I reached for my mug on the coffee table and took another sip.

I had made a lot of mistakes in my life, but this one proved to be one of the worst. I loved David. There was no getting around that and I knew he felt something for me. It was obvious or at least I hoped it was. Why else would he spend so much time helping me? And why else would he have been determined to put *something* on my mind and then kiss me. I had to admit in the beginning it had been about the sex, but even after we had finally made love David still came around and continued to help me. Then tonight when he saw me with Damien, I witnessed the dark look in his eyes and the jealousy brewing.

And it warmed my heart!

Returning my mug to the table, I rose and headed towards my bedroom. The moment I caught my reflection in the mirror, I frowned. I was being ridiculous. There was no way in hell I was going to spend the evening feeling sorry for myself. David had invited me to hang out with him and Donna and I planned to do just that. I raced to my room. It wouldn't take me but a few minutes to change back into my clothes and join them at Spanky's.

I had reached for the dress I had just rehung in the closet, when I heard the doorbell ring.

No, it couldn't be.

I tossed the dress onto my bed and raced to the door. When I opened it, I gasped. "David, what are you doing here?"

He leaned against the doorframe, giving me his most irresistible smile. "What does it look like? I'm here to see you. Can we talk?"

I stuck my head out and looked over at his BMW. "Where's Donna?"

"Donna is spending the night at a hotel. I told her I wanted you all to myself."

My pulse had increased. I needed to be sure before I got ahead of myself. "What about your date?"

David stepped forward until our bodies were touching. Staring down at me he replied, "I'm not interested in Donna. I'm interested in you." Without another word, David swept me up into his arms and carried me to my bedroom.

"I thought we were going to talk," I challenged as my arms slipped around his neck and my lips found the angle of his jaw.

He didn't pause on his way to my bedroom. "Calaine, sweetheart, I'm like a man dying of thirst and you're the only thing that will keep me alive. I've kept my hands off you since you left my bed. Don't ask me to wait any longer."

The passion in his voice turned my heart over and emotions overflowed. "I wouldn't dream of it."

Inside the bedroom, David lowered me to my feet and reached over to switch on a lamp beside the bed. Shrugging out of his shirt, he tossed it aside before pulling me back into his arms. I sighed with satisfaction as his strong arms closed around me. When he bent his head and moved towards my mouth, I met his kiss, returning it, sensing his need to devour me. It set my heart racing and my fingers clutched at him, trying to pull him even closer.

This was not like before. There was no slow sensual build. We had been apart too long, and the need was too great. Our hands dealt feverishly with clothes, discarding them in a staggered trail to the bed where, naked at last, we toppled onto the sheets.

The feel of him against me, the unmistakable evidence of his powerful need thrusting against my belly, scattered my senses. I moved against him with a moan. One of his knees pushed my thighs apart, allowing him to slip between them and enter me with one push. My body arched upwards in pleasure and my legs rose, locking about his hips as I drew him deeper inside me. David tried to slow down. I could feel the tension in his body, but the pleasure was too great. "David!" I cried and with a groan he thrust into me again and again, setting a rhythm I matched, driving us towards the satisfaction we sought so desperately. It came with explosive force, causing us to cry out and cling to each other. Waves of pleasure tossed us about until washing up on calmer shores where we lay until our heart rates returned to normal.

At last, David raised his head and looked down at me, a sober expression on his face as he brushed sweat-soaked strands of hair from my forehead. "Calaine, I'm through playing games. Without you, my life is a shamble. When I'm not around you I can't think, I can't sleep. You have unlocked my heart and soul...what I'm trying to say is I love you."

I couldn't believe my ears. He loved me! My eyes became misty, and my throat was dry, making it difficult to speak. I stared up at him leaning over me. There was so much I wanted to say to him.

My cell phone began to ring. As soon as I saw the area code, my heart began to pound. I pressed Talk.

"Hello?"

"Ms. Hart, my name is Robin Mitchell. I received a postcard in the mail today addressed to my aunt Eunice Roberts. Can we talk?"

Chapter 21

DAVID PULLED IN FRONT of the Delaware Hospital for the Mentally Ill and climbed out of the rental car. He moved around to the passenger's side and opened it for me.

"You ready?"

Nodding, I smoothed down the front of my dress, then took his hand.

We moved up the sidewalk, through the double doors and walked to a reception desk where two middle-aged women were answering a multi-line phone that was ringing constantly.

David scribbled his name on the sign-in sheet on the counter and waited for a chunky blonde-haired woman to acknowledge that we were standing there. I was starting to grow irritated by every passing second.

"Are we invisible?" I spat and before I could say more, David reached out and clutched my arm.

"Excuse me . . . Joy," David looked up from her nametag and gave the receptionist his most captivating smile. Slowly her large dilated pupils came up to study him.

"May I help you?" she asked while chewing loud and obnoxiously on a piece of bubble gum. Her eyes traveled from him to me, then back to him.

I stepped forward. "I'm here to see Eunice Roberts."

Joy popped her gum between her teeth. "Are you family?"

Am I family? That was a good question that unfortunately I was unable to answer with certainty. But I knew how to respond, otherwise I'd never get past this watchdog. "Yes, I'm her daughter."

Joy looked at me over the top of her glasses suspiciously.

David draped an arm around my waist. "Actually Dr. Williamson is expecting us."

She frowned and waved her hand. "Have a seat and I'll page her."

David lead me over to take a seat in the waiting room. We entered the deserted area where a large, flat screened television was mounted in the corner. While we waited, David watched the *Steve Harvey Show* and chuckled lightly as the talk show host lectured a man for giving birth to five children by four different women.

"Relax, everything is going to be all right," he assured me.

I waited for the nervousness to stop swimming in my belly. Guilt, tension and fear settled over me like a huge dark cloud. My heart was hammering from uneasiness and the fear I was feeling. Ever since her niece Robin called two days ago, my life had been in an uproar.

I tried to get as much information from Robin as I could. She was a sweet girl who was willing to help in any way that she could. She'd never known much about her aunt's past except that she'd had a nervous breakdown long before Robin was born. Her mother had been appointed by the state as her sister's legal guardian. Robin and her mother visited Eunice frequently and although Eunice sometimes acted like a stranger, she adored her aunt. When her mother died five years ago, Eunice was placed in a residential facility. I heard the guilt in Robin's voice when she admitted she had been so wrapped up in her career, she hadn't visited her aunt much nor did any of the other family members.

As far as Robin knew, her aunt had never been married and never had any children. She had given me the name of the hospital where she was residing and her physician's contact information. I took a deep breath trying to calm my nerves. In a few minutes, I hoped to have answers.

It wasn't long before a woman in a white coat came out to speak with me.

"Hello, are you Ms. Hart?"

I rose and walked over to her. "Yes, I am."

The physician nodded. "I'm Dr. Rachel Williamson. Robin told me to expect you." She gave me a friendly smile. "Why don't we go to my office and talk in private."

"Sure." David stayed while I followed her to a room down the hall and took a seat across from her desk.

"You're Ms. Roberts's daughter?"

I laughed nervously. "I don't know. I'm looking for my mother, and I think Eunice might be that woman."

Dr. Williamson stared over at me for several seconds, and instead of suspicion I saw the sincerity in her eyes. "It would answer a lot of questions."

My heart thundered against my chest. "What do you mean?"

"Ms. Roberts' been telling me she has a baby girl." She paused when she saw excitement dancing on my face. "Now please keep in mind, Eunice is diagnosed schizophrenic. She hallucinates and has the tendency to believe things are happening that aren't even true. Nevertheless, she had been trying to convince us for years of a little girl she lost."

"Has anyone ever corroborated her story?"

"No. She hasn't had many visitors. I've asked her family, but no one seems to know. The only friend she seems to have is Mrs. Jackson who visits her quite often and she doesn't even know."

I thought about how sad it would be to have been locked away for years unwanted or needed by anyone. "I would like to see her."

For a long moment, Dr. Williamson openly studied me until the wrinkles around her eyes evaporated and her expression softened. "I must let you know that Eunice also has terminal lung cancer. We're not sure how much longer she has left. But I have this strong feeling that she has been holding on, waiting for someone."

Terminal lung cancer. My stomach dropped. *Lord, no! Don't take her away from me again!*

Dr. Williamson rose and I followed her out into the lobby where David was waiting. Worry was in his eyes. I drew in a deep breath and signaled for him to join me. When he reached me, he took my hand.

"Everything okay?"

I looked up at him and whispered, "She's taking me to see her." He squeezed my hand, sharing his strength and together we followed.

Dr. Williamson took us down a secure wing where she had to swipe her badge to enter. Once through the double doors, I saw patients sitting in a lounge area watching television while others were seated at a long table putting puzzles together or playing a game of checkers.

We followed her down another long hall. Dr. Williamson stopped in front of a room. "Wait out here while I check and see how she's doing today." She moved to the desk and spoke briefly to one of the employees.

Large hands slid around my waist as David fitted his body to mine from behind. "Babe, how are you holding up?" He breathed against my neck, his warmth penetrated my clothing.

"I'm so nervous." That door was the only thing separating me from answers.

"It's going to be okay." David held me close, as he nuzzled the tender spot beneath my ear. I leaned into him and was so thankful for his love and support.

It seemed like ages before Dr. Williamson returned, opened the door, and instructed us to enter.

David caught me. I felt so uneasy. With his arm around my waist he led me into the room. I looked down at the frail woman sitting up in the bed, staring up at me with a look of astonishment.

"Ms. Roberts, my name is Calaine Hart and I'd like to ask you a few—"

"Calaine? Is that you?" Her eyes narrowed suspiciously.

I stepped away from David and lowered into a plastic chair next to the bed. "Y-you know who I am?"

Eunice nodded. Her eyes were brimmed with tears. "I always knew you would come back." She smiled proudly. "Wait until I tell Birdie, she'll never believe this."

I looked over at Dr. Williamson for help. "Who's Birdie?"

"Mrs. Jackson," she answered by way of an explanation.

Eunice reached over and squeezed my hand. "How have you been?"

My eyes misted as she smiled up at me. "I've been fine."

"Did they treat you right? I always wondered if you had a good life."

I nodded suddenly so choked up I was unable to speak. Tears streamed down my cheek.

Eunice leaned back on her pillow, studying my face. "I always knew you were going to be pretty. You were such a pretty baby. All my friends were so jealous." She chuckled absently as her eyelids began to close.

I smiled down at her warm friendly face. "Ms. Eunice, I have so much I want to ask you."

Her lids flew open in terror. "Where's your father?"

"He's dead."

"D-dead?" Her face softened with relief, then she began to laugh.

I looked to Dr. Williamson for help.

"Ms. Roberts, Calaine would like to ask you some questions."

Eunice continued to laugh hysterically until her laughter turned to uncontrollable coughs.

Dr. Williamson looked to us with an apologetic expression. "She has good and bad days. Maybe tonight isn't a good time. How about we try again in the morning?"

My heart sank. I didn't want to leave. There was so much I wanted to say to her, so much I wanted to know. I would have stayed and slept in the chair if I could have. Just to have been near her. *She's my birth mother.* I wanted to know everything I could about her life... before it was too late.

The coughing got worse. A nurse stepped into the room, urging us to leave.

I gave a robotic nod and allowed David to lead me out into the hall just as Eunice began to shriek with hysteria. Moving beside me, David's strong grip steadying me as we walked out to the car.

Eunice Roberts is my mother. I gulped, trying to push back the despair. Only this time it was impossible. Not only was my mother mentally ill, she was dying of cancer. I held on until we returned to the hotel. However, as soon as we moved into our room the tears started and I couldn't get them to stop.

David gathered me in his arms and held me close as I cried. I slumped against him, my face buried against his chest as heavy sobs consumed me. Warm wet cheeks dampened his shirt. "I don't know which was worse, never knowing who my mother was, or finding out she's dying."

David sat on the bed, pulled me onto his lap and cradled me. His hand stroked my hair as if I was a child while he whispered tender words in my ear. He laid me gently on the bed with my head on the pillow and lay beside me with his arm draped snugly around me as we fell asleep.

Chapter 22

I WOKE THE NEXT MORNING to find myself in bed, dressed, with David lying beside me, his arm draped across my waist. As I stared up at the popcorn ceiling, thoughts of the night before came rushing back.

This can't be happening again. I just found her.

I slid from underneath his arm and quietly moved into the bathroom, trying not to disturb him. I ran myself a bath, then slowly removed my wrinkled clothes and climbed into the tub before the water had a chance to fill. I leaned back and stared.

I found my mother.

Eunice Roberts. She seemed like a nice woman with a good heart. A sob ached at the back of my throat. *Daddy, why? Why did you lie to me all these years?* I needed answers. I also needed to spend as much time with Eunice as I could until I knew everything.

I looked down in the tub as the water reached my knees, my vision blurred by tears.

I had so many questions I wanted to ask her, so many things I needed to know. Hopefully, today I would have a chance.

Leaning back in the tub, I closed my eyes and tried to weigh the entire chain of events. Anger brewed on the edge and I had to take another breath and try to relax. How could Daddy have done something like that? I had never truly known my father, this I was certain of, because the man I remembered would have never done such a thing.

"Daddy, why did you take me away from my mother?" The question hammered at me. I wanted to put together all the pieces and my father was the only one who could do that. Unfortunately, he wasn't around for me to confront for answers. Deciding to raise me as another woman's child was one thing, denying me my mother, who obviously wanted to keep me, was another thing all together. I never guessed I could feel so much anger for a dead man.

I inhaled as the steam began to rise and tried to ignore a cynical inner voice in my head. *How could your uncle have not known what happened?* After all, he had taught all the women an anatomy course, and my father was his brother. The only connection my dad would have had with the students would have been Uncle Tad. He had been with him at the jazz club.

I was more certain than ever my uncle knew more than he was telling. Tonight, after I visited Eunice at the hospital, I was going to give him a call and demand the truth.

Tormented by confusing emotions, I tried to look at the bright side, only to realize there was no bright side. After a long and troubled night of soul searching, I realized I had to end my relationship with David. My heart swelled with emotions, but what else could I do? My biological mother has lung cancer as well as schizophrenia. She needed me. There would be no time for anything else. David deserved to have a wife and family. I couldn't give him either. And as much as it hurt me, I was going to have to break off our relationship.

I turned off the water and slid deeper into the water while trying to sort out my conflicting emotions. Momentarily, I was so lost in my thoughts and didn't hear a male voice cut through my thoughts.

"Calaine."

"I'm in the tub," I replied.

"May I come in?"

David was standing right outside my door. How could I deny him? I hesitated, then said, "Sure, come in." He opened the door and stepped inside wearing an adorable smile and looking so damn fine.

"How are you feeling this morning?" He lowered the toilet seat and sat down.

I gazed up at his waiting eyes and answered quietly, "The same."

"It can only get better now," he said with reassurance. "It seems that your mother has been waiting all these years for you to come back."

I met his positive smile, tears glistening in my eyes. I was hurting for losing all those years with her. I was also hurting for what I had to do. "I have to go and see her," I said in a low, composed voice.

David nodded and murmured, "As soon as you get out I'll take a quick shower, then be ready in a flash."

I looked down and studied my hand. "I want to go alone."

"What did you say?"

I looked at him; our eyes held for a moment until I found the courage to say, "I need to do this by myself."

"Calaine, you're in no condition to handle this alone. Let me go," he insisted.

"No." I rose from the tub and reached for the bath towel David offered me. "If I'm going to open this mysterious chapter of my life, I want to do it on my own." Wrapping the towel around me, I stepped out the tub and padded into the other room.

David followed. "All right. I respect that. Just know I have your back and I'll be here if you need me."

I stopped and turned slowly. "Now that we've found my mother, I don't know how long I'm going to be here."

David shrugged. "It doesn't matter. I want to help." He lowered onto the mattress as I reached for my suitcase and opened it on the bed beside him.

"I don't need your help," I snapped. "What I need is to sort out my life and I don't need you distracting me." I saw him flinch at my words, but I did nothing to soothe him.

Despite my gruff words, he leaned lightly into me, tilting his face towards me. "What are you saying?"

I planted a hand to my hips and spoke with as reasonable a voice as I could manage. "I'm saying that seeing Eunice made me think a lot about my own life. I still need to uncover who I really am and until I do, now is not the time for a relationship."

"So the gratitude is over," he mumbled sarcastically. "I guess that's why you felt compelled to keep thanking me."

"No, I... I really appreciated your help, but I can handle it from here."

His expression stilled. "So what are you saying?"

"Your services are no longer needed."

It hurt me to say those words, but it was the only way I could get him to let me go. If he knew I was breaking things off because I thought it was unfair to him to give up his dream of ever having a family, he would never leave. David would sacrifice his own happiness just to be with me, and I couldn't let that happen.

"So you want me to leave?" he asked, puzzled by my change in behavior.

"Yes, that's the way it has to be. My priority right now is my mother. Everything else has to come second, including you. I have to find out who I am and I'm going to do that no matter how long it takes."

Rising, David reached out and caught my hand in his. Catching me by surprise, I dropped the towel. He wrapped an arm around my naked form, pulling me close against him. "I told you we're in this together. I'm not leaving you until this thing is over."

I wiggled free and lifted my arms to shield my breasts. "This thing is already over," I replied with a ring of finality. "My mother has been found and is dying. I need to take the time to sort through my life and find some order." Considering the conversation over, I put some distance between us. I reached into my suitcase and removed matching undergarments and quickly slipped them on. With a phony smile, I met his eyes and said, "Come on, David. We both knew this thing between us wouldn't last. Instead, it was..." I purposely paused, then shrugged. "It was fun."

David ran a frustrated hand across his face. "What kind of games are you playing? One minute you want to be with me, the next minute you don't. You've been doing this from the beginning."

I shook my head. "I'm sorry, I didn't mean to mislead you."

David looked up to the ceiling as if asking for strength before his darkened gaze traveled to me again. "Then tell me what you want from me?"

I swallowed. "I'm truly grateful for everything you've done."

"I don't want your gratitude. I want your love," he snarled.

Looking up at him, my heart ached at the pain I saw in the depths of his eyes. It was because I loved him that I was doing this.

"I know," I paused, trying to find the strength to voice what I was about to say. I kept all expression from my voice and face as I said, "I'm sorry, David, but I can't return those feelings. Not now, maybe not ever."

I saw him flinch from the sting of my words, and I wished I could start laughing and pretend it was all one big joke, but I couldn't.

"You know what? I'm going to give you your space. I'm just tired of playing this game with you," he snapped as he reached for his wallet off the nightstand and slipped it in his back pocket.

"Who's playing? This is my life we are talking about!"

David was silent for the longest time as he slipped on his shoes. Part of me hoped he would come back with a snappy retort, something strong that convinced me I was making a grave mistake. "I'm going to go and take a walk before I say something that I'll later regret." He reached for his room key, then turned to me again, his eyes dark. "I hope you find all of your answers." With that, he turned and walked out the door.

I fell across the bed and cried until my head hurt.

Chapter 23

WHILE I WATCHED CALAINE, my heart pounded rapidly against my ribcage. I remembered holding her tiny body only seconds after she was born. Little fingers curled around my thumb while suckling hungrily at my breast. My heart had been filled with love as I stared down at a head full of curly hair, and exotic brown eyes identical to my first love.

A lump formed in my throat that I couldn't swallow. It was pride. And it was regret because the beautiful woman standing there talking to Dr. Williamson was my little girl. The little girl I hadn't seen since she was five days old. The daughter I'd never had a chance to know. Giving Calaine my grandmother's name was the only decent thing I had ever been able to do for her. An ache swelled in my chest with longing so profound I almost went to her. I wanted to hold Calaine in my arms while I begged for forgiveness. I wanted my daughter to tell me that everything was going to be okay.

I dropped my arms to my sides and released a long shaky breath. Regret assailed me. For forty-four years, I had been unable to put the pain of something missing from my life to rest. All along, I had known that pain was the loss of my daughter, Calaine.

I WAS ON THE VERGE of tears. After a brief visit with Dr. Williamson, outside of Eunice's room, she had informed me, my birth mother's condition had worsened. It was only a matter of time before her demise.

"I wish I had better news." She squeezed my shoulder comfortingly, promised to drop by again, then moved down the hall to see her other patients.

It wasn't fair! When would the despair in my life end? I found myself yearning for David's strength. But he was gone. I had been so self-centered and sent him away.

Taking another deep breath, I stepped into the room and stared down at her beautifully aging face. She was sleeping peacefully. I was glad. Eunice was on a great deal of medication for the pain. The staff was trying to make her last days as comfortable as possible.

Taking a seat in the chair beside her, I took her hand in mine. Eunice stirred and raised her eyelids long enough to see my face and smiled.

"Baby, I'm so glad you came back," she whispered quietly.

"Of course I was coming back," I said, forced around a lump the size of a golf ball.

"I'm glad. Now I can quit worrying... now I can rest," she whispered as she squeezed my hand. "I'm so very tired."

"Rest, we'll talk later."

Eunice nodded and drifted off back to sleep. I continued to hold her hand and watched her sleep while tears spilled from my eyes.

"It doesn't matter why you gave me up," I whispered. "All that matters is that we're together now." I continued to stroke her hand. This evening, I planned to call my office and let them know I was taking a leave of absence. I needed to be here with my birth mom and spend as much time with her as I could. I also needed to reach out to her niece and discuss arrangements for her final resting place. I didn't want to step on anyone's toes, but she was my mother and I wanted to be included in those decisions.

After several minutes of making a mental list, I had the strangest feeling that someone was watching me. I looked up to find a woman stick her head in from around the curtain.

From the moment I looked up at her, I felt an instant tug. Was it the look in her eyes? I recognized her. Tall and thin with wide brown eyes and long thick dark brown hair.

"Dorlinda?"

She nodded. "Hello Calaine." She stepped closer with a slight smile. "When Eunice told me you were here, I had to see you for myself. I-I feel like I am dreaming."

"I almost stopped looking for her. I-I thought she was dead."

Dorlinda pursed her lips and said softly, "No...she tried suicide thirty years ago and failed, so she is very much alive...for now." There was no mistaking the pain in her voice.

"How come...why did she...?" I wasn't sure where to begin or what to say. "I would have been here sooner if only I had known."

Dorlinda gave me an understanding nod. "Your being here now is what she'll always remember." She moved closer wearing a nervous smile. "You should have seen her face this morning. All she could do was talk about you."

I wiped fresh tears from my eyes. "How long have you been here?"

"Since early this morning."

I dropped my eyes to look at Eunice again. "My mother's dying." I knew Dorlinda was aware of Eunice's condition, but for some reason, I needed to say the words out loud. Part of me hoped that maybe, just maybe they weren't true.

"Calaine," Dorlinda said, drawing my attention. Stepping closer, she took a deep breath and said, "Eunice isn't your mother."

My eyes narrowed and before the words had even come out of her mouth, I knew. "You're my mother, aren't you?"

Chapter 24

"YES, I'M YOUR MOTHER."

"What?" I shot up off the bed. It was one thing to think a dying woman was my mother, but this was all together a different story.

I continued to frown as my eye perused the length of her. Dorlinda looked healthy and in wonderful shape. She didn't appear to have to worry about where her next meal was coming. Her hairstyle was from a beauty salon. Her clothes were off a designer rack. The large diamond solitaire on her ring finger indicated that she had married well. In fact, she didn't look like a woman with a forty-four -year-old daughter. I found it all too much for me to deal with.

Too much.

Dorlinda's top lip quivered. "I waited a long time for this moment."

I shook my head, disbelieving what she said was true. Blood roared through my ears. my heart thundered in my chest, my legs grew weak and wobbly. So I sat back on the bed again. Through my misty eyes, I stared at the woman who had just revealed herself as my mother.

Touching fingers to my lips, I whispered, "How could you...abandon me?"

"Calaine, baby. I know you have so many questions, so please just give me a chance to explain," she pleaded.

Baby? The way she'd said it, as if I belonged to her.

I braced my palms on the mattress. "Explain what? The reason why you left me all those years ago and never once came looking for me?" I shook my head vigorously. "I can't talk to you right now. I need time to think."

I rushed out before Dorlinda had a chance to speak. Through a rage of blind fury, I caught a cab and returned to the hotel only to find my pain had just begun. True to his word, David had returned for his things and was gone.

I fell upon the bed with my head buried in a pillow. I cried until no more tears came. When I had finally quieted, I forced myself to get up and wash my face, then drew in a deep breath.

My cell phone rang, and I reached for it.

"Calaine?"

"Donna?"

"What's wrong?" She sounded frantic. I didn't mean to scare her.

"Everything...everything!" I wailed, my voice was both fragile and shaky.

"Do you want to talk about it?"

I could barely lift my voice above a whisper. "Eunice isn't my mother."

"What?" I registered the surprise in her voice. "How did you find out?"

"Dorlinda's my birth mother. She came by the hospital today while I was visiting."

Donna gasped. "What did she say?"

"She walked in and literally said, 'Guess what, I'm your mother.' I was so pissed I walked out the room."

"Keke, why!" Donna screeched. "I thought you'd been waiting weeks for this moment."

"I know, I know. I just got so angry when I saw her standing there looking like a million dollars that I left. How could she have left me like that?"

Donna's soothing voice probed further. "Why didn't you ask her?"

Following a sigh, I mumbled, "I should have."

"Yes, you should have," she scolded. "Listen, I spoke to David and he doesn't want you to be alone. Would you like me to fly down in the morning?"

What I really wanted was for David to come back. However, not until I figured out my past and discovered what the future held for me. "No...I need to do this alone."

"You're never alone."

"I know Donna and I appreciate it. I just need time that's all."

"I love you, Keke."

"And I love you." I drew a sigh. "Can you water my plants before you leave for the airport? I might be here for a while."

"You know I will. Now go and get some rest."

EARLY THE NEXT MORNING I arrived back at the hospital. Dorlinda was already there sitting on the bed beside her closest friend. Standing at the door, I watched her care for Eunice with such tender care it brought tears to my eyes. *Why couldn't she have been there for me the way she was here for Eunice?*

I wanted, needed, to put all the pieces of the puzzle together so I could get on with my life. There was only one person who could provide me with answers.

"How is she?" I asked as I stepped into the room.

Dorlinda turned at the sound of my voice. There was no mistaking the tender warmth of her eyes. "She's been fading in and out." She gave me a nervous smile. "She's been asking for you."

I moved to the other side of the bed and took her hand. Eunice stirred slightly and gave my fingers a weak squeeze. "Hey, baby girl ...have you met your mother?" She spoke in a tremulous whisper.

I glanced at Dorlinda, keeping my expression blank and unreadable, then back down at Eunice and nodded. "Yes, we met yesterday."

A weak smile perched her lips. "Birdie's a good person. She's always loved you." Her eyelids fluttered close again. "Take care of her for me."

I simply nodded, then cast my eyes downward.

As Eunice slept, Dorlinda sat on one side of the bed and me on the other, both of us holding a frail hand. It was quiet except for the faint sound of the heart monitor and several other machines that were unfamiliar.

"Eunice always thought of you as her own." Dorlinda began, breaking the silence. "She'd had a biking accident in high school that damaged her pelvis, so you were the child she never had."

I just sat there and continued to say nothing.

"I remember when I first found out I was pregnant. I was scared. Going home wasn't even an option. My father was a strict Baptist minister who didn't believe in premarital sex. He would have beaten the tar off me, then thrown me out in the street." She gave a laugh that lacked humor. "As for your father...well, I knew he would never leave his wife, and the scandal would have ruined his career. But I couldn't bring myself to have an abortion and Eunice supported my decision." She paused and drew a heavy sigh. "I'll admit, I wasn't very strong. Weak actually, and I fed off Eunice's strength. She was always *so* positive. She told me, 'Birdie, we can get through this together.'" Dorlinda smiled with a far-off look in her eyes. "You weren't due until after finals. Eunice made plans for us to get an apartment at the end of the semester, and I deliver you before we returned to school in the fall. She made it sound so perfect that I almost believed it would work." She paused again long enough to catch her breath. "When your father found out I was pregnant, he gave me money to terminate, but instead, I spent it on clothes. Back then, I was a little woman, so it was easy to hide my protruding stomach behind those nursing uniforms. They were like potato sacks!" She laughed. "But you came a month early. Eunice and I tried to hide you, but our dorm mom found out and threatened to have us expelled. I was so scared I didn't know what to do." Her lips quivered. "So when your father told me he found a good home for you, I had no choice but to accept. I don't know what I was thinking except I knew I couldn't provide for you. I just never thought for a moment that I would never...never see you again." She stopped, tears filled her eyes, and took a moment to pull herself together before she began again. "I thought I could finish school, get a nursing job. and get you back. Instead, that summer I fell apart. I failed two classes that fall, lost my scholarship, and moved to Delaware with Eunice. While she enrolled at Delaware State, I was hanging in the streets strung out on heroin." She drew a breath and her eyes shifted to meet mine as she added, "Two years later, I met my husband when he arrested me for shoplifting. With his love and strength I eventually got myself together."

I shifted slightly on the bed. I still couldn't speak, only listen.

"Olivia hired a private investigator, who tracked me down a week before your forty-second birthday. All those years, I thought your father had given you away and there you were all along. All that time and all I had to do was call and ask him if I could see you." Her nostrils flared. "Olivia wanted to surprise you, so she invited me down. I was terrified and so afraid you wouldn't understand that I never showed up."

My brow rose. Olivia did that for me?

As if she could read my mind, Dorlinda replied, "Olivia was very understanding and told me to call when I was ready. While your father, on the other hand, was furious. He didn't want to see you hurt. He told me to stay away until I was ready to make you a part of my life." Dorlinda turned in her seat to make sure she still had my attention. Finding that she did, she continued, "I underwent counseling for almost two years before I finally felt strong enough to meet you.

But when I tried to contact Olivia, I was told about the accident." She sighed. "I wanted to give you time to get over your loss before I tried to step into your life. So I waited. Two weeks ago, I contacted Thaddeus and told him I was going to tell you the truth. He asked me to give him a chance to talk to you first."

"Wait a minute..." I couldn't have ...possibly heard her right. I rose from the bed, then asked softly. "You spoke to my Uncle Tad?"

Dorlinda looked just as confused. "Uncle?" She was suddenly still, an odd expression in his eyes. "Oh my God! He still hasn't told you."

"That you're my mother?"

She spoke, her voice troubled. "No. That...he's your father."

Chapter 25

MY KNEES BUCKLED. I lowered onto the bed just before they gave away.

I was speechless. I didn't want to believe the one person I loved the most had betrayed me. Not Uncle Tad! I dropped my head and closed my eyes before looking back up at Dorlinda who was watching me. Concern was etched in her eyes.

Dorlinda was staring at me in dismay. "He always did have his own way of dealing with things."

"Apparently, he's not the only one," I murmured sarcastically.

The color slowly drained from Dorlinda's face. "I guess I deserved that."

I rolled my eyes and looked away.

"Thaddeus never promised me anything. I knew he was married, but I didn't care," she explained.

"He told me he didn't know who my mother was," I said, shaking my head.

"Tad was trying to protect you."

Tad. The only people who used his nickname knew him well...or intimately. Prolonged silence surrounded us.

"Please, Calaine, say something," Dorlinda urged.

"What is there to say? I've spent weeks dreaming about this moment, only it's nothing like I imagined. Instead of welcoming you with open arms, I find out I've been betrayed not by you, but by the one person I've loved most in the world. On top of that, I can't understand how you could have known where I was and never bothered to contact me!"

She shook her head. "I didn't know what to say. I was embarrassed and afraid I would only hurt you more."

"I am a grown woman, not a child! You've had the last two years to tell me you were my mother."

Dorlinda's shoulders sagged. "You're right. There is no real excuse for what I have done. I thought I was doing the right thing. I made a lot of mistakes over the years, but I'd like a chance to finally make things right. I-I hope you can find it in your heart to someday forgive me."

I saw tears cloud her eyes. I looked away not wanting to feel anything for her. But that wasn't easy. There were so many things I wanted to know. "Do you have any other children?"

Dorlinda nodded. "I have a son, Michael, and a daughter, Kelly."

My voice was hesitant. "Do they know about me?"

She gave an audible sigh and said, "Yes, they always have."

LATER THAT EVENING I returned to the hotel with my mind reeling with fresh information. *How ironic.* I believed both of my parents to be dead only to find out they were both alive and well. I still have a mother and a father!

I slipped a pair of canvas mules from my feet and fell back against the bed. I had kept the "do not disturb" sign on the door so the bed had not been changed since I checked in. Bringing the pillow close to my face, the cotton still lingered with the scent of David.

I had been such a fool to send him away. I saw the pain on his face. There was no way he would give me a second chance. Not after the things I said to him. If anything, the breakup was probably a relief to him. Who would want to be a part of a dysfunctional family if they didn't have to be?

Family.

I had a family and a history. While Eunice faded in and out, Dorlinda spent the last several hours enlightening me.

She had been raised in a small town of Pace, Mississippi where everyone knew one another by name. My grandfather, a Baptist minister, had been a respected member of the community. Dorlinda had been the youngest of seven and with a fifteen-year gap between her and her youngest brother, she had never been close to the others. The reverend was a strict no-nonsense father while her mother was meek and passive. Like me, she grew up starving for love and began looking for it in all the wrong places. She met Eunice when she was fifteen and they both dreamed of someday becoming nurses. Her father had been dead set against it and wanted her to marry an older member of his congregation. For once, she stood up to him. However, before she left for nursing school, her father told her once she walked out that door, she would forever be dead to him. Heartbroken, she set off to Missouri determined to make something of herself. She fell in love with Thaddeus and despite the fact that he was her instructor and married, she did everything in her power to get his attention. When she finally did, they had an affair that lasted a month before he broke it off. She was devastated and had also contemplated suicide before she discovered she was pregnant. Since my Aunt Alma was unable to conceive, Dorlinda had hoped her pregnancy would have changed my uncle's mind about them being together, but it hadn't. Despite the indiscretion, Uncle Thaddeus loved his wife.

As a minister's daughter, she couldn't bring herself to have an abortion nor could she turn to her parents for help. Thaddeus had been furious, but he helped her financially. Once I was born, he offered to find me a good home. With stubborn pride, Dorlinda refused and kept me for a few days before she realized she was being selfish. There was no way she could have raised a child.

I quietly listened in fear of interrupting and missing something important. While Dorlinda spoke, I saw the torment in her expression when she told me it broke her heart to give up her baby. Despite my determination to harden my heart, I sympathized with her.

Shifting slightly on the bed, I stared up at the ceiling as I tried to make heads or tails of what I was feelings. I wanted to stay angry, but it was hard. Dorlinda was human. Humans were born to make mistakes. If she hadn't been strung out on heroin, there was no telling how much sooner we could have met.

I hugged the pillow to my chest and took a deep breath. What touched me most was the fact that Olivia had taken the time to track Dorlinda down and had intended to reunite us. My gaze clouded with tears. Why had Olivia decided to find Dorlinda? That was one question I might never find an answer. I would just have to accept that fact that Olivia loved me in her own odd sort of way.

Rising from the bed, I was headed to the bathroom when I noticed the red light on the hotel phone blinking, indicating I had a message. I reached over and pushed the button, hoping it was from David.

"Calaine, this is Uncle Tad. I'm sorry. I-I thought I was doing the right thing. I will be down in the hotel restaurant at seven if you want to talk."

I hung up the receiver and looked at the digital clock. I had five minutes to get down to the lobby.

I found my uncle sitting at a small table in the corner drinking cognac. He looked so sad and fragile. Had he lost weight since I'd last seen him? Despite every intention of being angry with him, my heart lurched at the sight of him.

I remembered all the times my mother had said no to the things I wanted and when she wasn't looking my uncle had bought them for me anyway. As I walked towards him, I thoughts of all the weekends I spent with him fishing or doing anything I had wanted to do. I remembered my sixteen birthday when my parents refused to buy me a car saying that I was too young. Uncle Thaddeus told them they were wrong and went behind their backs and bought me a Honda Civic. Neither of my parents had squawked at his actions and I never could figure out why. Now I knew it was because I was his daughter.

As I reached the table, his sad eyes came up to focus on my blank face.

"Keke, I'm so glad you came."

I ignored the yearning in his expression and pursed my lips. Taking a seat across from him, I leaned back and waited for him to begin.

"I'm so sorry. I spoke to Dorlinda this morning and had to see you."

I shook my head with disappointment and anger all rolled up in one. "How could you?" I choked on my voice.

He momentarily dropped his eyelids. "I can't make excuses for my past actions. I was wrong for lying to you, but please just let me explain." When I nodded, he proceeded. "I was stupid. I was just starting my career and on top of the world. I also knew I could have any woman I wanted. Alma and I were having a lot of problems, but instead of trying to work things through I sought comfort elsewhere. Your dad and I used to hang out at jazz clubs meeting pretty women. He remained faithful. But for me..." Uncle Thaddeus cleared his throat. "Dorlinda was so willing... I took advantage of her vulnerability. It wasn't until she became pregnant that I realized it wasn't a game." He stopped long enough to take a sip from the glass. "I asked her to get an abortion, but she refused. I was angry, but I had to respect her wishes. In exchange for me helping her through the pregnancy, she had agreed to give you up for adoption." He frowned. "Only when you finally arrived, she changed her mind. It took almost a week before she realized she couldn't do it alone. She called me and I came over right away. I had every intention of giving you to a young, childless couple I knew, but when I saw your precious little face I could not." His lips quivered before he cleared his throat and continued, "I remembered parking my car in a deserted parking lot with you in my arms, gazing up at me with those big eyes that I broke down. I knew there was no way I could give you up." He paused taking a moment to get himself together. Watching him, I could sense how difficult this was for him, but I couldn't say anything to comfort him.

"At the time, my brother, your father, and his wife were trying to have a baby and found it to be hopeless. He convinced Olivia to raise you as their child. I was forever grateful to them for such a selfless act. As long as I never told Dorlinda where you were, they promised to keep my little secret. I agreed."

I stared at him. Too afraid to even breathe.

"Dorlinda came looking for you when you were almost two years old. She was strung out on drugs and instead of offering to get her help, I sent her away," he confessed. "A few years ago, Olivia hired a private investigator who found she had cleaned up and rebuilt her life. We were all going to break the news to you last year."

I sat across from him; our eyes locked the entire time. How could I be angry and feel sorry for someone at the same time?

"How come you just didn't tell me the truth when I asked you? I've spent the past few weeks searching for clues that you already had the answers to."

He swallowed hard and replied, "I was scared of losing you. Everything had happened so fast. Your parents were killed and then you started asking questions about your birth and I panicked." He cleared his throat. "When you went to Texas to speak with David's mother, I assumed Wanda was there."

My brow rose. "Yes, she was."

He nodded. "I think the moment you left the house, she contacted Dorlinda and told her you were looking for her."

So that explains the looks she had been giving me. She had known the truth all along. I scowled. "Why has everyone been lying to me?"

Uncle Thaddeus hesitated before saying, "I paid them to be quiet."

"Paid? What do you mean by *them*?"

"Coletta, Wanda, and Eunice... they were never to talk about the baby." He must have seen the concern because he added, "she didn't know."

I breathed a sigh of relief. If David's mother had been in on it, I would have felt so betrayed.

"What about the dorm mom?"

He nodded. "She passed away two years ago."

"Does Alma know?" I asked, cutting to the chase.

He nodded, looked down at his glass, then back up at me. "I told her yesterday. She's angry and feels betrayed. I'm going to be sleeping on the couch for a long time, but I just couldn't lie to her anymore. If I had said something a long time ago, maybe things would have turned out differently. If my brother hadn't taken you, I would have found a way to keep you, because there was no way I could have given you away to strangers."

"Why did Olivia...my mom, decide to look for Dorlinda?"

"Because she wanted you to know the truth."

It was that simple.

I was quiet, unable to speak, needing time to pull everything together. "Where are you staying?" I asked.

"The Hilton," he answered.

Nodding, I rose. "I need some time to think. I'll call you when I'm ready."

Turning on my heels, I started towards the elevators. I had taken no more than five steps when I stopped to glance over my shoulder and found my uncle watching me. My heart tugged. "Uncle Tad...I still love you."

A single tear rolled down his cheek. "I love you, too, Keke."

Chapter 26

THIS IS THE WORST BIRTHDAY of my life, I thought as I stood near fresh dirt and watched as Eunice's coffin was lowered into the ground. The funeral reminded me far too vividly of the pain and grief of losing both my parents at once.

The last two weeks had been a time for growing and healing.

Dorlinda gripped my hand tightly as the tears fell from her eyes. She had lost her best friend seven months after losing one of her sisters to a brain tumor. I sympathized with her, wishing I could take away some of her pain. I leaned in close and did my best to comfort the woman who had become a good friend.

Only a few dozen mourners gathered at the grave. My eyes drifted to my half-sister, Kelly, an elementary school teacher. Her face paled and brown eyes shone with tears. Her ponytail and short bangs were adorable. So was her warm and loving personality. She rested her head on my half-brother, Michael's, chest as they comforted one another. Michael was a tall, mahogany-colored man; an officer and a gentleman commissioned in the United States Army. He was everything I could have ever wished for in a brother.

Tears pushed to the surface of my eyes. The two had accepted me, their big sister, as if I had always been a part of their lives.

My eyes darted over to the far left where Uncle Thaddeus leaned against a tree. As soon as I had called him to tell him Eunice had died, he had hopped on the first plane out. I loved him. Despite all that he had done, he was still my father and the man I would always call Uncle Tad. It would take me a long time—if ever—to forget what he had done, but my love for him allowed me to forgive. Two days ago, I spoke extensively to my Aunt Alma over the phone. She wanted to reassure me nothing had changed. She loved me and was looking forward to my return.

Dr. Williamson, Eunice's niece Robin, and a few other friends and family members were present. Otherwise, the service had been quite small.

It wasn't until dirt began to spill on top of the cedar coffin that the crowd began to turn and walk away. Still holding my mother's hand, we moved to where the rest of my family stood.

"Do you have to go?" Dorlinda asked.

I looked at the woman who had become a major part of my life in such a short time and nodded. "I've got to get back to work. Besides, I have some unfinished business to attend to."

I hugged my new family and bid my goodbyes, then taking Thaddeus' hand, I moved with him to the rental car. Once at the hotel, he waited for me in the lobby while I went up to collect my things.

I took the elevator up to the fifth floor and swiped my key in the door. Stepping into the room, I stopped and became utterly still. It seemed that even my heart had ceased to beat.

David was sitting on the edge of my bed. His shoulders appeared wider, and his hair appeared longer than when I had last seen him two weeks ago.

"How did you get in?" I asked around a large lump that was lodged in my throat.

"I still have my key," he answered in a quiet tone.

I stepped into the room and closed the door behind me. My mouth grew dry as I stared into his gold-green eyes. I couldn't figure out what he was thinking. All that mattered was that he had come back.

David stared across at me and I could feel his gaze penetrating my soul. I felt an overwhelming urge to simply throw myself into his arms, but I held back. I couldn't do that until I knew why he had returned.

"How was the funeral?" he asked, breaking the silence.

My brow furrowed. "Like all funerals. How did you know?"

"Donna called me."

"Then I guess you also heard about my mother."

He nodded. "And your father."

I stood there trying to pull my thoughts about him and our relationship to the surface. David also remained quiet as if waiting for me to speak. Brushing my pride aside, I decided to say what was on my heart.

"I had a lot of time to think while we were apart and I realized something," I said in a shaky voice.

David let out a breath. "And what was that?"

"I never told you I love you," I confessed as I wrung my fingers nervously in front of me.

"I love you, too." He rose and moved toward me.

I backed up and held up a hand. "Wait. Let me finish."

"All right." David lowered back onto the bed.

"The last few days I've learned I was wrong. Dead wrong. I was never alone. I've always had Uncle Thaddeus and Aunt Alma. And I had you. The love and support I've received from the three of you was enough to fill a lifetime, only I was so busy feeling sorry for myself to see it." I stopped long enough to catch my breath. "Having you in my life was the most wonderful feeling. Without you, I can't think, I can't eat, and I can't breathe. You are the fire in my soul," I told him as a flood of tears rushed my eyes. "For once in my life I have the confidence to let go of so many fears and insecurities and live my life. I have been blessed again with parents and an entirely new family with a brother, sister, and lots of cousins," I added with a laugh.

"What I'm trying to say is..." I drew a breath. "...I'm sorry and if you'll have me, I'd like another chance." I looked at David as he sat quietly staring at me.

He finally rose and moved to cup my face with his hands. "Only if you'll marry me?"

"W-what?" My heart thumped.

He smiled and leaned down to kiss me deeply. "I love you, Keke, even with all your flaws."

"Flaws!"

He chuckled. "Sweetheart, you're flawless."

David drew me into his arms, and I felt his heart beating as erratically as mine. Our kiss grew deeper but before things got out of control, I pulled away.

"Wait a minute, I have something for you." I said, stepping over to my suitcase.

"So do I."

I reached inside my bag as I spoke. "I found this card in the hospital gift shop and was planning to mail it to you when I got home. If that hadn't worked, I would have parked in front of your house until you'd forgiven me." I was giggling as I swung around then gasped, dropping the card from my hand. David stood in front of me, holding a small velvet box. "Oh my God..." I stared down at an exquisite diamond ring. "What is that?"

"What do you think it is?" David replied as he slowly lowered onto one knee and took my hand in his. Gazing deep into my eyes, he said, "Calaine Renae Hart, will you marry me?"

Before I had time to breathe, I burst into tears. For the first time in months, they were tears of joy. "Yes," I answered breathlessly. "Yes, I'll marry you!"

David slid the ring onto my finger, then rose to his feet. Sliding his hand down my back, he drew me closer. I stared down at my finger and fresh tears filled my eyes. *Could I possibly be any happier?*

With a smile, he reclaimed my lips, kissing me softly at first, then urgently with all the passion that had been pent up for too long. His body was hard and strong, his lips warm and gentle. I shivered at the tantalizing sensation. We kissed and held each other for several long moments.

David lifted me in his strong arms, and I laughed as he carried me over to the bed where he quickly discarded my clothes. When he began removing his own, my eyes widened. "Wait a minute! Uncle Tad is waiting for me."

Humor gleamed in David's eyes. "No, he isn't. After I asked him for permission to make you my wife, I gave him strict instructions to catch the next plane home."

I tossed my head back with laughter again. Beautiful joyful laughter.

He came to me on the bed, covering my body with his own. I closed my eyes and clung to him as I met another deep thrilling kiss.

Our love was complete.

Mind and body.

Heart and soul.

Other Books by the Author

SEDUCED INTO SUBMISSION- Curious (Interracial romance)
Seduced into Submission – Serve (Interracial romance)
Seduced into Submission – Obey (Interracial romance)
Seduced into Submission – Surrender (Interracial romance)
Beg for It (Interracial Romance) (Interracial romance)
Feinin' *Big Spankable Asses Anthology* (Interracial romance)
Talk a Good Game
When It Rains
A Delight Before Christmas
Love Uncovered
When I First Saw You
In the Company of My Sistahs
Trouble Loves Company
Careful of the Company You Keep
Misery Loves Company
Intimate Intentions
Hart & Soul
Time is of the Essence
A Will to Love
Endless Enchantment
Destiny in Disguise
The Second Time Around
The Playboy's Proposition
The Player's Proposal
For You I Do
Before I Let You Go

In Her Neighbor's Bed
Show Me
Any Man Will Do
Coming for My Baby
Strutting in Red Stilettos
Running to Love in Pink Stilettos
Say My Name
Every Second Counts
A Beau for Christmas
Do Me Baby
Naughty Before Christmas
Claiming What's Mine
Wicked Pleasure
Time for Desire (Interracial romance)
Stilettos & Mistletoes
All I Want

Did you love *Fire in My Soul*? Then you should read *Put Your Name on It*[1] by Angie Daniels!

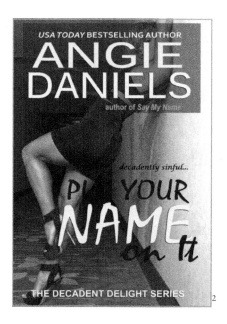

The Decadent Delight Series continues with this sizzling new addition... Claudia Winters is crazy about Maximilian James. Unfortunately, he's possibly the father of a baby by another woman, and despite how Claudia feels she doesn't do baby mama drama. She tries to resist temptation, only Max plans to prove to her regardless of the circumstance her heart belongs to him. As things begin to heat up in the bedroom, Claudia has to decide whether to stick to her goal, or go against every rule she has ever set for herself to have the greatest love of all.

Read more at angiedaniels.com.

About the Author

Angie Daniels is a free spirit who isn't afraid to say what's on her mind or even better, write about it. Since strutting onto the literary scene in five-inch heels, she's been capturing her audience's attention with her wild imagination and love for alpha men. The *USA Today* Bestselling Author has written over thirty novels for imprints such as BET Arabesque, Harlequin/Kimani Romance and Kensington/Dafina and Kensington/Aphrodisia Books. For more information about upcoming releases, and to connect with Angie on Facebook, please visit her website at angiedaniels.com.

Read more at angiedaniels.com.